THE CR

James Brighton
Roxton Manor
26th Jul '25

James Braxton
The Crocodile Stone

To my mother Linden Braxton (née Mosey)
Much travelled, much loved and much missed.

First published for the 2025
WIGTOWN
BOOK FESTIVAL

Front cover linocut © Annie Braxton
Cover design & layout © Annie Braxton
@aobdesign
annieobraxton@gmail.com

Thanks to Chas Parker, Sam & Alice of Tandem Publishing, Burlie of Custard Design, Guy Clutterbuck – gem hunter, Harry Collins MVO and Lucy Ritson of G.Collins & Sons, Royal Tunbridge Wells.

To my four children, Amelia and her husband Dave, their son Monty, Charlie, Ned, and Annie and her boyfriend Raphael for their support and just being delightful.

Finally, to my wife and editor Joanna, who has been both my fiercest critic and loudest champion. Without her love and patience I would never have written this second book.

Chapter 1

Hastings & London

Lionel sat at home in his tub-shaped Lloyd loom chair. Beside him, on a circular bamboo table, rested his mobile phone and a frothy coffee. The morning sun was on his back as he opened the *Antiques Trade Gazette*. The headline read,

'Important oriental ceramics and works of art sale in Hong Kong breaks previous record.'

He opened his banking app and there in green text read a credit: '*St James's Auctioneers* +£3,500,000.00.' His smile stretched further. After forty years of hard toil in the antiques trade he had finally struck a bit of luck. He swapped mobile phone for his cup of coffee and sat, half thinking and half daydreaming. Well, as much as a man in his late fifties can daydream, though he had been up since 6am. Dressed in his summer uniform of a navy-blue linen suit, paired with a white herringbone Turnbull & Asser shirt, he cut a good figure, a benefit of not owning a car. Everything was either a five- or twenty-minute walk away; each day he would clock up at least ninety minutes. A car in Norman Road, St Leonards-on-Sea, had become a bore. Traffic wardens, road tax and a lack of parking spaces had eroded the pleasure, and he was happy with the unintended consequence of a permanently flat stomach.

Should he stay in St Leonards on the south coast, or go away? Strangely for Lionel, he hadn't told a soul about his good fortune. After a long career in the antiques trade he had learnt to separate purchases from sales. Nobody wants to hear that an object he had just sold for £2,500 had cost him only £50. The smiles of others to his good news seemed to get thinner and thinner. The problem was that the vases hadn't sold for £2,500 but for over £4 million. It would test every fibre of his self-control. He also knew that the next four weeks would be the most difficult. His tongue might slip after a couple of white burgundies in the Horse and Groom pub at the top of the road, or with his great friend Barty after dinner service at the Imperial in Queen's Road. He needed to get away. Normally it's people with problems who run away, but in his heart of hearts he knew he should go. Autumn was fast approaching: he could go to South Africa. A lovely dry climate, but what about Sri Lanka? He and the second Mrs Lionel had enjoyed a lovely honeymoon in Mirissa, only an hour's drive along the coast from the old fort town of Galle. They had stayed for two weeks, one on the beach in Mirissa and one inland at Kandy and Nuwara Eliya, travelling between the two by a lovely slow train.

🐊

While Lionel was coming around to the idea of a 'little thinking space' in Sri Lanka, a rather happy Mercy Penfold was sitting at her new desk in the Gazette offices in London.

She had previously headed up the 'Stolen Pages' for the paper and had turned them from an odd if fascinating listing – much like 'looking for love' in a local paper – to a well-regarded industry recovery tool supported and read by the trade, insurance industry and private individuals. It was one such private individual who had been the catalyst for her promotion. Sir Roger Swotter of Kooling Towers in Norfolk had written such a generous letter of thanks to both her, and – more importantly – to the paper's editor, that her planned move from the 'Stolen' to the 'Auction Reporting' desk happened on very attractive terms. Furthermore, her hand was strengthened by a letter from Norfolk Constabulary, in which a certain Detective Inspector Kevin Smythe had stated that the 'Stolen Pages' under Miss Penfold had become a much-respected catalyst for the recovery of stolen antiques. The editor whisked her off to Hong Kong to assist in covering an important oriental sale – that scoop now covered the front page of the latest issue. The trip and auction had the excitement of a Bond film, the room packed with buyers surrounded on three sides with banks of telephones held by impossibly glamorous staff. Buyers unable to afford the time to both preview the sale and attend the auction; plus some who chose to be represented in the room by the telephone, rather than in person. A known dealer or collector rarely wishes to excite interest in a particular lot by bidding for it in person, as a younger bidder might be reassured to go higher by the interest of the respected elder. Auctions are two-handed affairs: on the one hand are the buyers trying to secure bargains and, on the other, the auctioneer trying to achieve the top price. It's a juggling act conducted in one time and in one place, pressurising the market to produce ever bigger prices.

Albert and Rose Penfold had shared the joy of their daughter's promotion. Just like their parents and grandparents, Mercy and her sister Grace had always worked hard. Their father's family had moved banking interests to a new country, but on their mother's side it was a more humble beginning. The two sisters' maternal grandfather's first job had been sweeping platforms on the London Underground and Overground. He didn't clean for long. Being well over 6 foot, hard-working and black, he stood out. He was quickly promoted to platform guard and it took a further three years to achieve his ambition of becoming a train driver. As Mercy and Grace's mother told them, 'you couldn't stop your grandfather going to work.' By the end of his working life he was responsible for all the drivers' rotas, still managing to rota himself in. Mercy and Grace never met their mother's parents; their hard work in establishing a new home had taken its toll. But their mother spoke of them daily, and by gradual osmosis Rose's parents had been very much a part of the two sisters' childhood.

On her return from Hong Kong, Mercy's new Head of Department, Anthony, marked up a previous issue of the paper's auction calendar. He highlighted five recently conducted sales and asked her to ring the auctioneers.

"What should I ask them?"

"I would start by asking, did anything surprise you?" he replied. "I'm sure I don't need to tell you, Mercy, how to get a story. After winkling out information on stolen goods, talking to auctioneers – who, incidentally, love talking about themselves – will be a breeze."

Anthony was right. Mercy soon found her line of enquiry. She enjoyed writing the reports, rigorously guarding them from becoming just a list of auction highlights. The 'surprise' items invariably had a strong correlation to the most inaccurate presale estimates. She soon started recording these inaccuracies in a table, which Anthony wickedly named 'The graph of shame'.

Enquiries done, she made herself a cup of black Earl Grey tea; after all, she had a figure to look after. She had really enjoyed her time on the 'Stolen' desk, and the Kooling Towers recovery was the right case to leave on. Had the generous Mr Barty Hix of Hastings, who had donated the first prize in the raffle at the Kooling Tower's fundraising cricket match, really replaced the stolen bronze to its original garden plinth? A large smile crept upon her face; a theft where all parties seemed to benefit. Much like musical chairs, maybe the bronze's temporary loss allowed all the associated parties to change place.

Mercy's new seat was in the job she longed for, whilst, in St Leonards, Lionel's new seat was very well padded with extra gilt trimmings!

Chapter 2

Hastings

Lionel was alright with technology. Like most of the antiques trade he used Instagram as a selling tool, but remained suspicious of comparison websites. Why, when he looked up the price of flights to Colombo, Sri Lanka on one site did it change after viewing another? And always upwards. Were most sites owned by the same holding company? He would normally address technical tasks and queries to one of his friends' children. His great friend Pru, a respected artist whose living came from dog portraits, had two very tech-savvy daughters, but on this occasion he couldn't risk explaining why he was going to book a flight to Sri Lanka with an open return; anyway, why worry about potentially paying too much when he was now rich ... in fact, *very* rich.

He decided the sooner he left, the better. The only call would be to his friend Barty Hix who owned the Imperial pub in Queen's Road, Hastings. Barty was both patron and chef, opening his cellar restaurant four days a week. By operating from Wednesday to Saturday he was able to give himself a good income, plus three days off and, when you're over sixty, you need those rest days. Whilst away, Lionel would decide how he was going to share his good fortune, but for now, it was better not to explain.

He placed a call to Barty.

"Morning, I have decided to go away on holiday, would you hold a house key for me?"

"Of course. Where are you off to?"

"I thought Sri Lanka."

"Bit out of the blue, how lovely. How long are you going for?"

"Three or four weeks, I haven't decided yet."

"OK."

"I know it's a long time, but I can't think of the last time I went abroad."

"Good for you."

"Would you like to come with me?"

"I would love to, but I can't. The restaurant is doing well and I know Polly and Phoenix need the money."

Polly and Phoenix were the Imperial's two regular waitresses. Lionel assured his friend that he quite understood.

"When are you off?"

"Tomorrow."

"Wow! Would you like a lift to the airport?"

"I was going to ask young Jack to take me to Heathrow."

"Are you going to get Jack to house-sit for you?"

"How silly of me, I didn't think of him. I've been too busy organising my flights."

"Jack would love to stay in Hastings. You know when we were away in Norfolk, he had such fun with Polly and Phoenix. He might even keep buying from your runners. Who's Norman going to sell to when you're away?"

Lionel had been buying antiques from the back of Norman's Austin Maxi car for decades, and it was Norman who had taken the pair of Chinese vases up to St James's auction house on his behalf.

"Don't worry about Norman! I know I'm one of his many buyers."

"But surely he gives you first dibs?"

"That's what he tells me, but I recognise you have to keep more than one buyer sweet."

"Give Jack a call. I'm happy to hold a key but I'm sure he will leap at the opportunity. Plus, that dog of his loves the beach."

"You're right. I'll give him a call now."

Jack was delighted to receive the offer. "I'm getting too old to still be living with my parents in Epsom."

"Well, while you are here in St Leonards why don't you look for a place to rent or buy?"

"I would need a lottery win to buy, though it's got to be cheaper than Epsom."

"Ooh, I don't know, Hastings is on the rise! Why don't you come down earlier and I'll show you how things work, like the fuse box."

"Let me pack and I'll call you when I'm on my way."

"Perfect, see you later."

Lionel went upstairs and dug out a small cabin bag for a spare shirt, trunks, rolled Panama hat, books, notepads, pens and headphones. In a larger hold bag he folded: sarongs, linen shirts, shorts, cotton squares, more books and one of life's essentials, flannels. He didn't own flip-flops. The nearest he got to casual footwear was a pair of racing green Gola trainers, which he had bought last summer when suffering from plantar fasciitis in his right heel. He really preferred his trusty Shipton and Heneage loafers; for everyday use the tobacco Wiltons had served him well. What he didn't have now he would buy once there. As long as he had 'standing-up' clothes he would be fine.

In Epsom, it didn't take Jack too long to pack, as he always wore the same clothes. A sort of uniform of white T-shirt tucked into sandy-coloured cotton trousers, threaded with a heavy brass-buckled brown leather belt, finished with his brown dealer boots. It was a simple look that needed a good figure. Luckily for him, however much he ate, his stomach remained wash-board taut. Two hours later he was standing outside Lionel's shop. After a guided tour of the 'mechanics' of 69 Norman Road, Jack, who had stayed before, resumed his room on the floor below the top-storey kitchen.

It might have been more conventional to site the kitchen on the ground floor, adjoining the sitting room, but the view from the top was just too good. It was even too good to install a dishwasher – Lionel enjoyed washing-up at his sash window, overlooking the many terraced roofs falling to the sea beyond. He decided to cook supper at home as he couldn't trust himself in the Horse and Groom pub: too many known faces.

While Jack helped himself to a beer, Lionel walked down to the shops on London Road. He popped into the post office and collected 150 American dollars, emergency money for an airport taxi. After the post office he bought spinach, tomatoes and a cooked rotisserie chicken at the food market. He didn't call into the corner shop run by the Sikh brothers, as goodbyes might lead to awkward questions. On returning he made straight for the kitchen and withdrew one of the three chilled bottles of white Burgundy from his Maytag fridge. Fridge staples for most households are milk, yoghurt, butter, orange juice, bacon and vegetables. His fridge had a less demanding owner. Three bottles of white Burgundy, two bottles of rosé, numerous lemons, limes, butter and eggs. Barty had taught Lionel that a colder egg holds together better when poaching. Jack observed Lionel from one of the two kitchen Lloyd loom chairs. He knew he liked to sit in the one facing the room with his back warmed by the sun and he also knew Lionel was a man of habit. The unspoken selfishness of living on one's own when one's needs are totally satisfied. Jack sitting in the wrong chair would definitely compromise that happy settled state.

"A glass of wine, Jack?"

"Yes please ... Cheers, and a very good holiday."

"Thank you. Do you have any plans while you're here?"

"Well, I will be messaging Polly tomorrow and hopefully meeting up with her and Phoenix after I've dropped you at Heathrow."

"You should be alright tomorrow, it being a Tuesday; remember they're at the Imperial on Wednesdays, Thursdays, Fridays and Saturdays."

"Is it just in the evenings?"

"It used to be, but now Barty's got busier they've been helping with the prep too, he likes to cook everything from scratch. He's lucky with Polly and Phoenix, their mother Pru is such a good cook and thankfully her girls have inherited some of her skills. One day you might be lucky and have one of Pru's quiches, they are sublime."

"I don't think I've ever knowingly had a quiche."

"You're joking," said Lionel.

"No, I'm pretty sure I haven't."

"Well for goodness' sake don't have one until you've had one of Pru's and then you can start at the very top. Like chillies are rated for their heat, measured in *Scovilles*, named after a Mr Wilbur Scoville, an early 20th-century American pharmacist ... Well, in my opinion, all quiches should be rated in *Pru's*, a full 100 being a Pru and a 10 being a Lionel! Talking of cooking, are roasted tomatoes, steamed spinach and chicken good for you?"

"Perfect."

"The oven is really easy to operate." Lionel pointed to the grill/oven selector knob. He turned it up to maximum heat and turned his attention to the tomatoes. First cutting them in half, then drizzling them with olive oil, seasoning them with salt, pepper and mixed Mediterranean herbs, hedging his bets: he never knew whether it was dried thyme, basil or oregano that went best with tomatoes. He should really ask Barty or Pru; they would know.

"Another glass?" Lionel proffered.

"Yes please, it's delicious."

"It's made from the finest Chardonnay grapes. You have to hand it to the French, they do know how to make wine. Like the Italians, they have been doing it for over 2,000 years."

"Time well spent in my opinion, this is the best white wine I've ever had."

"Take it from me Jack, this is mid-range, there are literally hundreds, if not thousands of bottles better than this. Here's to a lifetime of research."

"I'll second that," said Jack, raising his glass.

Next on the culinary job-list was the breaking of the cooked chicken. On cue, Jack's dog moved immediately to Lionel's left. Clive, a liver-coloured working cocker spaniel, had observed that Lionel was left-handed and as he started separating the cooked meat from the carcass he would be in the best place for titbits. Clive didn't bark or paw for attention, he employed his 'third' call, an intense stare broken only by the periodic licking of lips. It wasn't long before Lionel conceded. Bits of skin, some dark meat and even a little breast were dropped. He portioned most of the chicken onto a plate and a goodly amount into Clive's bowl, to which he gave an extra-large lick in acknowledgement. They sat down to chicken, steamed spinach, and lovely jammy roasted tomatoes.

"Something for the prostate," as Lionel generally acknowledged tomatoes. During supper he gave Jack details of his normal working week.

"Norman, the runner, offers his best stuff on Mondays. The fruits of the weekend car boot sales. Tuesdays and Wednesdays are a little leaner, normally items from charity shops. I would walk Clive on the circuit up London Road, along Station Road to Warrior Square station, doing one side of the shops there and the other side on your way home. They don't open until ten. Don't forget to cover the Old Town first thing on Friday morning, as you may catch the fresh stock for the weekend retail. Remember, everybody knows my routine so nobody will come to my shop before 11.30am. I normally stay in until 1pm, and after that they tend to call on the mobile."

"But they don't have my number," replied Jack.

"They will tomorrow. A text from me to Norman with your number and, within twenty-four hours, everybody will know! If you want to know anything in this town, just ask Norman."

"But I don't have your spend."

"I've thought of that too, here is a float of £3,000, would 50-50 be fair?"

"That sounds fair, but what about the unsold stock, do we split that too?"

"No, unsold stock will be subtracted from your half, remember it's only sales that make profits.

"Make a success of this and next time it'll be me driving you to the airport!"

Chapter 3

Hastings & Sri Lanka

Lionel woke up with the ring of the shop bell as Jack took Clive for a walk. Never comfortable on a lead, Clive dragged him down Norman Road towards the beach. Once through the queuing traffic on the coast road and safely on the promenade, Jack released the straining dog. An 8ft drop to the shingle beach was taken without hesitation, as he flew towards the sea birds feeding on the tide line. Unfortunately, his quarry seemed to lift just before he got to them. Undeterred, he spotted more birds so resumed another accelerated chase. Maybe, with more practice, he might finally catch a bird, but he must work on his approach. The crunch and crash of shingle was too loud an alarm for an already nervous avian. After fifteen minutes of frantic chasing, he returned to Jack just to check that he was watching 'his little boy'. Reassured, he sped off again. The great thing about birds is they are as game as their pursuers.

On Clive's next reappearance, Jack was able to motion him back towards a set of steps. He could see himself settling into a nice morning routine. He might even start swimming. He'd spotted groups of middle-aged women shrouded in dryrobes; beneath, they wore rubber swimming caps, goggles, bright

Croc sandals, and carried baskets containing thermos flasks, fruit cake and red plastic floats. If you thought swimming was about shedding clothes and leaping in, you would be so wrong. Once these ladies had made camp, they moved towards the water like a floating pontoon!

On his way back to 69 Norman Road, Jack called into the Sikh brothers for Lionel's newspaper and wine gums, and then to the bakery for a couple of fresh croissants. As he climbed the stairs he caught the heavenly smell of frying bacon, followed by happy barking from Clive as Lionel greeted his four-legged friend.

"Morning."

"Morning, Lionel."

"Good walk?"

"Clive managed to unsettle the local birdlife, I've got your paper, wine gums and some croissants."

"Many thanks, would you like a bacon sandwich?"

"Yes please, that sea air certainly gives you an appetite."

"You'll find the air on the coast is very different to that of inland Surrey."

"I'm hoping to add a morning swim while I'm staying here."

"You will enjoy it, just remember – give it a miss after heavy rains."

"Why?"

"Well, regrettably, our water companies now discharge raw sewage into the sea, if they believe their treatment works will be threatened by excess rainwater."

"Yuck," said Jack, wrinkling his nose.

"It seems while everybody else is becoming more conscious of our environment, the water companies, in the interest of their shareholders, are doing the opposite!"

After they had finished eating, Jack gave Clive his breakfast: a handful of dried dog biscuits, the remainder of chicken from last night and a splash of hot kettle water to make a rudimentary gravy.

"What time do you want to get to Heathrow?"

"My flight is at 20.20 this evening, and it's recommended that I arrive three hours before, the M25 will be a nightmare at that hour, plus I don't want to deal with Norman or anybody else who might come into the shop. Are you good to leave at 10? Then we will miss any callers and you should have a less complicated run there and back."

"That's good for me, I'm ready to go whenever you are."

"Well, let's have a coffee and these croissants first."

Half an hour later, the holiday party were in front of Jack's Mercedes Sprinter van. Jack driving, Clive in the middle with Lionel next to the passenger window. He hadn't told Jack that he had booked a business class seat, which entitled him to use a rather swish airport lounge. Time spent in the company of *free* food and drinks wouldn't be a hardship.

The drive up was without incident and after their farewells, along with a double-check that Jack had the house key, Lionel was off. He travelled with a Samsonite aluminium case on four castor wheels and an old game bag over his shoulder, in its outer knotted net he carried a cap, scarf and the day's newspaper. There was no queue at the business class Sri Lankan Airways check-in desk, and with a seamless progression through security Lionel found himself in the airport lounge.

He settled into the large quiet space with a glass of champagne and a bowl of cashew nuts. There is something fascinating about watching large planes being serviced by comparatively miniature buses, fuel tankers, chains of luggage trolleys and all the other vehicles necessary for the transfer of bags and souls. It was a marked contrast to the last time he had flown, with his knees wrapped around his ears in economy.

It was in Colombo's immigration hall that the preferred status of business class evaporated. The next shock was through the arrivals hall, where the cool of the terrazzo marble floor and air-conditioning gave way to hot concrete. Lionel made his way to the airport taxi kiosk, paid his money and took the lucky dip of fate. When his allotted taxi arrived, it did so in such haste that the driver managed to clip the kerb. After frantic clasping of his head followed by a well-judged kick to the plastic hubcap, cases were loaded and the front passenger door opened. Lionel was smartly pushed in, seatbelt extended, and the door slammed shut. Lionel half expected the driver to do a roll over the bonnet, but he chose to run around the back of the car to check that the boot was properly fastened. Before he even pulled away from the kerb, the driver ceremoniously presented a business card. It read: Akhila Anura, International Driver, then listed various contacts with a mobile number first, then email, followed by all manner of other platforms: Instagram, Facebook, Twitter, etc.

"Good to meet you, Mr Anura," smiled Lionel.

This was greeted with a blank face that could only be read as puzzlement.

"My name is Lionel."

Again the same blank and puzzled face.

Lionel tried a third time, with much the same result. For a man who proudly listed so many points of communication on his business card, Akhila Anura seemed strangely uncommunicative.

Suddenly, Mr Anura's mobile rang and the interior exploded with noise accompanied by random hand gestures, some involving the whole arm. Like an uncoordinated uncle at a family wedding, the driver used a sort of interpretive dance to add another layer to his shouted words. Silence was restored only when the phone was replaced in its dash-mounted cradle.

Lionel had two options: leave the car or show his phone with the hotel's address. He decided on the latter. It worked, the taxi sped off and joined the public road. The driver assaulted his task with the vigour of a man who allowed speed to cover for a total lack of craft. If a collision had occurred it should always be behind them. Thankfully, they were soon on a less crowded dual carriageway which allowed Lionel to loosen his vice-like grip on both seatbelt and seat edge. After another excited phone call, a calmer Mr Anura took over, and a certain tranquillity crept into the cab. Palms, granite hills and paddy fields became a sleepy blur woken by a violent swerve to the left, as no more than twenty yards away, a large red bus was heading their way.

Lionel turned to him saying, "That was close."

Anura replied with a broad smile. Adversarial driving must be his bag. For the remaining thirty minutes of their journey, he narrowly avoided anything that might be on tarmac. There were buses, cars, lorries, bicycles, dogs and cows to negotiate, mostly on his side of the carriageway, but many on the wrong side too.

Once at the hotel Lionel just stood with his cases for a moment, drinking in his new world. Before him was a long string of stepping stones floating in coarse green grass, and beyond this, Lionel glimpsed the sea. The sensory calm of cooling lush plants, the smell and sight of the sea making so marked a contrast to the chaos of the highway beyond the hotel's wall. As he mused, a man in a branded T-shirt and shorts approached and uttered in good English,

"Welcome, my name is Saman and I am the general manager of The Papers Hotel."

"Marvellous," Lionel replied. "I was rather expecting St Peter, as these stepping stones look like they might lead to heaven."

Chapter 4

London

Anthony, Mercy's Head of Department at the auction reporting desk, gave her the job of writing a special report on her recent visit to Hong Kong. After all, it was a record-breaking sale for both ceramics and works of art and, given the current political change, both buyers and sellers would be pleased to know that Hong Kong remained one of the best places to trade.

"Here are the top ten lots by hammer price," said Anthony, handing over a note. "I spoke to my contact at St James's, a certain Ollie Croyd, who told me he took out a pair of vases with him on the plane; surprisingly, they're on that list. I have highlighted them on your sheet."

"Number 8, at £4.5 million, that's a life-changing amount."

"The fact that Ollie took them on the plane with him suggests that they were both a late entry and worth the bother. My instinct is there is a story attached to those vases. I have rung Ollie and suggested you meet for a coffee."

"I will call him now."

"No need, it's already sorted. Ollie said he has back-to-back meetings all this week, but fortunately he's free today at 11."

"Thank you, shall I go to his offices?"

"No, he suggested Fortnum & Mason's tearoom around the corner from his office."

"I know the one, my sister meets her friends there."

"Good, well good luck and let me know how you get on."

"Anthony, how will I recognise this Ollie Croyd?"

"Easy, he is very tall with black curly hair."

"Ah, I remember him from the sale."

"Did you get the chance to chat to him?"

"No, all the staff were so busy."

"Can you remember the vases?" asked Anthony.

"I can, as they took so long to sell and I do remember they were very pink!"

"That's a start."

"It was just all so new and so busy in Hong Kong," Mercy continued, "the auction was an assault on the senses, just so much to process. I wish I'd paid more attention now."

"A lesson learnt. It would be good if the vases came from an ordinary home."

"Well, I'll give it my best shot. It's 10.30 now and I don't want to keep this Ollie Croyd waiting."

🐊

Mercy's timing was spot-on, her Uber dropping her at the Duke Street entrance. She walked into the large wedding cake of a room, decorated in the pastel shades of macaroons. A glorious sea of pinks, blues, oranges and greens. Once she had adjusted to her new surroundings, she scanned the room for Ollie. All the while, a mop of curly black hair started rising, and kept rising, almost threatening the lustre drops of an overhead chandelier. This must be her man, she thought, as she walked towards his table.

"Good morning, you must be Mercy? Tea or coffee?"

"Cappuccino, please."

At this, Ollie held up a hand and gave a nod to a watchful waitress. At 6 foot 7 inches, with another 1½ inches of curly hair, you tend to attract a level of attention not enjoyed by the majority.

"Congratulations on your sale in Hong Kong."

"Thank you. I did see you at the sale and I'm sorry I didn't spend any time with you."

"I totally understand, you were working and I was merely observing. It was quite a scrum."

"In the Far East a wealthy collector rarely attends a view day alone. He generally comes with sons, daughters, assistants, along with numerous dealers and, of course, the curious, who like the drama, drinks and nibbles."

"The large number of people in the room gave it a market feel."

"That's what we always hope for, a wave of interested optimism. As the sale proceeded, I noticed the smiles of collectors, with the penny dropping that their collections at home had gone up another 20 per cent."

"What might break the wave of optimism?"

"A series of unsold lots," replied Ollie.

"I didn't notice any unsolds, did you have many?"

"A couple, you always do, but none of the big-ticket items failed to sell, thankfully." To which Ollie, rather sweetly, clasped his hands in mock prayer.

"My boss, Anthony, said you brought out a pair of vases with you on the aeroplane. Were they a late entry to the catalogue?"

"They were, and the only reason I risked them after the

catalogue had been printed was that they are so fashionable at the moment."

"Why?" Mercy pressed.

"For a start they were large, undamaged and colourful, in fact not dissimilar to this room. They also had age. They were made in the Kangshi period, similar to our George III, i.e. late 18th century, circa 1780."

Mercy's forehead creased slightly. For an auctioneer like Ollie, who can register the facial changes of a single person in a room of fifty, it was as if Mercy had held her hand up.

"Am I getting too technical?" he asked.

"No, I'm fine, but it's always intrigued me how 18th-century dates start with a 17 and not a more logical 18."

"I suppose it's one of the anomalies of recording history, much like BC and AD. Mercy, who codified before and after Christ?"

"I haven't a clue," replied Mercy.

"It was the 7th-century writer and scholar, the Venerable Bede."

"There you go again," riposted Mercy. "Don't tell me late 600s."

"And early seven hundreds," said Ollie, smiling. He was beginning to like this pretty journalist.

"So a lifetime of scholarship is condensed into four letters."

"But what a legacy, a code which is used every day."

"Thanks for the history lesson ... but the vases, why are they so fashionable?"

"They had everything: colour, size, technicality and condition."

"I remember them, they were the most extraordinary pink, almost livid."

"Not only a pink ground, but with yellows, blues, greens and all the gold dragons chasing flaming pearls. They had everything the market regards as fashionable right now. The most extraordinary thing was that they had an undamaged second skin. It's hard enough, firing a large pot at over 1200°c, but imagine firing two identical vases. It's difficult to achieve now, just imagine doing it in the 18th century, when the kilns that they were using were fuelled by dirty coal, charcoal etc." Warming to his subject, Ollie continued, "To get a pair of vases, I would guess tens of vases would've been wasted and once past the initial firing, each colour is fired at a progressively lower temperature. Every time you close the kiln door you entrust the vessels to the kiln gods, who may or may not allow successful firing. Centuries ago, private bodyguards were exchanged for Chinese porcelain collections but now it's so much easier. You just need lots of money."

"Who bought the vases?" Mercy asked.

"A collector who is known to us."

"Was he Chinese?"

"Yes, Hong Kong Chinese."

"Does Chinese porcelain generally find its way home?"

"By and large. Yes. The same goes with Indian and Russian artefacts."

"How will the buyer display his new pair of vases?"

"They will be prominently shown in all their glory at his apartment or office, as a statement of wealth. The great thing about porcelain for the Chinese is it's literally in their DNA. So like all great art, it's easily recognised by your fellow man. For a collector, they're both a statement and a store of wealth."

"Was your seller happy with the sale price?"

"He seemed thrilled when I called him with the result."

"Have you not met him?"

"No, he consigned them via a third party." Ollie paused, and then continued, "When they were brought to me, I don't think the vendor or his carrier had any idea of how valuable they were. I certainly wouldn't have risked carrying such expensive pots to London in that manner."

"Why do you say that?" prodded Mercy.

"Are you interested in cars, Mercy?"

"Do you mean do I like cars? Well, I don't own one, does that answer your question?"

"Would you know what an Austin Maxi looks like?"

"I wouldn't."

"Well, it's a car that was made by British Leyland in Birmingham during the '70s and early '80s. It was the donkey of cars, a large hatchback, a sort of box on four wheels which was both ugly and uncomfortable. Probably the last time an Austin Maxi drove around Piccadilly would've been the late 1970s. That is until four weeks ago, when I was asked to go down to inspect two boxes in the back of a brown Austin Maxi."

"Christmas every day, eh," said Mercy.

"It certainly was on this occasion. There is a certain thrill when you look in any box and find not just one, but a pair of 18th-century porcelain vases."

"I bet the chap was thrilled?"

"Strangely, not really, he was more concerned about parking and getting back to Hastings!"

"Do you think he was a dealer?"

"Definitely, and it's my guess they were found in a house clearance."

"Have you ever dealt with the seller before?"

"Mercy, you do realise I'm bound by rules regarding client confidentiality?"

"I do, and you must know I'm new on the Auction Reporting Desk. In fact, truthfully you are my first ever interview."

"Oh what a shame," Ollie said, looking down at his watch. "I have a 12 o'clock meeting at my office, but we could continue this 'interview' if you'd like a drink after work this week? I hope that's not too forward?"

"Not at all, I'd love that," said Mercy with a reassuring smile.

"May I message you?"

"Of course." She opened her bag and gave Ollie one of her new business cards.

"Very smart," said Ollie, looking at it. "Where is the BA Hons from?"

"Bristol."

"What did you read?"

"English."

"I tried for Bristol but went to Exeter instead."

"What did you study?"

"History of Art."

"Useful?"

"It has been. Bye, Mercy, I will message you." She remained seated and watched as he exited, bobbing under the chandeliers.

Chapter 5

Sri Lanka

Lionel sat and pinched himself. Only when you come away do you wonder why you hadn't done it sooner. Too many lost years, fulfilling day-to-day demands and not making the break. Normally Lionel found peace in his top-floor kitchen, sitting in his chair with the sun on his back ... now swapped for a tub-shaped bamboo armchair with a companion three-legged coffee table. Saman was soon at his side with a beer – cold bottle and cold glass. He sipped and sat back. Directly in front, out at sea, bobbed a clutch of optimists, the collective noun for surfers forever waiting for the 'right' wave. To his left a man-made stone pier, constructed to stop beach erosion, and to his right was an island connected to the beach by a narrow spit of sand.

The island was a sleeping dragon; its hunched body rose some 50 feet, red with earth and green with tropical vegetation. The head was formed from random rocks left where the sea had eroded the soft red earth, its tail now gone and replaced by sand. Lionel could see people walking along its spine, to get a prime position for photos. The sun dropped quickly into the sea beyond the dragon's head. As it dropped, Lionel became aware of many floating bamboo lampshades, connected and hung from black wires strung between the palm trees. These large warm yellow bulbs magically turned the garden into a more intimate room. He felt at home amongst a combination of bamboo and teak furniture. How strange, he thought: in Hastings I spend my life searching for bamboo furniture and, after only one flight, I'm surrounded by it.

He ordered a rice and curry along with another beer. Five minutes later, Saman placed white porcelain before him. On it sat a neat dome of red rice, surrounded by a collection of small white bowls, the shape and size of rice wine cups. Saman identified their coloured contents: "Bean curry, pineapple curry, eggplant curry, dahl, and in the two smaller dishes, fried coconut potato cakes and mango chutney."

"It all looks delicious, is any of it hot?"

"Only a little chilli and a little mustard seed, you try, you tell me?" urged Saman.

Lionel broke the dome of rice with his fork and then poured the dahl into it.

"Delicious, so creamy."

"No cream here, sir, we are a vegan hotel."

"By choice?" Lionel smiled.

"Yes, sir, no tummies here."

"Could I lose weight here?"

"Of course, sir, no dairy, no meat: clears both your skin and your tummy."

"I'm nearly sixty years old and I'm happy with my skin but the older you get the more interested you become in your gut," said Lionel, stroking his flat stomach.

"That's age. Remember, happy gut, happy life," said Saman, tapping a little paunch. "What do you want to see while you are in Sri Lanka?"

"First, nothing but this view. Only when I tire of it do I want to explore what this country makes. Is all your furniture made locally?"

"It is, sir, and I know all the places where they come from."

"I really like those bamboo light shades."

"They are made here, sir."

"I love a workshop. When I started in the antiques business, every dealer of note had a restoration workshop."

"What's a restoration workshop, sir?"

"It's where furniture is repaired; replacing lost handles, polishing scratches out of tops and anything else that will help you get a better price."

"Our tables are teak. They are difficult to scratch."

"I can see that," said Lionel, pressing his thumb nail into the side of the table leg. More iron than wood, he thought.

"I will leave you now, just call one of my staff if you need anything." Saman brought out a phone from each of his trouser pockets, looked at both screens and then answered the ringing one.

Perfect, thought Lionel, Saman is a fixer!

🦎

Lionel made short work of the curry and repaired to bed. Eight hours later, he awoke to the rhythmic sound of crashing waves. After a couple of gulps from his bedside water glass, he was up and out, donning his swimming trunks. He walked through a small picket-fenced garden, over a connecting path, then squeezed between two beached fishing boats to arrive at the water's edge. It was a shallow bay with only ten yards between high and low tides. With the first wave Lionel stood still and then walked quickly with the pull of the backwash, just before a second wave sent him head over heels. He recovered on all fours before a third wave broke. Flopping sideways into this new wall of water, he swam under the wave, not daring to resurface, lest another separated his head from his body.

Once beyond the breakwater, Lionel could enjoy the relative coolness of the sea. Although powerful and constantly moving, the sea was crystal clear with a shell-strewn sandy floor. After a short swim he chose a weaker wave to come in on. Ascending the beach with as much dignity as the soft sand and crashing waves would allow, he found a powerful outside shower which removed the sand and salt from every crevice. Feeling very much alive, he made his way to the large palm-leaf-roofed pavilion that served as the restaurant-bar and general shady retreat. Seeing Lionel, Saman moved quickly from his bar stool and handed him a blue striped beach towel.

"Morning sir, did you sleep well?"

"Very well, only woken by the sound of the waves."

"Perfect, tea or coffee."

"Tea naturally, you must have some fine tea here?"

"We do sir, Ceylon tea is the very best."

A pot of tea appeared; this may have been achieved by a secret sign language or telepathy, as Saman neither spoke nor moved from Lionel's side. The tea was poured by Tahlina, a tall and smiley man in rectangular metal-framed glasses. There was no milk, nor offer of it, just lime. Lionel didn't always eat meat, perfectly happy with vegetables, but a day rarely passed without either egg, cheese or milk. The tea was lovely without a hint of bitterness on the finish. Breakfast was the choice of 'nut bowl', fruit and coconut yoghurt or bruschetta. His friend

Barty often served bruschetta, fondly saying, "Yesterday's bread with tomato, mozzarella, basil and olive oil. The Italian flag on old bread, surely a gift from the gods." He plumped for the bruschetta, again summoned without any verbal communication. Three minutes later a plate arrived with three pieces of toast; two with a mixture of finely chopped tomatoes and parsley and one with black olive tapenade. If this is what vegans have for breakfast, sign me up, he thought.

"Do you have any plans today?" Saman enquired as he passed Lionel's empty plate to the ever-present Tahlina.

"None, just a potter along the beach. Which way do you suggest: east or west?"

"We in the east often look to the west, I would say west, your path will be lit by the morning sun, the beach is wider and better that way."

"Right, to the west I will go."

🦎

Lionel didn't get too far before his path was interrupted by a wave intent on soaking him: not just his feet but his knees as well. He passed a restaurant with contemporary pink neon signs at odds with its beachfront, jammed with small working fishing boats. These fishermen provided live drama twice a day when they tackled the breakwater, judging the oncoming waves in their impossibly narrow boats with only a paddle for power and torpedo-shaped outrigger for balance.

On a wooden platform hung from a near-horizontal palm tree sat drinking fisherman. Ah, the players at rest. It would soon be the tourists' turn to provide the performance: walking, posing, swimming and surfing in their near-invisible beachwear. Up some roughly hewn steps, Lionel found himself on a raised coastal path behind concrete coastal defences on which were squeezed a couple of makeshift bars, boasting pizza ovens and glass-fronted fridges, but let down by 'sit-up and beg chairs', repurposed from wooden pallets ... ouch the splinters! Next, he walked beside the elegant grounds of a 1960s hotel with white-painted pavilions, teak porches and louvered blinds. To one corner of these grounds stood a large pavilion, held aloft by pairs of white-painted concrete pillars, the order of which is best described as Doric. Whilst he considered the elegance of this pavilion against the Vietnam vibe of its neighbouring bars his eyes were drawn to a poster.

'Now Yoga Begins' and pictured behind this statement a bearded man in T-shirt and shorts, striking a supple pose as befits 'enlightenment'. The poster read: 'Traditional yoga 8 to 9.45am' and 'Sunset yoga 5 to 6pm'. He had always quite fancied the idea of yoga but had never actually done it. His artist friend Pru and her two daughters were keen devotees, and they had lovely flat stomachs and elegant limbs to prove it. He considered the two options, 8 to 9.45am or 5 to 6pm; for a start, it might be best to go for just an hour, so the evening slot it would have to be. He continued west past the 'land-monitor' island. Beyond, suddenly the sand changed, finer and softer underfoot, stretching into a mile-long crescent-shaped bay, finished by another green headland.

He walked the tideline, his white skin attracting "hellos" from Sri Lankan men busily setting out sun loungers, tables and chairs. He walked all the way to the end, just short of a lush and rocky headland, before he was lured by an Italian 'Lavazza' coffee sign. He found a table under green shade, ordered a cappuccino, which arrived in a double espresso cup and saucer; it had just the right amount of bitterness. Within a day, he had chanced on the best positioned hotel and possibly the best coffee spot too. Luckily, they were at either end of a very long beach. He was definitely going to lose some weight here.

Chapter 6

Sri Lanka

Lionel arrived ten minutes before the evening yoga; he had managed to find a pair of red trunks with a little 'give' in them, and a T-shirt. He normally just wore linen shirts in the summer, but the T-shirt had been a present from the Brewing Brothers who leased part of Barty's Imperial pub. It was dark green with a stitched white monogram of BB on his left chest, the back printed with a stylised rainbow emerging from the Rolling Stones mouth, above which was printed 'Hastings Pride'. He nervously smiled at a small man sitting cross-legged on a yoga mat. To say cross-legged was to understate the position: he had seen Pru's daughters sitting cross-legged on kitchen chairs and had marvelled at their suppleness. But he had never seen a man assume one so similar to images of the Buddha. Toes, feet and legs all in unbroken straight lines. The 'lotus position' then spoke.

"Welcome. Please take a mat. Join me."

He pointed to a small pile of rolled plastic mats. Lionel chose a green one.

"You have the heart."

"I like the colour, the green green grass of home."

"In yoga, we speak of chakras and some have colours. Green is for the heart. Please sit now," said the bearded man.

As he struggled to lower his 6-foot 2-inch frame onto his 'heart'-coloured mat, he was questioned again.

"What is your name? My name is Kamal."

"My name is Lionel."

"I have never met a Lionel before, what does it mean?"

But before Lionel could answer, the beard continued, "Kamal is a Persian name, with a meaning: lotus, perfect or perfection."

Lionel pondered on how his parents knew he would become a yoga teacher, or was it a case of living up to his name?

"I know," an excited Kamal added with a huge smile, "Lionel Messi, football!"

Lionel smiled too: name-recognition certainly helped greatly by the world-famous Argentinian footballer. Before Messi, the best he could come up with was 'little lion', which seemed rather ridiculous coming from a taller than average sixty-year-old.

They were joined by two tall girls in their late twenties.

"Welcome," he repeated, "what are your names?"

Sasha said one, and Dasha said the other.

The two Russians rolled out their mats and straightened them without bending their knees. We haven't even started, and they are already bent double, thought Lionel. Kamal tapped the mobile phone next to him.

"It's 5 o'clock, let's start. Cross your legs, close your eyes and breathe through your nose."

As Sasha and Dasha folded their extremely long legs in a well-practised and perfect lotus position, Lionel felt a searing pain running along his left hamstring.

"Keep the open face and straight back," the beard said to

Lionel: crossing his legs and smiling was one task too many for him. Once he had vaguely assumed the desired position, he turned to see Sasha and Dasha: both perfectly still, eyes firmly closed. Lionel turned his head back to the beard and closed his eyes too. After what felt like an age, Kamal barked,

"Lionel, close your mouth. Through the nose only."

He had been too busy smiling, 'opening the face', to remember the breathing bit.

"The nose is for breathing and the mouth is for eating."

Again, he looked over to the perfectly formed Sasha and Dasha, and noticed small, rather smug, smiles. Smiles that he remembered from his school days, worn by the smarter children in the class who enjoyed the reprimanding of others. Lionel checked; his back, his mouth, his smile and his closed eyes. He was back in the game.

"Now we open the nose, short breath in and long breath out."

This, Kamal demonstrated with short sharp snorts, whilst reaching high above his head with his arms and grabbing the air with his hands. This was followed by pulling his arms down so his clenched fists momentarily paused either side of his chest. At first, Lionel tried to follow him, but Kamal was going far too fast. So he closed his eyes and found his own pumping rhythm, only stopping when he could no longer hear the snorts of others. He turned and saw the same smug smiles on Sasha and Dasha.

"Now with your right hand, close your first and middle finger," Lionel copied Kamal.

"Bring your open thumb to close your right nostril and breathe in and breathe out. With your next breath in roll your hand and block your left nostril with your third finger. The left nostril feeds the right side of the brain and the right nostril the left side of the brain. So we close the moon to feed the sun."

Lionel wanted to pick this up, but decided his question on the sun and the moon should wait.

Still sitting, Kamal then instructed the class to extend their legs straight and roll them from side to side to get the blood flowing.

Lionel went to unfurl his right leg, but it just wouldn't budge. He then tried the other one, but that wouldn't move either. He began to panic, he'd only been cross-legged for ten minutes, and now he had lost the use of both of his legs!

Kamal, reading the panic, rose with the easy action of a pair of scissors and pulled Lionel's legs straight.

"Roll them," Kamal barked.

As his legs moved, the pins and needles came. After a good two minutes, Lionel resumed the cross-legged position, but it was more dead dahlia than lotus.

"Close the eyes, open the face and empty the mind." *Empty the mind*, he thought ... with so many things to do – breathing through his nose, crossing his legs and all with his eyes closed – how long could an hour possibly be?

Chapter 7

London

Mercy left Fortnum & Mason's and headed for Piccadilly Circus. It was a bright day and the pavements weren't too crowded. After passing the Shaftesbury Memorial Fountain, with its legions of foreign tourists taking selfies, messaging 'in front of Eros'. Whereas they were, in fact, in front of Anteros, the god of selfless love. She wondered what the Victorian designer Sir Alfred Gilbert would have made of selfies in front of his 'selfless' bronze. She took a right by the corner of Lillywhites, downhill past the theatres on the Haymarket, across Trafalgar Square with its mighty column and even mightier passant lions. Unlike Sir Alfred Gilbert, Sir Edwin Landseer's lions have done exactly the same job since installation. Reminding a grateful nation of the heroism of Lord Nelson in defeating Napoleon's navy at the Battle of Trafalgar, as well as now providing climbing opportunities for foreign students.

Mercy walked down Northumberland Avenue, heading for the Hungerford footbridge over the River Thames. She was passed by numerous trains bearing people in and out of Charing Cross. Once on the south side she passed the National Theatre, Oxo Tower, Tate Modern, and lastly Shakespeare's Globe before turning south to her office in Southwark Street. Walking was normally thinking time but sometimes the sites of London were too distracting, especially on the rare occasions the sun shone on them. Only in the final minutes of her journey did she think of Ollie Croyd, the giant with curly black hair. He was certainly handsome – striking – impressive, even. He had a presence and a good sense of purpose. It was quite something to hold a record-breaking auction in a foreign land. She had met many junior bankers through her father and sister. Most were good-looking, all were ambitious, but for her, there was little mutual ground. She didn't use spreadsheets, she used words. She liked the fact that Ollie Croyd had read History of Art at Exeter rather than International Statistics at University College London. She also liked that he was forward with his invitation to 'a drink after work,' a busy man seizing opportunities. After all, it would've been easier for him to have deferred the pink vases from Hastings to a scheduled sale six months later, but both fashions and politics change quickly, especially in a place such as Hong Kong. Mercy knew her mother Rose would fuss over Ollie and that her father would be impressed too.

After a brief exchange with her new boss, Anthony, she sat at a desk and checked her messages. Two from her mother, one from her sister, and one from Ollie Croyd. Mercy read Ollie's first.

'Would a drink tomorrow, Tuesday, be possible? Will come near you.'

Mercy replied, 'Perfect will be free at 6.30pm.'

Almost instantly another message arrived, 'The Swan at the Globe Theatre at 6.45pm? Rgds Ollie.'

Holding her breath and counting to ten, she replied 'See you there.' Then she read her other messages.

'Good luck in your new job xxx sis.'

'Good luck my gorgeous girl xxx Mum.'

'P.S. Remember to eat!!! Mum.'

Mercy sent heart-shaped emojis to all three messages and then removed her laptop from a large, tan-coloured Mulberry bag.

The bag was a present from her parents and the laptop one to herself. After using only a laptop at uni, she was more at home with a flat keyboard, the knobbly keys of a desktop seemed too old-fashioned. She would use the desktop computer on her new desk for reference and the laptop for writing. She started to draft a report on the record-breaking Hong Kong sale, but wouldn't file it with Anthony until after she had seen Ollie Croyd again. He had already let slip that the pair of pink vases had come from Hastings, and suspected that they may have been part of a house clearance. This, Ollie inferred by the manner in which they were consigned, by a third-party in a rather awkward old brown Austin Maxi. Further, it was a one-off consignment from an unknown dealer. Ollie obviously knew the identity of the seller, but he had said he hadn't met him. She thought: I bet Barty Hix might know him.

🦎

Mercy was psyched about her after-work drink, or as her mother had excitedly informed her father, her 'after-works date'. Back at home and with supper over, she asked Grace and her mother to help her choose an outfit. First, a tailored black jacket and trousers.

"You're not off to an interview," said Rose. "You want to turn heads. Now, with your colouring ..."

At this, both Mercy and Grace groaned. Their mother had always seen her colour as an invitation to wear bright clothes.

"Come on, something hotter," urged Rose, meaning colour and not cut. The girls began giggling.

Grace held up an orange dress. "Now, *that's* hot."

Rose nodded in agreement. "Try it on."

Mercy removed the jacket and trousers and reached for the hanger.

"I'll do that. Come on, we want to see this dress on, you can't keep a mother waiting."

Mercy's beautiful brown skin seemed to intensify the orange, and the dress was definitely cut for her.

"You look fab," said Grace.

"Give your mother a twirl."

"Wow," said her father from the bedroom door. "Who is this man?"

Mercy had had enough.

"Come on, out," said Grace, gently pushing her mother through the door before turning to her sister.

"You know she is probably just as excited as you are."

"I know, but sometimes it's just suffocating."

"What's he like?"

"He's tall."

"How tall?"

"Basketball tall, he almost brushes the chandeliers at Fortnum's."

"Wow, that tall. Is he handsome?"

"He's striking, rather unusual, with a big mop of curly hair."

"He sounds like a Greek god. Remember it never ends well, when the gods play with mortals."

"I don't think he's a god, but who knows?"

"Remember," said Grace, "don't bring him back here too early. By the sound of him, mum won't let him go! She'll have you down the aisle before the week is out."

"Grace, it's just a drink after work."

"Sounds like a date to me, I'm with mum on this one."

"Should I wear the orange dress?"

"It's made for you. Good luck. Dad and I are off early to Bristol. He wants to chivvy up the team on some new trading software. I wouldn't hurry home tomorrow, too many questions."

"Good night sis."

The next day was busy writing up more sales reports. Most were easy: as Anthony rightly said, auctioneers do like talking about themselves. Mercy had spoken to one in Plymouth who seemed delighted with five lots making over four figures; a serpentine mahogany commode had made more than £5,000. One in Derbyshire had a string of four-figure lots and two which made over £10,000; a 4-carat solitaire diamond ring and a cased platinum and diamond tiara at £25,000. Both had come from a local lady, whose mother had lived a much more glamorous life than her daughter. As that auctioneer succinctly said, it was no longer required, or even advisable, to wear jewellery like that for dinner at the Midland Hotel in Derby. The day passed quickly, and soon it was time to leave. Mercy had managed to miss her school trip to Shakespeare's Globe Theatre. Although she had walked past it so many times on the Southbank, she had never actually made the time to venture in. There is something rather extraordinary about round buildings. She was yet to own a house, let alone build one, but she did understand why the Globe and the Gherkin were so unusual, as they were both in the round.

Ollie had arrived early to secure a table looking towards St Paul's Cathedral. He made sure that he had a couple of glasses of water and clear sight of the main door. When Mercy walked in, he saw the heads of others turn. She looked taller and wore a warm orange dress, revealing a figure that could confidently sashay through a restaurant.

Mercy's heart was pounding. 'Head up,' her mother would've said, 'round shoulders in that dress just aren't going to work, shoulders back girl.' She kept walking through the tables until a mop of curly black hair started rising and rising. Then she saw his broad smile and suddenly everybody else in the room faded away.

He greeted her formally with an outstretched hand; after all, it was 'after-work drinks'.

"What would you like to drink?" asked Ollie.

"A glass of wine, please."

"White, red or rosé?"

"Rosé, please."

Ollie looked towards the bar, and met the eyes of one of the two waitresses watching. When she approached, he handed her a drinks menu, pointing at an item at the bottom of the list.

"Have you written the auction report yet?" he asked as they sat down.

"Almost, but there are a couple of questions I wanted to ask you."

"Fire away."

"The vases you say were delivered to you in an Austin Maxi by a man from Hastings and you mentioned a house clearance?"

"My world, although international, is an extremely narrow one. Collecting Chinese and Japanese porcelain and works of art, be they swords, suits of armour, lacquer etc., has generally been the preserve of the very wealthy, and these items are normally housed in palaces, country houses or city mansion apartments. Only on death or in straitened times do they fall into the hands of museums, auctioneers or dealers, but occasionally items have been given to family, friends and old retainers."

"Old retainers?" Mercy asked.

"Servants and staff, people who are paid to look after other people. They tend to get attached to those who look after them, especially the elderly, as they may be the only people they see day in, day out."

"Do you think the vases came by this route?"

Ollie was about to reply, but was interrupted by the waitress holding a shiny chromium-plated ice bucket and two glasses. She then showed Ollie the bottle. It was unusual, mallet-shaped. After four years at the *Antiques Trade Gazette* Mercy was beginning to pick up descriptive terms. After cutting the foil and pulling the cork, the waitress gave a little to Ollie to try.

"Perfect, pour away," he said, turning back to Mercy.

"To your new job," Ollie toasted.

"This is lovely."

"It's Mireval, made in the south of France by Brad Pitt. When I say made by Brad Pitt, I mean he developed the winery on the Mireval estate, and I'm sure he has had a hand in making this."

Style as well as looks, Mercy mused.

"Is it rare to find something so special, such as a pair of multi-million-pound pink vases, in a house clearance?"

"It certainly is in a pub."

"Pub?" Mercy said with a hidden smile. She was beginning to get a strap line for her auction report.

"Yes, the seller found the vases in a pub. Why are you so interested?"

"My interest lies in Hastings; may I tell you a story?"

"I'm intrigued, go on."

"The story is about a stolen bronze from a country house in Norfolk. It was a quarter-sized bronze of a real-life racehorse and jockey, and I'm sure the owner won't mind me revealing his identity. The owner was, and remains, Sir Roger Swotter of Kooling Towers near Holt. He contacted me when I was working at the 'Stolen' desk of the *Gazette*, first reporting the theft and soon afterwards offering a reward of £1,000 for information leading to its recovery. Following the thefts publication I received a call from a man in Hastings who wanted to check the bronze's measurements."

"That sounds odd."

"It was odd, enough for Brighton's Police Antique and Stolen Goods Squad to question him."

"Did anything come of it?"

"Yes, but not in the normal sense of recovery. I was so intrigued that I went with my mother up to an annual charity cricket match at Kooling Towers, and during the course of the day, we discovered that the bronze had been returned to its original plinth."

"Remarkable."

"It certainly was, but the most extraordinary thing was that the first prize in the raffle, a Magnum of rosé wine, was given by the same man in Hastings."

"Does this man have a name?"

"Yes he does, a Mr Barty Hix."

As Mercy gave the name, she carefully watched Ollie's face; it didn't alter. Not the reaction she had hoped for. But maybe now was the right time to give Barty Hix a courtesy call, to say that the stolen bronze had been happily returned to its Norfolk country house. Hastings seemed to be busy again!

Chapter 8

Mirissa

"Have you finished your breakfast, sir?" Saman inquired. "It's cookery lesson time, I have arranged a tuk tuk. Jazzy will take you to the teacher lady. The lady owner mixes and sells spices. She is a good cook and very fast."

"Fast is good. I have a friend at home in England who is a chef. He makes me food all the time, it would be good to surprise him and return the favour."

No sooner had Lionel lowered his coffee cup then a hovering Tahlini removed it. Saman made sure no Tuk tuk drivers, delivery men or tradesmen were allowed beyond the till area, lest they stood and stared at his scantily-clad hotel guests.

"Mr Lionel, this is Jazzy."

Jazzy shook Lionel's right hand whilst he gently touched his upper arm with his left hand. Lionel had noticed this before; it seemed to be a courtesy extended to foreigners.

"Good to meet you sir," said the driver. Unlike Saman, he was unusually tall, with a darker complexion and shaved head. He might have made a good Bond villain if it wasn't for his broad smile.

Saman spoke quickly to Jazzy in Sinhalese, and Lionel was ushered towards the tuk tuk's rear bench seat, through an opening that could be confused with a food hatch. The yoga lesson had been timely. He took a deep breath through his nose and eased himself in with the partial grace of Sasha and Dasha.

"You are going to spice lady? You will enjoy the food there."

"She will teach you well, and remember to eat some meat!" said Saman with a smile as he patted the roof of the tuk tuk, much as you might a horse's backside. Before Lionel had the opportunity to reply to either party, he was whisked away up the pink granite drive, through the opening of the hotel's pink walls and onto the busy high street. Tuk tuks are lowly vehicles in the pecking order of Sri Lankan roads, above dogs, pedestrians and bicycles, and below scooters, cars and lorries, but all are below the primate of the road, the bus. Whereas in England buses are seen as something to pass, buses in Sri Lanka do the passing, and they do so at a frightening speed.

Jazzy kept a steady path on the nearside, allowing tooting buses and cars to overtake whilst the scooters swarmed all around. Both sides of the road had various shops and restaurants. The shops principally for clothing: T-shirts and voluminous yoga pants, oft seen on returning gap year students. The roadside restaurants announced rice and curry, grilled fish and prawns alongside lurid pictures of sweating burgers.

After five minutes, Jazzy pulled off the high street outside what could be best described as a gap between two small plate-glass fronted shops, one boasting whale watching trips, the other an abandoned restaurant. As Lionel unfurled himself from the back, Jazzy beckoned him into the ten-foot-wide-gap-cum-driveway, its white-painted concrete block boundary walls softened with jasmine hedging and climbing pink bougainvillea. On the crushed grey granite drive stood an old-fashioned sit up and beg bicycle and a modern black and white Honda Navi motorbike, a modern version of the classic Monkey bike.

"Come this way, sir," Jazzy urged, as he walked through an enclosed area furnished with three rectangular hardwood tables and brown plastic chairs. Beyond was a white porcelain sink with matching pedestal stand, a sort of domestic 'eye-catcher' at odds with the lush green garden. You can't argue against the merits of hand washing; it's obviously an outside activity here in Sri Lanka, thought Lionel. Before the garden and its freestanding sink was an open door beside a large shop window. A circular table dominated the interior of the shop, on which stood an industrial chromium plated grinder; the interior of the mixer was stained with a red powder ... chilli, thought Lionel. Behind the table was a dresser base on which was a range of thirty or so lidded plastic jars, reminiscent of an old-fashioned sweet shop but. each containing different spices. As he marvelled at their range, a woman with a broad smile approached. She looked to be almost sixty, well dressed in a red and black floral printed skirt and low-cut red top. A pair of black framed glasses and gold knot earrings completed her look. She had clearly dressed up for Lionel's cookery lesson.

"Come, come, I have three kitchens," she said.

Jazzy bid Lionel farewell. "I will be back in two hours, sir."

"Come, come," the lady beckoned Lionel to the rear of the spice shop. Through the door, he was confronted by a bare set of concrete steps. Open on both sides with no handrails or tiles to the treads, it just floated to another storey with no obvious signs of support, having a 'builders just upped and left' vibe. The layout of the kitchen was simple: a concrete worktop housing a sink with a white enamel mixer tap alongside a free-standing two-ring gas burner connected by orange hose to a 15kg blue gas bottle on the shelf below. The rest of the top shelf was peopled by a variety of pans, bowls and other cooking implements, some of which were clean. After finding Lionel a glass and a cold bottle of water, the lesson began.

"Vegetable curry," she almost shouted.

Lionel was unsure whether this was a statement or an action. On a shallow chromium-plated metal dish, similar to a 1960s car hubcap, lay a rather forlorn bunch of vegetables: green beans, carrots, a white cucumber, white radishes, and a long white/green thing, similar to a rigid snake.

She pointed to the green beans and carefully broke them in two, discarding any spoiled ends. He, unlike his best friend the chef, wasn't a natural cook but was methodical and enjoyed simple tasks. His instructor now cut carrots with a rather unusual steel blade, held at either end on a heavy rectangular stand, like a Regency boot scraper. She then tackled the white cucumber, taking out the seeds, then grating the radishes. Lionel had to step aside, pressing against the floating steps as she moved from blade to gas ring. She placed a clean, rounded pan on the burner and turned the knob to ignite the flame, taking a plastic bottle and pouring in a measure of cooking oil.

"Best coconut oil," she announced.

Then she took a jam jar, unscrewed its lid and sprinkled in half a teaspoon of a dry mixture.

"Mustard seed with cumin." She did the same with another jam jar.

"Fenugreek, good for the heart." Saying this whilst tapping her chest to confirm the heart's location. She squeezed past Lionel again, as he filled the tight space between the steps and the concrete kitchen worktop. She gathered the cut vegetables and started pushing her items into the pan. In went the carrots, tomatoes, green beans, ten or twelve curry leaves, half a red onion and four bruised garlic cloves, finishing with half a teaspoon of salt, curry powder, mustard powder and turmeric. "Turmeric is for the colour."

She mixed all the contents of the bowl with a coconut spoon on a high heat. After no more than three minutes, she added half a cup of water. On the rare occasions Lionel cooked at home, he always steamed his vegetables in a sieve above a pan of boiling water, adding only a pinch of salt. As far as he could work out, she had added at least ten different elements to the pan. She was making curry as one might make a stir fry, fast and furious. After another three minutes, she added some 'best' coconut milk, then checked progress by lifting a section of carrot with her coconut spoon, dabbing it onto her open left palm, then licking it up before deciding to add more salt.

"You like to try?" she asked, lifting another piece and placing the scalding vegetable in Lionel's left hand. The carrot was cooked to perfection and the sauce was so creamy.

"Amazing, so quick and perfectly cooked."

"I learnt this style of cooking in Singapore, I was a nurse there for four years."

"I thought it had a touch of stir-fry."

"Cook quickly, keeps both taste and colour," she said with a broad smile.

Lionel thought of his friend Barty. He always cooked by the colours of the Italian flag. Well, in Sri Lanka they add another colour, the yellow of turmeric; as he mused, his cookery teacher was on to the next dish.

"Okra, you like okra?"

Lionel had no thoughts on okra, probably because he didn't know what it was. It looked like a geometric courgette. She cut it into diagonal sections, using her sharp bladed 'boot scraper.' She placed a deeper, rounded-bottom bowl on the gas ring and turned it to high. As before, in went the coconut oil followed by the okra, tomatoes, half a red onion, four garlic cloves, curry leaves, plus all the same spices except for the mustard powder. He was about to ask why, but thought better of it, as she was moving so fast.

"Cook for only five minutes."

Although everything went very quickly, Lionel was left pulverised as he had tried to record all the various steps by both pen and paper and phone camera. He hoped he had it all, if he was to successfully repeat this at home. Like all good cookery lessons, the proof is in the eating. It was heaven on a plate; Barty might be impressed.

Chapter 9
Mirissa & Kandy

It only took a couple of days for Lionel to fall into a slower routine. The normal start of 6am became 8am. The walk to the Hastings shops for his daily newspaper and pork pie was replaced with a swim. The breakfast bacon sandwich became a plate of fruit and coconut curd. Morning walks and negotiations with Norman to buy antiques metamorphosed into tuk tuk journeys to potteries, furniture makers and fabric shops. Lunch at the Horse and Groom with one of June's pies was now rice and curry on the beach among palm trees and the barely clothed. Even the white Burgundy was swapped for cold bottles of Lion beer. The newspaper and *Gazette* were exchanged for tomes of P. G. Wodehouse. At home on the south coast, he always had a bedside book on the go, but by the time he was ready for bed he could barely keep his eyes open. On the rare occasions he couldn't sleep, he might manage a chapter. Saman was looking after him far too well, steering him to hidden shops in the larger neighbouring town of Matara, but there was something missing, and that was culture. He needed to get to a city where he could wander amongst temples and parks.

"Saman, I think I need to travel, a bit of your culture and sightseeing."

"There is Colombo, our new capital city, sir. Sigiriya or Anuradhapura, and then there is the Royal City of Kandy."

"Why Royal City?"

"It is where our last king lived before he was overthrown by the British. It's built around a lake and there are many temples, shops and hotels. My brother is the general manager of an old hotel in Kings Street. You will like it, sir, it is called the Royal Bar and Hotel and it's very British. After school my brother and I left Sri Lanka to work in Dubai. We had little at the beginning, but willingness to learn. Dubai was growing quickly and we worked for ambitious men who entrusted us with ever greater responsibilities. We ended up as heads of concierge desks, it was difficult for Sri Lankans to become general managers then. It was good pay, we soon learned to turn requests into reality, the tips were fabulous. My brother Lysanta will look after you well up there and point you in all the right directions, sir."

"Is Kandy far?"

"It's four to five hours by taxi, and longer by bus."

"I don't think I'm built for your buses."

"When would you like to go?"

"Today, please."

"I will arrange it sir, maybe travel after lunch to arrive at 7pm?"

"Perfect Saman, arrange away please."

"It's what I do best, sir." Saman left, pulling both phones from his back pockets. One for 'general manager', one for 'concierge' thought Lionel, returning to his room to retrieve a couple of books – a Lonely Planet guide and a historical tour of Sri Lanka. Properly prepped, as Barty always extolled, one might get the most from any trip. Having read the relevant chapters, he was looking forward to seeing the city built by the last king, Sri Vikrama Rajasinha. A builder of palaces, just like our Prince Regent but bloodier. Lots of impaling on sharpened stakes and heads crushed by elephant's feet!

At lunch, Saman talked Lionel through the arrangements made on his behalf. "Your taxi will come at 3pm, sir. I would pack for three days. Would you like me to store your other bags?"

"That would be kind. Tell me Saman, is Kandy hotter or cooler than the beach?"

"It's in the hills, so cooler, sir. Take a jacket — it being a Royal City, it's more formal. I have asked my brother to lend you an umbrella. It will be useful under the rain trees around the lake as there are many shitting fruit bats and birds, sir. Also the umbrella will be useful against the sun and street vendors!"

"Luckily, I have my Panama hat too. In England we have a saying, 'if you want to get ahead, get a hat'."

"Very true sir, but for me, it is the beard." At which he gave a broad smile and a loving stroke of his manly growth.

Lionel had intended to gently doze in the back of the taxi, but what was happening outside was just too fascinating. When on small roads, it was the people, the shops, the temples that drew his attention, but on the relatively empty two-lane express ways it became the ever-changing landscape. All plants and trees seemed to bear fruit and every paddy field was worked by people, oxen and white cranes. He thought this must have been what life was like before tractors. On their approach to the city, the streets got busier with more shops and people. The rather monosyllabic taxi driver alerted Lionel that they were very close now to the hotel.

"Before we get there, would you drive around the lake?" asked Lionel.

"Of course, sir. Have you come to visit the tooth?"

Lionel had read that Kandy was an important place of pilgrimage for Buddhists, as within the former royal palace there is housed the final resting place of their 'sacred tooth'. History relates that it was snatched from Buddha's funeral pyre and smuggled in the hair of a Sri Lankan princess to Kandy where this sacred relic has been since the 4th century.

"I'm here to sightsee," replied Lionel, as the taxi crossed a set of traffic lights and turned right. To his left he could now see the white-painted frilly wall that enclosed the lake. As they travelled around, he got his bearings, noticing the many hotels on his right, with large rain trees shrouding the black waters of the lake on his left. They circled the top end, returning towards the large palace complex with its distinctive Queen's Bathing House straddling the water. Onwards they went, taking the road around the old palace and the Anglican church of St Paul's, a little piece of England with its castellated church tower sitting amongst the domes of the white and golden temples.

As the taxi drew up outside Lionel's new hotel, a guard in brown trousers and lighter brown shirt complete with military-style shoulder cord moved towards his door.

"Welcome to the Royal Hotel, sir. Please, I will attend to your luggage."

It was lucky that Lionel had already paid and tipped the driver as the security man was directing him with the sort of irritation that a regimental sergeant might inflict on a lowly recruit.

Lionel walked up three shallow steps with polished brass noses on to a shaded landing from which led four arched doorways. Three served a downstairs bar, and the fourth took him past a long hall table into a large open courtyard, surrounded by a string of white-painted columns supporting a balconied first floor. The stone-floored courtyard was shaded by two large trees that climbed above the sloping roman tiled roofs. Lionel's acclimatisation was interrupted.

"We have one of our best rooms for you, sir, reserved by my brother." said a small bald man with no beard.

"You must be Lysanta. I have heard only good about you."

"My brother, sir, talks too much. Here in Kandy we are more careful," he said with a smile just like Saman's. "Follow me please, sir."

Lysanta led Lionel across a courtyard, through a large archway, passing a 'Hotel Guests Only' sign. Up a flight of steps to an open corridor with a run of red-painted bedroom doors. They stopped at number 7.

"We call this room '007', the James Bond suite, sir."

"Your hotel has that feel, Lysanta."

"Thank you, sir."

Lysanta unlocked the red door with a large brass key. Neither too large nor too small, the bedroom had a high double bed hung with white mosquito netting.

"In here, sir." Lysanta beckoned Lionel through a narrower pair of panelled doors.

"A bath!" exclaimed Lionel.

"Next best thing to a swimming pool, you might need this after a day at the temples. Would you like dinner with us, sir?"

"Yes, that would be good, but first I must unpack."

"No need, sir, the houseboy will do that."

"Marvellous, well in that case lead me to your bar. What do you Kandyans drink?"

"The Arrack Attack, sir. Arrack, ginger ale and fresh mint, but here at the Royal we mix it half with ginger ale and soda, then it's not so sweet."

The restaurant was an airy square room centred around a white baby grand piano, beyond which were four arched openings, on which hung pairs of part-glazed doors below fan-shaped lights, and to his left was a well-stocked bar, above which hung a pair of British army officers' swords between a pair of circular mechanical dial clocks; both had engraved brass plaques, one titled 'Ceylon' and the other 'Great Britain'. Plus, for the avoidance of any doubt that this was once a hotel serving Sri Lanka's old British community, there was a series of Union Jack-carved wooden panels above the bar's brass foot rail.

Lysanta, who had been following his eyes, said, "Welcome home, sir."

Chapter 10

Kandy

Lionel didn't sleep as well in Kandy as he had by the coast. Whether it was a lack of sea air or physical exhaustion from swimming, or possibly the two Arrack Attacks and wine at supper, he awoke at 5:30am dressed and was out before 6am. Lysanta had left a rather smart Malacca-handled black umbrella outside his room. On leaving the now quiet hotel, he exchanged a formal greeting with the ever-present uniformed security man.

"Good morning, sir. For the lake, turn left out of the hotel and take the first street on your right."

"Good morning. How did you know I was heading to the lake?"

"The umbrella, sir. Best raised under the rain trees, as there are too many bats and birds," he said, with the most cautious of smiles.

Touching the brim of his Panama hat, Lionel strode off, assured he was properly equipped for what lay ahead. Following his nose, he walked along lightly peopled pavements, crossing the road at the corner of the Queen's Hotel. Once through the bag-searching security of the gatehouse he was literally carried by a tide of pilgrims, monks and tourists towards the temple complex. He found an empty bench by a moat that guarded the octagonal library, built by the last King, Sri Vikrama Rajnsinha.

Everywhere there was a different-shaped building, all painted in white, some with golden finials, mostly devotional, some for pleasure. Like the Queen's Bathing House, an extraordinary building with an oversized tiled roof supported on fluted columns rising from the water. He passed the gold-roofed temple housing the sacred tooth, through more security and then onto a more 'secular' path around the lake. It took him an hour to complete the entire circumference and return to his hotel, where he exchanged greetings with Lysanta.

"It's quite a walk around the lake, no?"

"It certainly builds an appetite."

"Shall I bring you fruit and eggs?"

"Perfect."

"Fried, scrambled or poached?"

"Like James Bond, scrambled please, and some tea."

"Coming straight away, sir."

After a lovely plate of fruit with buffalo curd and honey, which included the most glorious mango, Lionel made light work of his scrambled eggs on toast.

"My brother tells me you are here for culture and antiques. So I have arranged for a senior tuk tuk driver to show you the very best of our Royal City. I have asked him not to take you to any tourist traps, is there anything in particular that you would like to see, sir?"

"Yes, your Botanic Gardens, and the antique shops of Kandy, not necessarily all today!"

"I would suggest shopping in the morning whilst it's cooler and the gardens in the afternoon. Would you like some coffee before you leave?"

"Yes please."

"Americano or cappuccino?"

"Something frothy please, a cappuccino."

"When you have finished, please come down to the courtyard, and I will introduce you to your driver, sir."

Lionel briefly returned to his room to change his rather heavy polo shirt for a lighter linen one. He found Lysanta talking to a tall man with a David Niven-like moustache who wore a white linen shirt over a pair of navy-blue trousers and leather sandals. He had a simple elegance.

"Mr Lionel, this is Chris. He will show you our city."

Lionel extended a hand, which was taken gently but firmly.

With the weather set fair, Chris had removed the rolled-up plastic doors of the tuk tuk, which denied taller passengers a passing view. Once Lionel had rearranged his legs in the back, Chris turned around and spoke.

"Lysanta has suggested we go to a large antique shop near the Botanic Gardens in Peredeniya, it's a twenty-minute journey and we can stop off at the Kandy War Cemetery?"

"I'm in your hands." Lionel replied.

"Very good, sir."

Chris moved off at a steady pace; his tuk tuk was basic, but his engine had a steady rhythmic sound. There were no crunching of gears or occasional engine gasps that Lionel had heard in other tuk tuks whose drivers were generally smaller, potbellied and quite often sullen. There was an assuredness in Chris that elevated him from most three-wheeler drivers. After turning off the Kandy Road they wound their way down a quieter one, before Chris pulled over, cut the engine and turned towards Lionel.

"Here, sir, is the tamarind tree."

Lionel unravelled himself from the back seat through the narrow opening.

"You must try this Mr Lionel?"

He took the squashed, cherry-sized fruit and tasted it. It was strong. Something that Barty would turn into a jam or chutney.

"A sharp taste and delicious."

"Look, here on the trunk, Mr Lionel."

Chris pulled a vine from the trunk, and beneath a veined oval shaped leaf was a 3-inch tail of tightly packed green seeds.

"Guess what this is?"

"No idea."

"This is black pepper, sir."

"Extraordinary. Do you know I don't think that I have ever seen a growing pepper before and it's the most widely used spice in the world."

Lionel had occasionally accompanied Barty on foraging expeditions at the upper end of Hastings' Alexandra Park, picking baskets full of wild garlic and sometimes chanterelle mushrooms, but he had never pulled off the road and tasted such fruit or seen a glossy green pepper pod. This was a truly extraordinary country that seemed to have it all.

After another couple of corners, Chris crossed the road. To Lionel's right was a metal railing fence guarding a very well-tended cemetery.

"Here, sir, brave men lie."

Lionel walked through a black-painted wrought-iron kissing gate and stepped onto a well-mown lawn in the shallow fold of a hill. Arranged before him were rows of white headstones, each carved with the recipient's regimental badge, their name, their regiment's name, date of death and age. It was the sobering ages that drew Lionel's attention, twenty-three, twenty-one and even twenty years old. But it was the unnamed headstones that prompted gulps from Lionel: 'Known Unto God,' those three clever words, phrased by the great author Sir Rudyard Kipling, hastened his departure. It was a regardful man who furled back into the three-wheeler. Chris decided not to speak and eased the brake off to use a rolling start to bump the engine back to life. They descended the hill and crossed slowly over a metal suspension bridge. Once over the river, Chris again pulled over and turned to Lionel.

"There are men on the rafts today, it is unusual."

"I didn't see them," said a bemused Lionel.

"Come with me, Mr Lionel, please."

Chris led the way to the middle of the bridge, and there in the distance before a bend in the river were two rafts.

"What are they doing?"

"They are digging for sand."

"In the river."

"Yes, sir. Can you see they have a long pole?"

"I can."

"Well, at the end of the metal pole is a triangular shaped bucket with which they scoop for sand and hopefully, gemstones. There are many gems on the riverbed, but they are generally small."

"How many men are on each raft?"

"Normally four men; one scooping, two sifting the sand, and one to punt the raft."

"What do they do with the sand?"

"The sand is sold as building sand because the river water has no salt, unlike the beach."

"Hard work sifting sand."

"Dangerous, Mr Lionel, as there are many crocodiles in the river."

"What sort of gems do they find? Any sapphires?"

"Rarely, mainly topaz. I can take you to a gem store and they will show you all the different gemstones you might find here."

"Sounds like a tourist trap, Chris."

"It is, but it is very interesting, and it's just up the hill here."

"OK, I would like to go and see this gem store, but first I'd like a king coconut."

"Very good, sir."

Minutes later, Chris and Lionel were drinking the largest and cheapest king coconut without a straw.

"This is how we drink them now as too much plastic with the straws, sir."

Duly refreshed, Lionel was delivered to the reception of a large industrial building to take part in a well-practiced routine. First came a ten-minute video, showing the mining process, digging a vertical shaft 10 to 15 metres, and then following the sedimentary seams, i.e. old riverbeds. It starred a rather pleased owner, supervising the work of thin and sweaty men. He was wearing large gold jewellery, his men were bare chested with muddy knotted sarongs. Next, Lionel was ushered into the gem-cutting and setting rooms, finally up to another floor, a large windowless showroom. At its entrance stood glass cabinets, each with semi and precious stones graded by colour. Then on to a vast jewellery store with many illuminated counter display cabinets, all manned by smiling sales staff, randomly dotted by excited women making noises over tray upon tray of bright but small stones sitting with rather anxious-looking men.

"Chris you're right, it was interesting, but much too new, let's move on to an antique shop now, please."

Chapter 11
Kandy

The antique shop was a ten-minute ride in the direction of the Royal Botanic Gardens in Peradeniya. The outside looked promising, with many items on the pavement. The neighbourhood was busy but scruffy; mechanical and electrical repairers, vegetable stores, poultry shops, a kaleidoscope of shops meeting the needs of its people. Back in England, antique dealers are often the colonisers of rundown areas; way before an artisan baker opens, there will be at least two or three antique shops taking advantage of cheap rents and freeholds frequently opening in former hardware stores, butcher shops or pharmacies. Maybe it's the mosaic thresholds that call these decorative dealers. The shop in front of Lionel was no different. It had three large metal-shuttered openings from which spewed random objects. A stack of massive aluminium pans measuring a good three foot in diameter with brightly polished brass handles, big enough to boil sheets and possibly, he thought, the odd missionary! There was a row of doors: at home, these would be four- or six-panelled painted or stripped pine doors. Here, the doors were hardwood with many fielded panels or louvered. In Europe a door's principal purpose is to secure a space, and its secondary job is to exclude draughts.

In Sri Lanka, draughts are deemed imperative and seen as good ventilation. Whilst Lionel picked his way through assorted baskets of china and metalware, he noticed a small elderly man in a sand-coloured tropical suit, the sort with bellow pockets and study buttons. This was the kind of clothing that would survive a day's trek through a jungle or a rummage through this jumble. The tropical suit smiled at Lionel.

"Have you come from afar?"

"Yes, from England."

"Where in England?" enquired the man in almost perfect English.

"Below London on the south coast in a town called Hastings."

"Very good, I have been there, many years ago. 1972 with my mother visiting her sister. My aunt was an ayah to a family in Rye, they had once been shippers with a presence in both Colombo and Trincomalee."

"Can you remember your visit?"

"Like yesterday. My aunt's family lived in an old house in West Street, it was full of antiques. It may have been the reason why I'm immersed in them today. Would you like some tea? I have a rather special one sent to me from the Mackwood estate in Nuwara Eliya."

"That would be lovely, but I don't want to put you out."

"Not at all, it's nice having a customer from England in my shop." He rang a rather large hand bell.

"Let me introduce myself, my name is Lionel, and I'm also an antique dealer."

"My name is Ashok, and this is my granddaughter, Amelia."

Unbeknown to Lionel, a young woman had silently approached.

"She helps me in the shop after school. It works well, when the shop's quiet she can do her homework, and I have precious hours with my granddaughter. It means her mother, my daughter, can work without rushing back home. It's good old-fashioned teamwork, we look after each other whilst my daughter can do her own job, without the worry of being somewhere else. Would you like milk or lime in your tea?"

"I will try the lime, please."

With this, his granddaughter left as silently as she had come.

"Are you looking for anything in particular?"

"Bargains, of course!"

"What do you sell in Hastings?"

"I sell items that would look good in grand houses. Items often collected from abroad that show guests they're in the company of worldly people. I have sold many silver souvenir dishes in the shape of Ceylon and quite a few porcupine quill boxes."

"We have many of those, but first please have a rummage, as you English say."

"I will, is everything on this floor?"

"Yes," he said with a smile.

Lionel turned away and switched into search mode. He normally went around a shop clockwise, but there was no easy path in this store. What surprised him was that everything was so clean. Normally, an elderly dealer went down with his stock, often clinging to both prices and goods that were no longer relevant. Here, probably because everything was so well-polished, it all looked like fresh stock. He felt the weight of a pair of louvred doors by carefully tilting them off centre. They were very similar to the doors in the Royal Bar and Hotel and would make splendid internal doors to his house back in Hastings. He picked his way through baskets, bamboo tables, rattan lights, all manner of metalware. While he weighed an

8-inch bronze figure of a girl in his hands, he became aware of a silent figure.

"My grandfather would like you to join him for tea," said this very poised girl.

"You have good English."

"Grandpa has spoken only English to me since I was born. Please, come this way."

Lionel followed her as she glided through the shop, passing her grandfather's desk, then through a pair of doors where he was immediately enveloped by the cooler air of a courtyard. It had the feel of a cloister with shallow arched openings held aloft on circular teak pillars, between which were robust teak benches. She led Lionel to the shady side where Mr Ashok sat in an old rattan chair. It was well worn, and obviously comfortable; without standing he motioned towards a similar chair for Lionel.

"I have a good side and a bad side with my hearing. On this side, I have the ears of an elephant, but on the other I have the hearing of a husband who doesn't want to listen."

"Is your wife here?"

"No, she died some years ago."

"Oh, I'm sorry to hear that."

"Please don't be. We had a great life together, along with the bonus of having a daughter. She is the one who cleans my stock and is occasionally helped by Amelia. I'm very lucky, three generations under one roof."

"You are indeed. I have no children," said a momentarily thoughtful Lionel, who was warming to this generous man.

"But, you have been married?"

"Yes, twice, but stupidly I put work ahead of home. I wish now that I had struck a better balance."

Lionel had only just met this man, and yet he felt suddenly confessional. It was probably the shared interest in antiques ... or was it his gentle listening manner? Lionel had always fancied himself in a tropical suit, so many useful pockets. While he was ruminating which pocket would house his phone, they were joined by Amelia, who poured a light brown tea into her grandfather's white porcelain cup, dropping a thin slice of lime in afterwards. This was followed by a plate with a small slice of golden-coloured cake and silver cake fork. After repeating the same for Lionel, she stood beside her grandfather.

"You will love this. My daughter makes the best ginger cake in Kandy."

"Grandpa, I should keep an eye on the shop."

"You should stay, surely you want to hear a real Englishman speak?"

"You two can chat now, maybe Mr Lionel might like to come back another day when mother is here."

"I would like that very much," replied Lionel, in case there was any indecision.

She kissed her grandfather on his forehead, and slowly walked away.

"Goodbye Mr Lionel."

"Goodbye and thank you for the tea." Lionel called out as she disappeared around the cloister.

"I sometimes worry what will happen when I go," Mr Ashok confessed.

"Would they like to carry on the business?"

"I'm not sure. My daughter is very good at cleaning and presenting the stock, but she's shy and is reluctant to sell, she's also never bought, always referring that to me."

"It will come, you have good stock."

"You haven't seen anything yet," he said with a wily smile, "How long are you staying in Kandy?"

"I have booked three nights at the Royal, but I have no set plans."

"In Kandy your hotel is known as the Royal 'Pub'. I go there to watch the cricket, they screen it on a projector in the courtyard, it's more fun to watch sport with others."

They spoke easily of antiques, life, England and family. It was good for Mr Ashok to brush up on his English and time flew by.

Lionel checked his watch, 6 o'clock. Poor Chris was still waiting outside.

"I should really go now, but before I do, I've noticed that you have a bronze female figure, about eight inches high."

"Was it in the far room on the round table? Next to a globe?"

"Yes, but it has no price label."

"Nothing does, I keep prices in here," said Mr Ashok pointing to a thick head of hair. "Come for dinner tomorrow and I will tell you the price of the Rodiya girl. Here is my card. Come for 6pm."

Lionel retraced his steps to the shop, and thanked Amelia for the tea and cake.

He found Chris happily watching the cricket on his android phone. Slipping the wires of his earphones into his shirt pocket, he asked, "To the gardens, sir?"

"No, back to the Royal, please. The gardens will have to wait."

On their arrival, Lionel agreed to meet Chris after breakfast again, paid him and made his way to the ground floor bar. As he spoke to the barman he was joined by Lysanta.

"Did you have a good day, Mr Lionel?"

"I did, very interesting, thank you."

"Did you buy any bargains?"

"No, but there's always tomorrow. Chris took me to a fabulous antique shop not far from the Botanic Gardens."

"The one with the big saucepans outside?"

"Yes."

"Mr Ashok is a very well-known antiques dealer in Kandy. He has two lovely ladies, they often eat here."

"He told me he likes watching the cricket in your courtyard."

"He does, and when he comes, he always wears his safari suit."

"He was wearing it today. He has asked me for dinner tomorrow."

"Sir. I believe he has a fine house, built for an old Burgher merchant with gardens."

"I had tea with him in a shaded cloister, but I didn't get to the gardens, I did hear some running water."

"You were honoured. Whenever an important person dies in the city, they always call him first."

Chapter 12

Kandy

Lionel was woken early by the 'call to prayer' and lay listening to the rhythmic words. He got up, showered and dressed. This time he decided to walk anticlockwise around the lake, saving the sacred temple complex till last. Passing the competitive chanters, in their respective mosques and temples, he wondered ... were they calling out votive chants or making public announcements or perhaps, as he had been told by Saman, thanking various worshippers for their offerings of cinnamon cake and help? "Many thanks go to Mrs Ajith."

Walking past the grand Queen's Hotel, over the road to the frilly wall bordering the lake, Lionel once again raised his umbrella as the rain trees still had some clinging bats and cranes. In spite of the early sunshine the lake's water remained a sinister black; no wonder Kandyans believed large snakes and dragons dwelt here. Twenty minutes later he turned around the narrow end of the lake; the traffic vanished as the main road veered away. The pavement now ran along a much quieter road serving the temple complex, dotted with bicycle-wheeled stalls selling offerings of lotus flowers, food and drink. He passed through security and was instructed to take off his brown Shipton and

Heneage docksiders. Everyone took off their shoes, he felt there was something rather charming about this common courtesy. Today, he chose a different bench to drink in the extraordinary complex. With his back to the lake, he scanned this architectural landscape and stopped, as amongst all these white-painted, shaped and moulded buildings was a brownstone English church. It looked like it had been taken from the Kent countryside, and thrown into this foreign land. The whole held a calming contemplative atmosphere as if each religion was nodding to one another. An hour later he returned to the ritual of breakfast.

"Fried, scrambled or poached sir," enquired the ever-present Lysanta.

"Fried today, and watermelon with mint please."

Lysanta made a tic tac signal to the watching waiter and resumed his enquiries.

"Do you have any plans for today, sir?"

"I'd like to go to the Botanic Gardens first and see how the day evolves."

"Very good, sir."

Lysanta left Lionel to his breakfast, returning with a cappuccino and a small plate of biscuits.

"I asked the chef to make some ginger and lime biscuits. I know Mr Ashok likes them."

"That's very thoughtful, and I would like to take him a bottle of wine, please."

"He likes our Chablis, sir?"

"Biscuits and wine, perfect. Lysanta, tell me about the gem diggers on the river. The men on the rafts."

"A very dangerous job, sir."

"Why?"

"The crocodiles."

"Oh."

"National Rangers come and catch them, but generally, only after somebody has been taken."

"I counted four people on each raft, why so many when there is only one man dredging?"

"It takes one person to dig, two to operate the sifter and one person to hold their position."

"Do they ever find big stones?"

"Rarely. Do you know your royal princess Catherine's engagement sapphire came from Sri Lanka."

"From the river?"

"No, most likely from a mine. Although coloured gemstones are hard, they are worn down by the constant movement on the riverbed, remember coloured stones are a lot softer than diamonds."

"Thank you. I'd like to go to the gardens now. When I cross the river, I will look out for the men on their rafts."

As Chris took Lionel across the bridge, he spotted three rafts in the distance, two in the middle of the river, and one by the bank offloading sand. It was at this moment he wished he had a pair of binoculars.

"Next to the Royal Botanic Gardens is our university. Would you like to see it? The university is also on the banks of the Mahaweli River, the students and the gem diggers have very different lives. Only the children of the rich come to study at Peradeniya University."

Chris drove slowly through the campus, pointing out the various faculties, then he stopped to show Lionel a giant Java fig tree with a canopy of switching branches with an amazing system of large roots running like snakes along the ground.

"This is the best Java fig tree in Kandy, better than any you will see in the Botanic Gardens."

On arrival at the ticket office Lionel was directed to the 'Tourist' kiosk: at which there was no queue. The incentive for the longer 'Locals' queue turned out to be a considerably cheaper ticket. The officer unashamedly left people waiting, whilst more expensive tickets were sold to foreign tourists.

Ticket secured, Lionel gently moved through that adjoining locals queue. And wandered down the main plaza.

He wasn't alone for long, a small family of monkeys wandered ahead of him.

With a true sense of fun, they inspected plants and trees for anything edible, and suddenly stopped for a little concentrated grooming. The main plaza was broken by an enormous circle, a sort of green roundabout. He took the second exit, straight ahead, onto a long avenue of giant palms. At the end, he turned left and followed the river, whose bank fell away on his right. He passed giant clumps of bamboo, some green, some yellow, and a fabulous cannonball tree, whose trunk was randomly hung with cannonball-sized fruit. A dappled path led him on to a yellow painted monument, its domed top held aloft on what looked like six stylised elephant trunks. Lionel read that it had been built to commemorate an early superintendent of the gardens. A George Gardner, who had successfully searched every part of the island to build this great collection that stands in 147 acres and attracts over one million visitors a year. Many of whom are local courting couples: he had been alerted to this practice by a shrill whistle from a moustached and uniformed warden, who then chastised a young couple for lowering their umbrella for a quick kiss.

"Oh, to be young again," he thought.

After what seemed to be most of the day, Lionel retrieved Chris from his phone cricket and headed back to the Royal to bathe and change for dinner, choosing a blue linen jacket with open white shirt. On his departure Lysanta handed him a chilled bottle of Chablis wrapped in newspaper, and the chef's ginger and lime zest biscuits, smartly boxed. Shortly before 6pm Lionel walked past the large two-handled 'missionary' pans and found Mr Ashok seated at his desk. He rose. He was neither tall, nor short, maybe 5 foot 8 inches, but immaculate in a buttoned, collarless gossamer-thin white linen shirt with a striking blue Nehru-collared long-sleeved coat.

"These are for you."

"How very kind, a bottle and..." he gently shook the white waxed box, "not the Royal's famous ginger and lime biscuits? My favourite. Now come and meet my daughter."

He led Lionel through the shop into the cool cloister behind. They walked round to a different cluster of tables and chairs, where he motioned Lionel to an armchair on the elephant-ear side.

"After dinner, I will show you one of my storerooms, but first, we will have drinks."

As he finished speaking, he could hear the girls approaching. Following his lead, Lionel stood up as the daughter laid a tray of champagne bowls on the table.

"This is my daughter, Sanchini." As Lionel's eyes met those of Sanchini, his jaw dropped. He hadn't been introduced to many Sri Lankan women, but he had seen some walking around. Sanchini was different – arrestingly beautiful, almost otherworldly. As she handed her father a bottle of champagne, Lionel was struck too by the precise, calm elegance of her movements.

"To our English visitor and fellow antiques dealer," toasted Mr Ashok.

"To you," they replied in unison.

"Delicious," responded Lionel.

"It should be, I cleared this from the home of the once principal judge in Kandy. He was a great collector of European wines. Beneath us is a cellar built by a wealthy merchant in the 18th century. All over Sri Lanka, the Dutch built large houses to live and work in. Goods were valuable and it was best to keep an eye on them. I bought this old merchant's house shortly after my wife, Piyumi, and I were married. We were very happy and secure here."

After drinks, they moved around the courtyard, through a pair of louvered doors into a small square room with an airy high ceiling. In the centre was the circular table, just over three feet in diameter, and around it stood four elbow chairs.

"My daughter will take the seat nearest the door, and you can sit by my good ear."

Whilst one member of the household staff lit the candles on the table, another brought in the food. Four warm plates were set with numerous white porcelain bowls laid in the centre. As Mr Ashok poured Lionel's Chablis, his daughter talked him through the bowls.

"Red rice, chicken curry, bean curry, beetroot curry, cashew curry..."

"My favourite," interrupted Mr Ashok with a smile.

"Dahl, roti, pineapple chutney, and curd. Just in case anything is too hot."

"Take the rice first, and then give it 'fair wind' as you say," Mr Ashok advised, reaching for his cashew nut curry.

"Father, guests first, please," Sanchini interjected. Her father gave Lionel a smile, and then passed him the cashew nut curry.

The food was deliciously fresh and the four merrily chatted. Sanchini worked as a personal assistant to a wealthy widow, who lived up above the valley to the east of the lake, whilst Amelia was studying hard for her final exams, which would decide her university.

Plates cleared, Mr Ashok rose and beckoned Lionel to follow. "Would you like to see my cellar?"

Chapter 13

Kandy

The cellar was secured by an impressive metal-strapped dark hardwood door. Mr Ashok brought a bright steel key from his coat pocket, the sort of ancient key that would have warranted a bronze stand in a Pimlico Road antique shop. The door swung towards them to reveal a wide set of stone steps. This wasn't a cellar, it was a magnificent undercroft where the pillars and arches were made of limed brickwork. There was a central colonnade from which many recessed metal-barred gates secured individual rooms.

"This is where I keep my wines." And with that, Mr Ashok pushed an unbolted gate and flicked on a brown Bakelite light switch. Lionel hadn't seen one of these since his school days. The sort of cupcake-shaped switch that would have been installed when the house was first converted to electricity. The rectangular room had a barrel-shaped roof and the walls had a single run of thick dressed stone shelving at waist height, supported by beehive-shaped niches. All joyfully peopled by loose bottles along with wooden boxes.

"I have a friend in England who has a cellar, not nearly as splendid as this one, he uses it as his dining room and he would love this," said Lionel.

"I have never bought a bottle. These are all from the houses of rich men, whose widows are always keen to rid themselves of their late husbands' cellars. I will never drink it all, but I do enjoy the choice."

Lionel looked around the bins; there were some great French, Italian and American wines.

"As you know, you find many things in house clearances."

"Don't I know that," agreed Lionel, thinking of his pair of Chinese vases. "Do you ever sell any of the bottles?"

"Only to one man who lives in Colombo. He runs a wine club, and he tells me what delight he gets from keeping 'his source' a secret. He often rings, relaying how surprised his fellow members are when he produces yet another unseen bottle from a famed vineyard."

"Come, now I show you some Sri Lankan silver."

As they walked out he flicked off the switch and pulled the metal gate to. Crossing the central colonnade and unlocking a gate directly opposite, he flicked the lights on and the room came alive with reflected bulbs bouncing off many silver dishes and vessels.

"My girls clean all this twice a year. It takes them two days, fortunately for you they only did it last week."

"Apart from the London Silver Vaults I have never seen so much silver in one place."

Mr Ashok picked up a green baize bag, and untied the black cotton drawstring. "My wife made all these."

From it he took a ten-inch pear-shaped dish.

"It's shaped like the island of Sri Lanka, look at the top, Jaffna, then on the top right is a notch for Trincomalee, at the bottom is Galle, on the left is Colombo, and in the centre is Kandy."

All around its 'coastline' was a wide border embossed with elephants, within narrower guard borders of scrolling flowers.

"You take it, it's quite light?"

Lionel felt it.

"These were produced in their thousands to take back to your country as souvenirs."

"Funnily enough, I have one at home. I came here many years ago for a honeymoon with my second wife, and I have always kept an eye out for them. I bought a particularly fine one five years ago from a fellow dealer opposite me in St Leonards. I paid £40 for it."

"You will need to pay a lot more now, silver and gold have risen. Would you like a ginger tea and maybe a little arrack before you go? My daughter keeps a close eye on me. She is concerned I drink too much, but when you get to seventy-five without illness you begin to feel invincible. Come, let's go and find the girls."

Out of the cellar, he carefully locked the heavy door, returned the key to his coat pocket, and led his guest back to where they had previously had their champagne. Lionel sat and tried to make out the garden within the cloister. As his eyes adjusted, he recognised the white flowers of the frangipani trees, along with the silhouette of the palms against the night sky.

Shortly afterwards they were joined by both women.

"Lysanta organised those biscuits," said Lionel.

"He is an outstanding general manager, and in the last five years he has truly brought The Royal back to prominence. Here, institutions ebb and flow, and it's generally the person at the top who alters their courses."

"So true. This morning, I was talking to him about the river diggers, the people on rafts."

"When Amelia was at her Montessori school, she was friendly with a boy whose father was later taken by a crocodile."

"He was the brightest boy in the class, he could read and write way before me," said Amelia. "He had a natural gift for learning, and our teacher was quick to recognise the talent of this poor boy in his too-large second-hand shoes. His father was killed when he was at secondary school. He was in a different school by then, but a friend told me that his lights went out, and he had to leave school as soon as he was able. In a better system he would have been a scholar, when I cross the bridge, I always look out for him."

"That is the legacy of a Royal City, there will always be class and snobbery. Now, Lionel, I must sell you something."

"May I see that bronze again?"

"Of course. Amelia, would you get the Rodiya girl, it's in the far showroom next to the table globe."

"That was a truly delicious dinner," said Lionel, turning to Sanchini.

"Thank you. We have a good cook at the moment."

Amelia returned and handed the bronze to Lionel. It was 8 inches high, modelled with both her legs and arms crossed in a rather demure manner. On her right arm, above her bicep, she wore a serpent bracelet with a similar bracelet on her left wrist along with an elaborate chain around her neck.

"It's exotic."

"To save you any embarrassment. Give me 80,000 rupee, and it's yours."

"Thank you. I will take it, may I pay you tomorrow?"

"Of course, come for coffee, and if you've nothing better to do, I can be your guide for the day."

Chapter 14
Kandy

The next day, in the interests of variety, Lionel decided to walk clockwise around the lake. So far, he had managed two uneventful and pleasurable strolls, but today wasn't to be so lucky. It was a warm morning and he had unthinkingly left both umbrella and Panama hat back at the Royal. He managed a quarter circuit, passing the Queen's Bathing House, before he felt a heavy thud on the crown of his head and a warm slow dribble slide down his neck. With creeping dread, he investigated with his right hand. The poo was enormous, thick and smelly. He had occasionally been splattered by seagulls in Hastings, but this tropical offering was a different beast entirely. As a Sri Lankan curry has an intensity, so do their bird poos. It's hard for a gentleman to maintain any sort of dignity on a morning walk with a bird turd on his head. Fortuitously, he had his polka dot cotton square, a present from Barty, which removed the worst of it, before he turned and retraced his steps to the Royal. Once past the ever-vigilant security guard, Lysanta appeared in the courtyard.

"Oh dear Mr Lionel, the cranes have found you."

"At home we say it's lucky to be splattered, but in reality, it never feels that way!"

"In Kandy also, sir," agreed a smiling Lysanta.

"I'm gasping for a pot of tea, I might just have a shower first."

"I will organise one for you now, sir."

The tea arrived promptly, so as not to disturb Lionel's shower. It was back at breakfast that Lionel decided against variety; different choices hadn't served him well today!

"Eggs, sir?"

"The same as yesterday please, Lysanta. I couldn't have any more of those ginger and lime biscuits, could I? They went down a storm."

"I will ask the chef, I think we have some left."

After breakfast he was handed another smart white patisserie box of biscuits.

"With our compliments, have a lovely day sir."

Lionel could get used to this service.

On the way to Mr Ashok, Chris took him to a favoured bank.

"Low charges in this one, Mr Lionel."

He wrestled with the not-so-logical English/Sinhalese instructions on the ATM's screen and finally managed to withdraw 100,000 rupees.

"That was protracted and virtually impossible, now we can go to Mr Ashok's. And then on to the Royal Botanic Gardens, please."

Once Mr Ashok had joined Lionel in the back seat of the three-wheeler, he suggested, "Coffee in the gardens and then we will see my jeweller friend, Lal. You can ask him all about the raft men, and afterwards would you like to join me for lunch."

"Perfect."

Mr Ashok directed Chris past the sign saying 'No cars, No tuk tuks' through the garden's wrought iron gates. As a security guard approached, he emerged from the cab resplendent in his trademark suit. Wagging fingers turned to broad smiles, and after a formal exchange of greetings and discreetly passed rupees, Mr Ashok and Lionel were escorted past the ticket office.

"The superintendent is a friend, and we will probably catch him having a coffee at this hour."

The two made an odd couple: Mr Ashok in his sand-coloured suit with a mop of thick hair and Lionel, a foot taller, with his Lock's Panama hat and carrying a rolled umbrella. After the morning's accident, he was taking no chances with Kandy's flying friends. The coffee stand was next to a large glasshouse. Whyever would you need a glasshouse in this heat, he mused. But maybe they had colder nights, or the enclosed space was monkey-free. The superintendent was there with some colleagues; nonetheless, Mr Ashok was received like an old friend. After brief introductions, the two sat and chatted.

On returning to Chris, they made their way across the river to Mr Ashok's jeweller friend. At the bridge he tapped Chris's shoulder, bidding him stop. There were two rafts out, one on the bank offloading sand, the other one in the middle of the river. In spite of being on a busy bridge he proceeded to hop out of the three-wheeler and remove a small pair of binoculars from one of his bellow coat pockets. Lionel joined him and was promptly passed the pair.

"I can't see Amelia's friend today. The raft is probably out of sight around the river's bend."

"The one who lost his father?"

"Yes. An awful death."

After returning the binoculars, he gave the final directions to Chris. His jeweller friend had a large building just over the bridge, near to the one Lionel had visited the day before. Chris pulled up next to two white Mercedes limousines.

Inside, the security man quietly gestured them into a lift, pressing the top button. On arrival, the doors opened to two good-looking young men.

"They are my friend's sons," said Mr Ashok to Lionel, "He has many. These two work here and the others look after the mines."

The taller of the brothers spoke.

"Hello, my father will be pleased to see you, but he is currently in a meeting. Would you like to see our newly decorated reception area, our Russian buyers have little interest in tea and coffee, so we have installed a bar." As the brothers opened a large pair of double doors, Mr Ashok led Lionel into a room swathed in suede. It looked like a first-class airport lounge with clusters of camel-coloured suede armchairs broken up by a gilt brass standard lamp and a circular polished teak drinks table. Beyond these stood a horseshoe-shaped bar, the front of which was upholstered in a shade darker sand-coloured quilted suede. Behind the bar stood a Sri Lankan pretending to be a French waiter. The uniform was right, but his beaming smile just wasn't 'typique'.

The brothers beckoned them to sit facing the windows with the view of the river beyond. Immediately the waiter brought glasses of cold water and bowls of cashew nuts, and returned with two glasses of champagne.

"My friend here is an antiques dealer in England," volunteered Mr Ashok before tasting his drink.

"How are you finding Sri Lanka?" said the elder of the two brothers.

"It's like a tropical Europe, with both the benefit of history and beauty, and everybody has been so helpful, especially this gentleman."

"We like the British too. They gave us railways, cricket, tea..."

Bang! Suddenly, the double doors were flung open, and five menacing men walked in, the smaller of the five sitting down immediately, whilst the other well-built men patrolled their new space.

"I think my father will be free now," said the elder brother, politely beckoning them out of the now hostile room.

Lionel was about to say something but was stopped by Mr Ashok raising a finger to his closed lips. The two brothers held open another pair of double doors and followed their guests into their father's office. It was as large as the 'Airport Lounge' and similarly furnished, but instead of a bar it had a gold-finished jewellery counter, housing velvet trays of multi-coloured stones.

"Mr Ashok, how lovely to see you, and who is this?" said a slight and beautifully-tailored man.

"This is Mr Lionel, a fellow antiques dealer from England."

He extended a polished hand. "Whereabouts in England?" he asked with a well-practised smile.

"South of London, on the coast, a town called Hastings."

"I don't know Hastings, but I have family in London with a business in Hatton Gardens. Please, sit down. Would you like some tea or maybe something stronger?"

He didn't wait for an answer, and spoke in Sinhalese to his younger son.

"I haven't seen you since you sold me that jewellery from old Mrs Sinnha. A fabulous sapphire necklace, I sent it to London. Do you have something for me now?"

"Nothing today, but I want to introduce Lionel here to you as I'm showing him around. He is intrigued by the raft people. Do you buy their gems?"

"They find, I buy. Every stone from the Mahaweli river comes to me. Most are worn to small stones, but I've had the occasional good topaz and a decent sapphire once, with such an intense colour. Over the years, I've made good money from them."

"I hear the crocodiles take the men on the rafts."

"They do, but there are many families involved, and like me, they seem to be lucky with sons."

At this point, one of them arrived with a bottle.

"I know you like this champagne, Perrier Jouet."

The jeweller stood up from his leather chair and raised his flute glass,

"To our English friend, may he never meet a crocodile."

Chapter 15

Kandy

Mr Ashok and Lionel found Chris parked between a white Mercedes limousine and another car.

"My friend does business with people that you and I wouldn't dare deal with. The buyers upstairs care only for money, and you don't want to be perceived as an obstacle in their path. In my experience they are best avoided. See no evil, hear no – *Sugar*" Mr Ashok swore as they heard the scrape, that aching sound that never seems to end. Chris was reversing the tuk tuk looking over his right shoulder, but had forgotten about his front wheel. Before they could inspect the damage, the Mercedes's alarm started urgently bleeping.

"Drive on, Chris. There is nothing to be gained by appealing to their better nature, as I'm pretty sure they don't have any."

Just as Chris was about to nose onto the road the flat front of a speeding red bus missed them by inches.

"Stop!" shouted Lionel. "We have just scraped a car and now narrowly missed a bus. When the third thing happens, which it will, I want some control. Chris, you and I should stay, but Mr Ashok must leave now. Walk quickly to the coconut stand and find another tuk tuk. Chris, park up and I will try and head them off inside."

"Shouldn't I..." started Mr Ashok.

"Go now."

Lionel managed to make it to the reception area just as the lift doors opened and gulped at the size of them.

"My tuk tuk has hit your car."

They didn't register, they just moved, like tanks to some unseen territory.

Luckily, there was no sign of Mr Ashok, only a rather sheepish Chris, standing by his three-wheeler. First the driver clicked the key fob, then inspected the damage, before turning towards him.

"Explain."

Why use more words, thought Lionel, especially if accompanied with a special sort of scowl.

"Our tuk tuk was reversing between the cars and turned too early."

The driver then traced the 12-inch scratch on the offside rear door. It didn't help that the limousine was very white and Chris's vehicle was blue. The scratch stood out like ink on a page. He checked the other panels including the rear on an otherwise immaculate car.

"Come, you must pay."

The driver took the lead whilst his colleague filled the immediate space behind him. Lionel could feel his breath, best described as meaty with notes of alcohol. If breath could be sweaty, this is what it would smell like. As they travelled up in the lift, Lionel noted how similar they were: same haircut, hedgehogy, same black clothing with seams straining to keep muscular frames hidden, and Prada high-top black boots. A little luxury that said more about their employer's wealth than their personal preference.

The Russian buyer had remained in the reception area, seated and drinking, with two of his bodyguards behind him. His caramel suede jacket merged well with the armchair, only his face and legs were of note. His driver bent down to whisper in his ear, but before anybody spoke, the jeweller and his two sons entered the room. All were now assembled for the kangaroo court.

Lionel couldn't bear the silence, "I'm sorry this has happened. It was a lapse of concentration and I'm here to make it good."

There was a long pause.

"You will," said the Russian. "Where are you from?"

"England."

"Where in England?"

"Hastings, south of London."

"Why are you here?"

"To learn about Sri Lankan gemstones."

"Are you buying or selling?"

This was turning into a verbal sparring match, and the Russian was throwing all the questions.

"He wanted to know about the raft people on the river," interrupted the jeweller.

"Why? They're your people."

The jeweller, had heard enough. "I will settle the repair bill."

"Why should you do that?"

"Because it's easier and the owner of the Merecedes dealership is a friend."

"There was another man? A small man in a safari suit?"

"Let this be an end to the matter," said the jeweller and, turning to Lionel, announced "My son will show you out."

Lionel didn't need to be asked twice. He moved quickly.

Chris took a rather pale passenger back to his hotel.

"Mr Ashok is the courtyard sir."

"Marvellous, I see you're still walking," said Mr Ashok, smiling, "Did Lal look after you?"

"He did, but I'm not sure we've seen the last of them."

"Sit down and let's not worry about what may not happen. May I choose for you?"

"When in Rome." Lionel replied.

"We will both have the coconut and prawn curry, please. Do you have saffron rice?"

"Yes, and would you like some coriander roti?"

"Perfect, and a bottle of white, please."

Without referring to a card, Lysanta reeled off the choices.

"We'll have the 2018 Chablis, please."

Mr Ashok caught Lionel worriedly staring into space.

"Did my friend satisfy your curiosity over the raft people?"

"He was certainly matter-of-fact about them being killed by crocodiles. As one is taken, another will fill their place. Not a lot of compassion there."

"It's our way, people have jobs and stations, and it used to be hard to alter your course. Once, if you were born in the fields, you were most likely to work in them, but that has changed with compulsory education. Same goes for Kandy's raft people. You're just lucky if you are born the son of a jeweller."

"In Britain, we have social mobility through education, and in America it's education and sport that provide springboards for change."

"In Sri Lanka, like any country, it still helps to be from a rich family to go to university or play cricket seriously. Once the only chance of mobility for the children of poorer families was to work abroad, but they were generally exploited in low-wage jobs where it's difficult to save money. All too often, the only chance of change is luck."

With those sobering words, the wine arrived.

🦎

While Mr Ashok was chatting and his companion was worrying about scratched cars and Russian mobsters, Amelia was opening the shop in Peradeniya. The three arched openings to the pavement had electric metal shutters, which never failed to delight her. The buttons were simple, up or down arrows indicated the shutters' direction of travel. You had to keep the button depressed and then, when released, the shutter shuddered to a halt. After all three shutters had been opened she automatically slid the nest of three 'missionary' pans out onto the adjacent pavement. To her knowledge, they were the largest pans in Kandy, made to feed a regiment of soldiers who had held exercises in the surrounding hill country twenty years ago; whilst pawnbrokers had their three balls, they had three vast pans. When all was shipshape, she returned to her grandfather's desk and picked up her set book for English literature: *Bleak House* by Charles Dickens. After reading a couple of pages she had a feeling that someone had entered the showroom. This wasn't a shopper announcing their presence with a cheery 'hello'. This was a quiet shadow, tall and thin, whose details were blurred by the sunlight from the street outside.

"Can I help you?" Amelia enquired in her clipped English.

"Hope so," said the shadow. "Please don't be afraid. We were friends at school."

As he spoke, she realised it was the boy from her Montessori school, who had been in their dinner conversation only the previous night. It's amazing how the brain can both record and retrieve patterns of speech.

"Manoji?"

"It is, Amelia."

With that brief exchange, tears rolled down Manoji's cheeks. He was the little hopeful boy again in the company of an old school friend.

"Come, sit down, I will get us tea and cake if you promise not to leave. Will you promise?"

He couldn't speak, the best he could do was nod. He wasn't going anywhere; for the first time in a long time, he felt secure.

Amelia opened the door to the cloister and left it ajar. Once in the kitchen, she switched the kettle on. It was a family courtesy that whoever used the kettle last made sure that there was a good teapot measure of water for the next person, today was the day that courtesy would really pay. As the water boiled, Amelia quickly assembled cups, saucers, plates, teapot, sugar, the Royal's ginger and lime biscuits, and two slices of cinnamon cake. Once boiled, she poured the hot water over the loose leaf black tea and returned to the showroom. To her relief Manoji was still sitting down where she'd left him.

She first handed him a paper napkin, something for the tears, followed by a slice of cake and black tea. Physically, he had changed greatly: he was tall, just under 6 foot, thin, but not weak, taut and wiry. After he had hungrily devoured the cake, she offered him some biscuits. He took one, hoping that that was the polite thing to do. She refilled his cup, he normally took sugar, but decided this may not be the correct thing either.

"I'm so sorry that your father died. Aisha told me that you left school soon afterwards. You do know we all thought you were the brainiest boy in our school."

Instead of nodding, this time he smiled.

"You look well," added Amelia, who was struggling to find the right words. She stopped trying, stood up and hugged him. As he cried, she started to cry too ... a lot had happened in eleven years. They both wiped away their tears, as the playing field seemed to have levelled up again.

"Now, how can I help you?" said Amelia, in a now-clear voice.

"I would like to show your grandfather something."

She knew where her grandfather would be: if he wasn't in the shop at 11am, he would be having coffee in the Royal Botanic Gardens, and if he wasn't here at lunch, he would be at the Royal.

She rang her grandfather's mobile twice; it rang and rang and then went to voicemail. Next, she phoned the Royal and asked to be put through to the general manager.

"Good afternoon, how can I help you?" answered Lysanta.

"Lysanta, it's Amelia Ashok, is my grandpa with you?"

"No, he has just left with Mr Lionel, they are walking to the Sacred Tooth Temple."

"I have tried ringing him, but he has probably accidently switched his phone to silent ring again. Could you possibly retrieve him? I urgently need him at home."

"Is everything alright, Miss Amelia?"

"Yes, it's fine, but something very important has arisen. Tell him he can bring Mr Lionel, if he wants."

"I will find him now."

Amelia put the phone down and smiled at her former school friend.

"He's on his way."

Chapter 16

Kandy

Lysanta recognised the request from Mr Ashok's granddaughter as one of utmost importance, and of such delicacy that he alone would exercise it. Having transferred the chain of command, he walked outside to find Chris chatting to the security guard.

"Let's go," was enough for Chris. At the temple gate, Lysanta hopped out in search of a Panama hat. Easy to find a giant amongst men, but at any one time the complex can host some 30,000 people, so the physicality of moving through the crowds was difficult. He pressed on and eventually found the two sitting on a bench overlooking a moat.

"Mr Ashok, sir, your granddaughter has called. She asked you to return home immediately please?"

"Is everything alright?"

"All is good, sir. I have Chris waiting by the entrance."

"Lionel, I must leave you now," said a concerned Mr Ashok, looking at his mobile phone registering several missed calls.

"Sir, she said you may bring Mr Lionel."

"Well, you must come too then, as my girls generally know what's best!"

Lysanta carefully led the two older gentlemen through the crowds to Chris before departing with a "Good luck, sir."

On the short journey home, Lionel tried to make conversation, and jolly things along. Mr Ashok was worried. He had never been urgently called home before. He stared ahead, willing Chris to go faster.

When they arrived all looked normal; the shutters were open, the giant pans were outside. Mr Ashok rushed in alone, only to return a minute later, somewhat calmer.

"Come in, all is fine, she's in the cloister. Would you help me close the showroom?"

"Of course. Chris, would you mind coming back in about an hour? I'll send you a WhatsApp message."

Whilst Lionel pulled in the missionary pans, Mr Ashok closed the metal roller shutters. All sealed, he led Lionel to the group of chairs in the cloister. Beside Amelia sat a slim young man; although seated, Lionel could see he was the sort who could easily climb a gymnasium rope, probably with his hands only! He was about to spring to his feet, but Amelia touched his arm and bid him stay.

Lionel took the empty chair next to Amelia; Mr Ashok sat next to Manoji and addressed him in Sinhalese.

"Firstly, let me say how terribly sad we all were to hear of your father's tragic death. Every time we cross the river we look out for you."

The response came quietly and in perfect English. "I know you do. As whenever a three-wheeler stops on the bridge, I look for the gentleman in a safari suit."

"I need binoculars to see you, how on earth can you see me?"

"I have good eyes, sir, trained to see the slightest glint of a gemstone."

"My granddaughter says you have something to show me?"

Without a word, the young man reached into a smallish brown paper bag and handed him something wrapped in a banana leaf tied with rough brown twine.

"It's surprisingly heavy," said Mr Ashok, weighing the package with one hand. He placed it on the circular table in front of them, untied the twine, peeled away the greeny-brown banana leaf, and revealed a large egg-shaped stone. Its rough surface hid its inherent colour so he licked his index finger and brushed a spot, revealing deep blueness. He picked it up and leant back in his Lloyd loom chair, holding the 'egg' up to the light of the sky. What all four present saw was an incredible intensity of colour. A dark pure blue that almost seemed to have its own light force.

"Well, that's the largest uncut sapphire that I have ever seen," said a smiling Mr Ashok. "It's bigger than a hen's egg. Here, feel the weight of it, Lionel."

Mr Ashok handed the stone over. It was much heavier than he'd anticipated and truly magnificent.

"What a blue," said Lionel out loud.

"I will get us all a drink, and then, young man, you can tell us how you happen to have this extraordinary gem. Amelia, would you get us a large jug of water and lime, and I will get us some proper drinks, this needs celebrating."

As the two departed, Lionel was left holding the gem. He smiled at the young man, who returned his smile with interest. He was very dark-skinned, as befits somebody who spends their daylight hours in the middle of a river, and he wore a brilliant white T-shirt tucked into a pair of sandy-coloured cotton trousers with a wide brown leather belt around his small waist. On his feet, he wore black flip-flops. He had a simple elegance that reminded Lionel of Jack back in England: a tropical version, minus Clive the dog.

"Here we are," said a returning Mr Ashok, placing a rather splendid ice bucket on the circular glass-topped bamboo table whilst Amelia offloaded a large jug of water and numerous glasses. The bottle was popped, glasses filled, and Mr Ashok toasted Manoji's change of luck. "And now it's your turn to speak..."

Chapter 17
Kandy

Manoji paused, he wasn't the nodding or gesticulating kind of young man; he remained calmly still, just as Amelia remembered him at school.

"Each day, at sunrise, I wake, my mother cooks rice and curry for the whole family – my grandmother, a younger brother and my two younger sisters. Then my three uncles arrive, together we walk to the river. We work on the same raft every day, not Sundays. Our main business is building sand, but the gemstones provide the difference between meat or vegetables with our rice. We tether the raft to the bank then we offload the sand into small trucks. River sand is cheaper than buying from the builder's merchants and our customers hope to find a missed gemstone! As the sun catches our side of the bank in the morning, the raft will be amongst resting crocodiles, and some are almost as long as the raft. My uncles were on the raft when my father was killed, it was caught and then released in a national park up country, to the north of the island. There are now many crocodiles in the river, as it is now years since the Rangers last came to catch them. My uncles ask the gem buyers for help, but they don't listen. They don't care for us, they know if someone dies, a job is made! My uncles have looked out for me since then, they tried to keep me in school, but I knew it was me that would have to pay the bills."

"Stop for a minute. Some water?" interrupted Amelia. Manoji duly drank before returning his water glass to the table and continuing.

"We gently push the raft off the bank, so as not to disturb too many crocodiles. Then we pole out to the middle of the river, as the constant current draws both sand and loose stones to the bottom, which is naturally in the middle of the river. So, when you see the rafts from the bridge, we are generally in the same place, as the river's current brings both the sands and gems to us."

"I never thought of that," said Mr Ashok, "but you're right, the flow of a river is a ceaseless force."

"Well, the day before yesterday we were returning to our midstream position after shovelling a second load of sand into a waiting truck. When we dig, we do so with a metal scoop on a long metal pole. It's hard work so we rotate as a team of four; one dredging, and two people sifting. The sieve is rectangular, like a small stretcher, and requires a man at each end. After working together for such a long time, we do things instinctively, that's why the raft teams are often family. It's all about trust on the water. When you are hard at work, you almost forget that there are any crocodiles ... then one gently floats up to the surface and reminds you, 'One slip, and you're mine!'

"I was one of two sifting, when we felt a thud. It's normally always a rock, but my uncle said, 'It's blue!' We balanced the sifter on the pile of sand below, and there on top of the mesh, sticking above a layer of unsifted sand, sat a huge blue stone. My eldest uncle, who had been digging, said, 'Manoji, quickly put it in your pocket and carry on working. It's very important nobody sees any change.' We carried on digging, sifting and unloading sand. Nobody dared speak, but we were all thinking about it.

"At the end of the day we offloaded our last pile of sand, whilst my eldest uncle negotiated the price on some small gemstones. The jewellers come to us at the riverbank, sometimes they frisk us, but that day they were in a hurry as some important buyers were expected. On our way home, we stopped and bought our king coconuts, my eldest uncle insisted that we keep to the same routine, as everywhere there are eyes. Being the least important on the raft, I was to keep the stone, and we would discuss what to do with it once out on the river the next day. I didn't sleep that night, nor it turns out, did my uncles. I hid the stone in my grandmother's room, my mother never cleans it. Not because she doesn't want to, but more to give my grandmother her independence.

"The following day, and only when we were out of earshot in the middle of the river, it was decided that I should show the stone to you. My uncles said that my father spoke of the girl that had won the kindness cup in my class and always said that her grandfather would be the man to go to if we ever had this chance, as he thought you would be fair. We worked normally today; same patterns, same loads of sand, and then, with all their blessings, I came here."

Silence.

"My, what a story," said Mr Ashok.

"Wow," added Amelia.

"Try the champagne," said Lionel.

Manoji took his glass, leaned back in his chair and, for the first time in thirty-six hours, he breathed.

"I'm going to fetch my torch and jeweller's loupe. It's about time we had a good look at this stone."

Mr Ashok returned, picked up the gemstone and rubbed it with a wetted cloth. He turned on the torch and handed it to Manoji.

"Hold this under the stone, and let's see what its story is. I will describe to you what I see with the magnification of the jeweller's loupe. There are silks running through the stone, much like trails of cigarette smoke. These are the gem's unique fingerprints. I'm now looking for consistency of colour, ideally we want a deep royal blue, nothing too dark neither too pale," he continued, turning the stone in front of his loupe.

"It cannot be cut in Sri Lanka or India, as my jeweller friend has long arms. I don't wish to scare you but this stone is of a size and colour that people might kill for. It should be sold and cut in Europe."

"But isn't that smuggling?" interrupted Lionel.

"In Sri Lanka, things aren't so clearly cut. This is a life-changing opportunity sent by Buddha, to right a wrong. As Amelia often told me, Manoji was the brightest child in her class, and through family tragedy he was denied the opportunity of a university education. Remember, it is never wise to question the gods, this stone 'arrived' to make amends. Here we call it karma. It's very important that this is not spoken of beyond this room."

"Hello, what's going on here? Champagne in the afternoon?"

Both Lionel and Manoji sprang to their feet.

"Who is this young man?" asked Sanchini.

"He's Manoji, mother," said Amelia. "The boy we spoke of last night, who went to school with me."

"But what's he doing here?" she demanded imperiously.

"He has only found the largest sapphire I've ever seen," said her father, holding up the stone.

"Amelia, come with me now," was her only reaction.

On their departure, Mr Ashok turned to Manoji. "Would you prefer a beer instead of champagne?"

"I would rather just have water. Thank you, sir."

"More for us, Lionel, pour away. As we drink champagne, this young man can walk on water."

Chapter 18
Kandy

"Amelia, what are you doing bringing this poor young man into our house? It's not good for him or for us. It complicates the order of things."

Amelia just watched and listened. She would never contradict her mother. If her family had a behavioural timeline, her grandfather would live in colonial Kandy, but her mother would be even further back, somewhere between the last queen of Kandy and British rule, and she saw it as her job to carefully manage the elitism of both eras. It was the structure of rules her mother liked; everybody in the right place, and this young man in their cloister wasn't in the right place.

"He can't stay for dinner."

"I understand, mother."

"Your grandfather likes to go off with his discoveries. I think sometimes, that's why he wears the British explorer's suit."

"What do you think of the sapphire?"

"I would like to discuss it with your grandfather first. There is obviously opportunity, but there is also risk, and with risk comes danger."

"May I ask Manoji to call on Sunday? I know he doesn't work then."

"Amelia, it's not for you to ask. I will ask him."

Amelia followed her mother back to the cloister. As Sanchini approached, both Lionel and Manoji sprang to their feet.

"Young man, this stone, however large, beautiful, and possibly important, also presents danger for us all. We, as a family..." (she looked carefully at her father, who knew when to be silent) "... must first decide if we can help you. Would you leave the stone with us and return on Sunday? Be assured it will be safe with my father."

"My uncles and I have discussed this, they all trust Mr Ashok. They will be relieved that you are keeping the stone, and they would want me to thank you for your kindness."

Manoji knew it was time to go. He thanked a seated Mr Ashok, a standing Lionel, and followed Sanchini and Amelia through the cloister into the shop. As Sanchini operated the metal roller shutter, Amelia flashed an 'It'll be alright' smile.

On the girls' return, Lionel was quick to his feet to offer a glass of champagne.

"Thank you, Lionel. I think you need to stay for dinner."

"So do I," said Mr Ashok, handing his daughter the stone.

"It is beautiful, there really is something magical about gemstones. Is it really very special?"

"Yes, I think it might be very special," said Mr Ashok.

"Amelia and I will check on how dinner is coming on, while you two work out what you are going to do with it. "

When the two women had left, Lionel spoke. "Does he own the stone?"

"Who knows," replied Mr Ashok, "but what I do know is the stone found him, and for me, that's good enough. Before our country was known as either Ceylon or Sri Lanka, it was called Serendip. I think it was an 18th-century English gentleman, Sir

Horace Walpole, who coined the word serendipity. The action of making happy and accidental discoveries while looking for one thing and finding another. Manoji and his uncles were dredging for building sand and found a huge sapphire. That must surely qualify as a happy and accidental discovery."

"Wouldn't it have been easier for him and his uncles to have sold it to your jeweller friend?"

"I know how my friend works. He would have given them the equivalent of three months' wages and instructed his buyers to cut the price they give for the smaller stones. He would then claw back the three months 'advance'. Manoji has recognised his chance. Do you know much about jewellery?"

"I don't but I do know somebody who does. What about you? Your jeweller friend spoke of a sapphire necklace you sold him; did he give you a fair price?"

"He did, as he wants to keep me onside, but he has no regard for those raft people. In Kandy we have grown up with gems, but this stone is beyond me, the colour is a fabulous royal blue, and when cut, with hopefully no major flaws, it could be between 40 to 200 carats, if so, we aren't talking millions of dollars, but tens of millions! This most definitely is no ordinary stone."

"Blimey."

"Don't worry, one step at a time," Mr Ashok murmured as they both sank into their thoughts and glasses.

🦎

Sanchini had bought a chicken on her way home from work; while she filleted and cubed the breasts into one-inch pieces, her daughter put a large, rounded pan on a medium heat, adding coconut oil, a mix of mustard seed and cumin, and another mix of her mother's fenugreek, curry leaves and cinnamon before adding the finely chopped onions, peppers and bruised garlic. Sanchini had taught her daughter to work quickly: "Speed brings both better colour and better taste."

She now took over the rounded pan, pushing in the cubes of chicken, giving them a stir for a for a couple of minutes, adding turmeric, a little chilli powder, and second coconut milk, as she would use the first and best press of the coconut milk to finish the dish. Then she turned the heat down to a simmer and looked at her daughter.

"You know rich girls don't marry poor boys."

Amelia didn't say anything but dropped her eyes.

"I fell for your father because I felt sorry for him, I didn't know his mother was wealthy. It may be in our blood, but you must try and resist feeling sorry for boys."

Amelia's mother rarely spoke of her father. He had died when she was just three years old, killed in a tragic road accident in Burma. He had been a gem buyer. If only he were here now.

"You do the rice, and I will finish the chicken and dahl," instructed Sanchini.

Amelia was always intrigued why other cooks seemed to spend so long in the kitchen.

"Heat is speed, just turn the gas up," her mother would say.

🐊

Mr Ashok and Lionel had finished the champagne and were now in the cellar searching for a white wine.

"I cleared a large house belonging to a retired German lawyer.

His family owned vineyards in the Mosel, and he was sent an allocation of cases every year. His cellar was lovely, cut into the rocks under his house: the deeper you go in Kandy, the cooler it becomes. They used dynamite for cellars then, but with neighbours now it's no longer possible." Lionel thought of his friend Barty's Victorian house on the hill in Hastings. His cellar had been dug by hand and lined with bricks. If they had used dynamite there, a good proportion of West Hill might have slipped to the bottom of Queen's Road!

The chicken curry was delicious. This goddess is a polymath, thought Lionel; he had always said the third Mrs Lionel would be a chef, but he never imagined beauty might also be included. During dinner they talked of Manoji and the sapphire. From the Mahaweli river in Kandy to cut stone in Europe seemed like a huge mountain to climb.

"Mountains are climbed one step at a time," said Mr Ashok, as he bid Lionel good night.

Chris took Lionel back to the Royal Bar and Hotel. It had been decided that all four parties should sleep on it and brainstorm the following day. Lionel tried to sleep, but his mind kept alternating between the sapphire and Sanchini. Both extraordinarily beautiful but one was living and breathing.

🦎

As Sanchini tried to sleep, she couldn't stop thinking of her late husband Dinish. He would have known what to do. Would Lionel?

Chapter 19

Kandy

The mosques and temples' competitive chanting woke Lionel at 5am.

"Do these people ever sleep?" he muttered as he made for the shower. He would do a circuit of the lake – walking always helped him make better decisions. After his now customary greetings with the ex-military security man, he strode to it, clutching both hat and umbrella. It was a cool morning and there was little traffic. His only hazards on the pavement were monks walking in earnest clusters towards the temple complex from their monastery on the other side of the lake, clad in their blood-orange robes. Once past the monastery, the pavement cleared, and Lionel was able to properly think.

He had come for a holiday, a little thinking time, a break from the routines of the everyday. There can be no greater thinking space than an empty beach, but he was now in Kandy with only a lake. Whereas the sea reflects the blue sky, the lake's inky water seemed to absorb it; nonetheless, he found the process the same, walking and thinking. Was it the legs pumping the blood that gave the brain the edge? Often, difficult conversations and good decisions are helped by the process of walking.

Lionel tried not to dwell on his two failed marriages. The second Mrs Lionel had left him through his own selfishness. He'd become too set in his routines, there was little room for another person, but it was an overriding sadness that had eroded his first marriage. They had married in their twenties and soon become pregnant. All was happy until the birth and when the boy was born, after too long a labour, the hospital staff whipped him away before they heard his cry. They never heard his cry. Lionel and his wife had done the crying. In those quieter moments – alone in the car, at home with a mug of tea, and always when they saw another baby boy. Would he have smiled like that? Would he have laughed like that? Despite trying to forget, they never did, and as each year passed the void got bigger. It was the slow exhaustion of grief that prompted their parting. She, thankfully, found work and became in time a much respected, and feared, television producer. Whilst he needed a change of scenery and headed for the south coast. He chose Hastings as it was considerably cheaper than Brighton, enabling him to buy a new home without causing his ex-wife the further upset of having to sell the marital home.

His road to recovery was on the promenade, breathing sea air, and watching the smiles of others. It wasn't too surprising to him that he liked the company of Jack. His boy, had he lived, would be in his mid-30s, Jack's sort of age and probably an antiques dealer too. Manoji reminded him of Jack, they both had an enthusiastic air of purpose and both stood well in clothes. Lionel would do what he could for them, as he had found every action of kindness helped him to reduce this terrible chasm of sadness.

Sitting down on a bench, his thoughts returned to the sapphire. He understood that he was being lined up to deal with the stone's European entry. He knew items were sold by stories. A

Victoria Cross medal without a citation is just a piece of bronze, and a large gemstone without provenance is just a coloured stone, albeit a large one.

"I'm racing ahead," he said out loud, raising the eyebrows of a passing couple.

"One step at a time," he continued for the benefit of nobody bar himself.

Its shape reminded him of the decorative stones popular in the 1970s. The stars of the English sitcom *The Good Life*, Margot and Jerry, would have had a bowl of turned hardstone eggs and a bowl of potpourri, both being 'must haves' in a fashionable interior. At home in Hastings, he always kept an eye out for these, especially the green malachite ones, as they didn't seem to date ... and there he had it.

"Where do you hide a person? In a city.

"So, where do you hide a stone? With hundreds of others!

"Thank you God, thank you Buddha."

After Amelia had left for school, Sanchini brought a cup of coffee to her father. The cloister with its four sides had different clusters of chairs: rattan, teak, wire and paper; all, most importantly, comfortable. In the mornings Mr Ashok sat in the east cloister, as the sun illuminated the courtyard garden. This was Sanchini's preserve; creative people are often good cooks and interested gardeners. It was a great joy for him to watch his beautiful daughter plant and prune this little piece of paradise.

The garden centred on a rectangular pond; in its middle rose a circular shallow bowl, made of white marble and carved with a girdle of stylised stiff lotus leaves. The water gently toppled over its edge into the larger pond, whose corners were planted with forever flowering lotus plants. You couldn't hear the traffic on the road beyond the shop, but you could hear the muffled hubbub of the city. The continuous plink-plonk sound of the spilling water cleverly cancelled the noise intruding on this oasis. Mr Ashok and Sanchini's late husband had built the pond together, to her design. Mr Ashok had found the materials: rectangular granite blocks, 20 inches long and 8 inches by 8 inches in section, while the marble bowl and baluster-shaped pedestal had come from the foyer of a now redeveloped hotel in Kandy. It was Dinish who had done the hard work: digging the pond and barrowing the soil away, he had poured the concrete on the reinforced steel bars to form the base, then laid the walls and skimmed the interior with water-resistant render. He had capped the walls with the granite blocks and erected the baluster-shaped pedestal on which the wide marble bowl stood. Mr Ashok could still clearly remember the moment when he turned on the electric pump; seconds later the water fell for the first time. He watched Sanchini kiss Dinish in thanks; it was then that he knew, if asked, he would give his consent for this man to marry his only precious daughter.

He had been a wonderful son-in-law who had devotedly loved his daughter. It was such a shock when they heard of his death. He had been on one of his quarterly buying trips to Burma. He'd called the day before saying he had bought some amazing rubies. The next day, he and his regular driver, the eldest son of a prominent Burmese jeweller, were killed instantly by a mining company lorry travelling on the wrong side of the road. It had seemed so surreal that both he and Sanchini never really believed it. Neither of them went to Burma, leaving Dinish's father to bring back the body. The water pump was never turned off, except of course for the daily power cuts: it was their very own eternal flame.

"You know, whenever I sit in the cloister and hear the water I think of Dinish."

"I know father," Sanchini said, touching his shoulder and handing him a cup of coffee.

"Do you think London George might help us?"

George had been Dinish's main buyer in Europe. They had worked for ten years together, and Dinish naturally became George's counterpart in Asia.

"If Lionel can get it to London, and that is a big if, I'm sure George will organise the cutting and sale of the stone. Let's hear what Lionel has to say first. After all, he may not want to get involved."

His phone beeped, announcing the arrival of a new WhatsApp message. "Lionel is outside."

"You go and get him in, and I will organise some coffee."

Once settled Lionel announced, "I think I've found a way to get the stone to England."

Chapter 20

Kandy

Lionel was bubbling with excitement as he explained to Mr Ashok and Sanchini how he could ship the sapphire to England in a container.

"I can help you fill one," said Mr Ashok, "but it must be filled with recently made items like bamboo furniture or clay cooking pots, as it's illegal to export antiques from Sri Lanka."

"Now you tell me! Where does a 'once in a lifetime' sapphire stand regarding export?"

"Don't worry, Lionel. We will fill a container with so many things, it'll be like looking for a needle in a haystack."

"I know I can sell bamboo back at home, as I do it all the time."

"I feel a trip to Galle coming on."

"Why Galle?"

"The Galle area has always been the centre of furniture-making in Sri Lanka. I think we should all go," said an excited Mr Ashok. "I haven't been on a buying trip for years."

"But we must tell Manoji of our decision on Sunday," said Sanchini, "and Amelia will need to stay at home. She has only eight more weeks before her exams. Why don't you both go and I will look after her and tell the young man of our decision."

"Are you happy to leave Kandy today?" asked Mr Ashok.

"Yes, very happy."

"Well go and pack, and I will pick you up in two hours' time."

When he left, Sanchini helped her father pack.

"You're not going to drive, are you?"

"Of course I am. Remember it's not me that drives the car, it's the car that drives me!"

"When did you last take it out?"

"I picked up Amelia from school last Friday."

"Ah yes, she told me, she was so embarrassed."

"Don't be silly, she loved it. I put her in the back, and I even wore my chauffeur's cap."

🐊

This was just the sort of arrival that the hotel's security guard loved, a grand 1930s Rolls-Royce drophead coupe. As soon as he had brought all traffic in the street to a halt with his whistle, Mr Ashok applied the handbrake, and without looking opened the latch of his door. Unbeknown to him, the security guard had rushed to open said door, but the outside handle was not where he had expected to find it. Suicide doors have hinges to the rear, and handles to the fore, so the heavy swinging door caught him squarely on the chest and the poor man rebounded onto his bottom, much to the amusement of the tuk tuk drivers. Just as Lionel and Lysanta arrived, Mr Ashok was helping the much-embarrassed guard to his feet.

"What a car, and what an entrance!" Lionel said in an aside to Lysanta, who, ever the professional, quickly guided Mr Ashok to the safety of the steps, blissfully unconcerned by the chaos he had caused.

"All packed Lionel? We are going to have a great trip."

Lionel said his goodbyes and generously tipped Lysanta and the still slightly dazed guard. Mr Ashok released the handbrake and off they went, leaving a waving Lysanta and a saluting security guard.

Lionel had often wondered why these old cars were sometimes referred to as 'land yachts', now he knew why. Mr Ashok didn't drive, he sailed through waves of cars, tuk tuks and scooters, even the buses gave them a respectful berth, and policemen waved them through junctions and roundabouts. The Mulliner Park Ward chassis with its black and white livery cut an unusual figure amongst the chaos of Kandy's traffic. Once on the expressway, Mr Ashok trimmed the throttle in the centre of the steering wheel, and the car seemed to float.

"We should arrive in Colombo before the traffic hots up at 5pm, Sanchini is ringing now to book us into the Galle Face Hotel. It's a marvellous grande dame of a hotel established in 1864, whose ethos is 'yesterday's charm with tomorrow's comfort'."

Once they got off the toll road and into the outskirts of Colombo, Mr Ashok re-employed the sailing principle, and it wasn't long before they tacked into the entrance of the hotel. Unlike the Royal Bar, with its the one security guard, half a dozen bellhops swarmed around in their smart blue Nehru-collared suits. After Lionel and the bags were removed, Mr Ashok parked the car; it would take half an hour to explain that you didn't depress the button at the end of the handbrake, let alone how to operate the throttle. Reunited in a cool marble-floored reception hall, Mr Ashok went off with the general manager to inspect the rooms, then took Lionel on a guided tour of the hotel. They passed through two pairs of double doors – a sort of airlock, not to keep heat in, as you might in England, but to keep it very firmly out. Beyond these doors it was very hot with a long wide polished-tile corridor and central coconut mat runner; above them were not just a couple of enormous gilt-metal-framed and alabaster bowled lights, but a string of eight. To the right of this corridor was the dining pavilion, held aloft by three rows of white-painted columns, just like the pillars of a multi-tiered wedding cake. This central pavilion was enclosed on three sides by this vast four-storey hotel. The south-facing open side was laid out with a large 'chess board' mown lawn with a bar, swimming pool and endless Indian Ocean beyond.

"May I get you a drink?"

"Marvellous," replied Mr Ashok, as he strode to the beach club. "Two long Arrack Attacks, please."

The barman looked blankly.

"Two long Arrack Attacks?" repeated Lionel.

Again, the barman stared blankly, then smiled, and stared blankly again.

"Allow me," said Mr Ashok, moving towards the bar's high counter.

He then held up two fingers, spoke rapidly and nodded his head a bit.

It was like a starter gun had gone off. The barman leapt into life. He was a whirr of glasses (long), ice, fresh mint, arrack and ginger beer.

"Wonderful," said Mr Ashok, raising this perfect Sri Lankan cocktail.

"Cheers or as we say on the south coast, bottoms up!"

"I have forgotten how hot Colombo is, no wonder the Kings lived in Kandy. Tonight we are in for a treat, an author friend of mine's daughter is a jazz singer and she's playing here. I have booked a table for 7.30, just enough time for a swim."

Lionel couldn't wait to see the rounded figure of Mr Ashok in trunks. Twenty minutes later he watched him walk down the terracotta-tiled path to the pool, resplendent in a hat, a long-tailed sandy jacket more appropriate for a souk than a colonial hotel, and a pair of coral-pink trunks. As the arabesque jacket swung open, Lionel couldn't fail to notice a straining waistband. On the approach to the pool, Mr Ashok tossed his hat and coat on a sun lounger and literally fell in. There was no attempt at either a dive or a jump, just a fall. When he finally surfaced, he elegantly propelled himself with a very precise breaststroke. After covering two lengths he returned to Lionel's end and called out, "Come on, get in. It's just what the doctor ordered."

"I didn't pack any trunks."

"Look in my jacket, my daughter packed an extra pair. She thought you might not have any with you, the ladies are always one step ahead. Go and change, it's lovely."

Lionel obeyed, as it's difficult to contradict the owner of a Rolls-Royce. The pool was saltwater and colder than the air temperature, but the real joy was afterwards – standing under the cold freshwater shower overlooking the sea.

The jazz bar adjoining the 1864 restaurant was thankfully air-conditioned. They sank into low banquettes, much loved by the young, but jolly difficult to get out of if you are over sixty. The singer was stunningly beautiful, singing everything from Aretha Franklin to Sade. She shimmered in a silver satin dress beneath an exotic head of curls. To silence two old boys for half an hour is quite an achievement. After enthusiastic clapping they tried to get up. On their fourth attempt, they managed to rock themselves on to their feet.

The restaurant's vibe was 'Scottish Modernist', with white linen-covered tables below antler-branched chandeliers. An interesting combination in the tropics thought Lionel, as they sat in black-painted open elbow chairs with shepherd's crook arms and black and white tartan upholstery.

Almost as soon as they were settled, a complimentary cheese and spring onion tart arrived, followed by another treat, and then another ... or was it their starter, there were too many courses to properly allocate. When the main course arrived, lobster with wide ribbons of fresh pasta, Lionel reckoned he had eaten more cream and butter than he would normally have in a fortnight! His thoughts turned to his own waistband.

Chapter 21

Colombo

The day started as it should, with a breakfast worthy of such a grand hotel. The oblong restaurant pavilion was stepped and divided into two tiers to accommodate the sloping fall of the ground. This also cleverly circulated cool air from the silent ceiling fans to all four rows of tables. Lionel descended the wide and shallow steps to the lower tier to find Mr Ashok already holding court.

"Good morning, these gentlemen are Scottish freemasons here to install a new Grand Master."

Lionel, who was hoping for a quiet coffee and coconut water, was plunged into vigorous handshakes. Mr Ashok continued, "Hamish is on a tour of Asia. He was in India last week, and after he's set Colombo on the right path, he's off to Perth in Australia."

"Aye, our work is rarely done."

"I thought it was just aprons and jewels," said Lionel peevishly, departing in search of his drinks.

"My friend finds the heat difficult," apologised Mr Ashok.

"Nay bother," said Hamish, "he's an Englishman!" To which the other Scottish freemasons laughed.

On his return, Lionel found Mr Ashok sitting alone.

"Was I rude?"

"A little," replied Mr Ashok, "but nay bother! Before we get on the coast road, I have booked us on a guided tour of the home of one of Sri Lanka's heroes."

"In this heat!"

"Don't worry, you'll like this one. It's possibly the coolest house in Colombo, it's the home of the late Geoffrey Bawa, architect and father of 'Tropical Modernism'."

Lionel found it difficult to limit himself to just one course at buffet breakfasts. The choice was just too much, here on seemingly endless white-clothed tables stood: tropical fruits, continental cold meats and cheeses, sticky patisseries, an English cooked section and smouldering Sri Lankan curries. Some of which should have a warning sign: 'Caution, this may burn.' Luckily, the string and egg hoppers were quite benign, but generally anything red in colour, stings.

As Mr Ashok went for the full English, Lionel headed for the cold meats. Funny how when you're away, you try something less familiar. As he looked at Mr Ashok's chicken sausages in awe, so did Mr Ashok view his slices of beef pastrami. The stomach is a marvellous thing: after the full assault at breakfast, it still manages to remind the owner of both lunch and dinner!

It was a heavier pair who climbed into the car, and were waved off by the general manager, chief concierge, Emmanuel, and most of the livered bellhops. It really was the way to travel, combining yesterday's charm with tomorrow's comfort. The final approach to Geoffrey Bawa's Number 11 was down a narrow residential dead end. Dominating the outside of the house were a pair of James Bond-like garage doors. Their large teak frames had a diagonal patterned lattice infill, running on large brass wheels.

Suddenly, one door was slid behind the other to reveal a similar Rolls-Royce.

"Snap!" cried an excited Mr Ashok. "Many people have told me I have the pair to Mr Bawa, and here it is!"

"You are very welcome. Have you come for the tour?" asked a man of about sixty, looking comfortable in both vest and white short-sleeved shirt. "Come in, it's much cooler than out. May I ask how long you've had your splendid Rolls-Royce?"

"Almost twenty years. I handled the estate of an old Scottish tea planter in Nuwara Eliya. Thankfully, he had retained a driver who ran it out every week, even when the old boy was bed-bound. The driver told me that his employer had difficulty sleeping towards the end, so he would take him on long drives with his nurse in the front passenger seat. The driver and nurse spent so much time together that they fell in love and subsequently married. The great thing was that the old Scot left the car to his driver in his will. I bought it from him, and the proceeds helped them buy a house on the south coast. Sorry, I'm carrying on."

"No, not at all. It's not every day we get a matching pair," replied the guide. "My name is Mr Laxman, I'm a retired architect and passionate follower of Mr Bawa."

As Mr Ashok took his phone from one of his bellow pockets to record the nuances of this matching Rolls-Royce, Lionel started breathing through his nose. For the first time in Colombo, he was beginning to feel comfortable – this really was a cool house. Parked behind him were two classic cars, and in front him stood a small tree shading a little garden furnished with a black-painted metal chair, a Dutch ebony and cane sofa and a rectangular coffee table. Lionel thought, "I could do this in my ground-floor shop at home, forget houseplants, let's use house trees."

"Please follow me. Look how the corridor and floors are painted white. This is done with an epoxy resin. A liquid material that hardens due to a chemical reaction between the resin and hardener, leaving a durable and high gloss surface used by Geoffrey Bawa extensively, it allows the falling cold air to roll, friction free, around the property. As we move through the house you will notice many small gardens, not only signalled by plants, but by their floors too. Some being just pebbles, others paving stones and then there are pools of water. All these pocket gardens are open to the sun and rain. There is no watering done here, as Shiva looks after our gardens." Lionel nudged Mr Ashok and mouthed, "Who's Shiva?"

To which he whispered back, "Our God, I'll explain later."

As they walked down the corridor they were drawn to a larger lightwell with a shallow rectangular pool of water, screened by four columns.

"Mr Bawa bought these teak columns from the Chettinad in Southern India, almost opposite Jaffna. He believed in the principle of 'Bricolage', incorporating architectural salvage in new buildings. He was a master of bringing together different architectural elements, furnishings and works of art. The Germans have a word for it, 'Gesamtkunstwerk,' which translates as a 'total work of art.'"

Lionel could think of quite a few total 'Gesamtkunst...!' at home in England, but thankfully he hadn't met any in Sri Lanka yet. Although the Russian jeweller could be a candidate.

The gentle Mr Laxman continued. "Can you feel the air here?"

They looked at each other.

"It does feel cooler?" Lionel ventured.

"Correct, this is not only the lightest part of the house, but also the coolest. The gently moving water draws the hot air down, and once cooled, it spills over the brick kerbing onto the floor."

"As the air falls, so the hot air rises," chipped in Mr Ashok.

"Correct," said Mr Laxman, "there is little or no wind to cool the building as this property is surrounded by the high walls of its neighbours. This passive system of ponds and plants has served this house well since the late 1960s."

"Remarkable," chimed in Lionel. They thanked Mr Laxman in the entrance hall next to Mr Bawa's car and reversed theirs down 33rd Lane, onto the Galle Road, bound for pots and bamboo.

Chapter 22

Colombo

"Who is this Shiva?" asked Lionel.

"Shiva is very important to all Hindus. Shiva and two other gods, Brahma and Vishnu, are responsible for the universe. They believe Brahma is the creator of the universe, while Vishnu is the preserver of it, and Shiva's role is like a wrecking ball. Destroying things, so they may be recreated better, as Hindus believe in beneficial change."

"What, like an 'Act of God'."

"Yes, as the buildings will be better considered in reconstruction."

"What about the loss of life?"

"It's Shiva's will."

Lionel paused, he was old enough and wise enough not to pursue subjects he only had a glancing knowledge of.

The Galle Road in Colombo was busy with men on either side, some alarmingly with guns and some with hard hats. The guns were carried by the military attachments outside the US Embassy, Indian High Commission and other official buildings, and the hard hats were for the many construction workers labouring on the skeletons of huge new skyscrapers.

"There's a lot of building work going on," commented Lionel, "could you live on a 42nd floor?"

"I'm very happy to be on two floors in Kandy. But once Dinish took us all to Bangkok. His jeweller friend had got us a deal at the Peninsula Hotel on the river. We had three rooms on the 33rd floor, and after two days I was gripping the walls! I had never suffered vertigo before. I understand the penthouses of these tower blocks go for millions. It's no wonder nobody lives in them, they're all too frightened to!"

As they moved farther away from the city, the shops and crowds became thinner, it was only then that Lionel took in the elegance of the car's interior. The well figured burr walnut dashboard was peopled by numerous black-faced dials, some obvious and some not so. There seemed to be lots of them, with oscillating hands reading amps, volts and temperature. The bigger fellows, the size of bedside alarm clocks, indicated revs, miles per hour and time itself. What fascinated Lionel was the governor in the bull's-eye of the steering wheel: it had three knobs, ignition, carburation and throttle. It was the latter that acted as the cruise control, having an indicated range between 'fast' and 'slow.' The other unusual thing he noticed was there was no gear lever or handbrake between the passenger and driver; these were to the right of the driver's seat. Not that they troubled Mr Ashok, as once in third gear he seemed to stay there, rarely stopping long enough to engage the handbrake. As had happened yesterday on their journey from Kandy to Colombo, policemen generally waved them through roundabouts and busy junctions. The only obstacle to progress were traffic lights, but he tempered his speed to arrive only on greens. As soon as Lionel saw his first tethered roadside cow, he knew Colombo was beginning to ebb away.

The plan was to stay on the coast road and stop at roadside stalls displaying anything of interest. Lionel was looking at a pineapple stall on the other side of the road when the car suddenly veered off and stopped.

"Here is our first call."

Lionel looked to his left: a small Sri Lankan man sat cross-legged weaving a shallow rattan basket. Above and beside were baskets of every conceivable form: shallow, deep, round, square, with looped handles and some with lug handles.

His car quickly drew attention; and soon they were surrounded by women holding back the enquiring hands of small children, men looking at the dash and dogs cocking their legs on the car's vast tyres. Mr Ashok marched into the stall, quickly followed by its owner.

"Lionel, what do you think you could sell in England?"

"Definitely light shades, wastepaper baskets and rectangular paper trays."

"What about these?" said Mr Ashok as he held a gourd-shaped lampshade over his head.

A tropical lamp standard, very mid-century modern, perfect.

"Marvellous, how much are they?"

Mr Ashok relayed this question to the owner in Sinhalese, and after much nodding and shaking of heads, augmented with theatrical hand gestures, he reverted to English.

"Three thousand rupees."

"That's under £10, that sounds like a great price."

"It is, but you need to take at least fifty."

"I'm happy with that. I'm sure I can stack them in the container.

How long will he take to do fifty?"

"Probably forty-eight hours, if I asked! But there is no hurry. Is this our first purchase?"

"It jolly well is."

After more smiling, vigorous handshaking, they continued to scrutinise the man's stock.

"Great," said Lionel, holding up a rattan wastepaper basket with a circular wooden base, "they need a more robust top edge though. I know from experience once the top edge goes, the cane all too quickly unravels."

Mr Ashok engaged the owner again, and through the power of both speech and mime, including sitting on the basket, biting the rim, and finally a small re-enactment of weaving the top edge.

"All sorted, he'll reinforce the top. They are 3,000 LKR each, and you need to take thirty. I think he's beginning to worry about his impending workload!"

They carried on, walking further into the cave-like interior. There was so much. At the back, he held up a circular table with three bamboo legs, twisted on the diagonal to form a tripod. After he had imitated a pixie sitting on a toadstool, it was agreed that they were the correct height to be useful, and after the now familiar buying ceremony, it was established the tables could also be 3,000 LKR.

"Is everything the same price in this shop?"

"I don't think our owner wants to complicate things. But I can assure you he will be doing alright. He's asked whether you'd like a king coconut or a Coke?"

"The former, please, I will just have another walk through the stock."

Lionel managed to find some small straw boxes, which would

make perfect packaging. They were formed from two different-sized sleeves that came together to form an adjustable box woven from multi-coloured ribbons of straw. They looked useful and were hopefully cheap; happy that he had seen everything, he joined Mr Ashok who was now sitting and chatting with the owner on one of the stools.

"I love the stool, 3,000 LKR?"

"We can do better than that," he replied.

A list was agreed, and assurances were repeated that they didn't need everything in forty-eight hours. Lionel gave the owner a goodwill payment of 60,000 LKR, and it was a beaming owner and his extended family that waved them both off.

As Mr Ashok engaged first gear and drew onto the road, he said, "They'll always tell you that they can do it in forty-eight hours, seven days is much more realistic. The expense will be the collection and we only want to do that once."

The buying continued: stopping, viewing, listing, negotiating and drinking king coconuts. Once back in Galle, Lionel reckoned they'd already filled half a 20-foot container, and they hadn't even seen one ceramic pot!

"This might be the lightest shipping container load in history," said Lionel.

"Don't be too concerned, tomorrow we will do the potteries but tonight I will show you Galle Fort."

Chapter 23

Galle

The approach road to Galle was as busy as Colombo's, but being only single-laned it seemed even busier. Shops, stalls, people, scooters, tuk tuks, and amongst it all their coupe, which incidentally comes from the French 'to cut.' Although lorry-sized in length and height, the cutting of the cabin gave the Rolls some elegance. There was no compromise to the comfort within the cab, which included a small cushion, not for Mr Ashok to sit on, but for his back.

"I need to get my feet to the pedals," he said, "every year I get shorter, the pedals seem to get further away!"

The shops and stalls on the coast were replaced with trees, along with roosting and shrieking birds. Lionel's eyes were caught by the food market opposite with displays of great branches of green bananas, rows of pineapples, and stacks of terracotta-potted buffalo curd. The next landmark on their approach to Galle was the large cricket ground, where its spectators face the ramparts of this 300-year-old fort. Built by the Dutch to protect Sri Lanka's principal port, the goliath-sized brown stones were fixed in sandy-coloured mortar. These sloping ramparts have a real permanence that was tested in the 2004 tsunami: they saved not only the fort's buildings but its people too.

Mr Ashok guided the Rolls through the new gate and turned right.

"Let's get our bearings before we find a hotel."

Keeping the walls of the fort on their right, they passed the colonnades of merchant houses, army barracks, temples and white-painted buildings. To Lionel, it had the intimacy of Rye in East Sussex, a cinque port town along the south coast not far from Hastings. The interior of the fort was a grid of streets with cobbled floors and two-storey buildings. The architecture was a pick and mix of nations: Moorish, Dutch, Portuguese, English, and even the whiteness of Greece. After they had completed a circuit Mr Ashok steered into Church Street, passing the very impressive Amangalla Hotel.

"Too much for me, just the sort of place our Russian jeweller might go to," said Mr Ashok, briefly glancing at a now worried passenger whilst sailing straight past and on to the Galle Face Hotel. With handbrake applied, he skipped out of the car straight up the steps to the restaurant. Lionel had noticed he always liked to initiate actions with a vigorous start, which gently dissipated until suitable seating could be found, and then once seated Mr Ashok liked to hold court. After decades of searching for goodies, he now allowed things and people to find him. This was one of the reasons why he firmly believed that the 'Crocodile' sapphire had found Manoji.

After the security man had alerted the general manager to the arrival of a rather stately motorcar, they were received with high accord and promptly offered fine rooms at an extremely preferential rate with the suggestion that they leave the car outside. "It's good to remind the Amangalla that we are the principal hotel in this fort," thought an ever-so-slightly-proud general manager.

"My only concern is that enthusiasts might try and lift the bonnet, and bad men might try and take the mascot. If I'm to leave it here, would your man guard against this?"

"Of course," he replied.

"When we're all asleep?"

"Doubly so," he assured them. "Please relax. May I offer you some tea?"

They stayed on the elevated veranda, happily watching the world go by. Tea moved to drinks and then to dinner.

"Sometimes the grass isn't greener. Let's have a wander after dinner."

"I agree, what's the smart money on in Galle?" said Lionel, looking at the menu.

"I'd have the crab, we're on the south coast."

Two crab curries with a bottle of rosé were chosen. The water and wine came quickly, and on their second glass of wine the curries arrived.

"Oh, my word," said Lionel, looking at a reddish crab poised as though about to attack.

"My days of wrestling with claws are over," Mr Ashok said, waving at the general manager. "Lionel, would you like yours dressed too?"

"No thank you. I'm happy to wrestle with this one."

"I can't afford to do battle in my suit. One splash and it's game over."

Once Mr Ashok was reunited with his crab, Lionel attacked his own with vigour. By the time he was breaking the third claw he was looking enviously at Mr Ashok's dressed one, but by the fifth claw, Lionel had got into the groove, deciding it wasn't a battle but a pleasure.

Replete and in need of exercise, they set off.

"We have streets to explore and fort walls to walk. You know what we really need are lots of egg-shaped stones."

"I do."

"Well, there's a retired geologist who may just be the man to turn some for us."

Mr Ashok walked ahead of Lionel, like a lead plane in formation, showing the way, but not too far to lose communication. They were an odd pairing as they made their way down Church Street. After turning left into Pedlar Street, they walked a further 50 metres to a two-storey terraced house with an arcaded front. Mr Ashok knocked on the closed louvered door.

"You are going to like this man, he is my late son-in-law's father, Jacintha."

Before Lionel could reply, the door opened to one of the tallest men Lionel had ever met.

"Ashok. Come in, come in."

Mr Ashok pressed forward and looked over his shoulder to reassure a very confused companion.

Lionel could now see where Amelia got her looks from. She was a genealogical combination of the beautiful Sanchini and this man's late son.

"Come, come," he bid them, walking up two flights of stairs to a terrace with a mid-thigh-height parapet.

"Have a seat. How lovely to see you Ashok, and who is your friend?"

"This is Lionel, he is an English version of me, just slightly taller."

"So, Lionel, you are an antiques man?"

"I am."

"It's been too long," Jacintha suddenly burst out. "I should have come and seen my Dinish's daughter and her beautiful mother. I just find it very hard to summon up the courage, when I see them, I know I will cry. I cry for my son, and his extinguished happiness. I know in time, I will be more able to share their lives, but for now all I do is cry. He was a lovely son. He only studied gemmology to share my passion. As our only child he was our total focus. I must stop, it's too much for you."

They were joined by a young man dressed in white, punctuated with a red fez on his head.

"Three arracks, and plenty of ice please."

The 'fez' silently nodded and disappeared down the steps.

"From my rooftop, you can see all over this historic fort. When my dear wife saw this house, she was pregnant with Dinish. What do you say in Britain, 'New baby, new home.' We were lucky as many houses in Pedlar Street are low, but she said to me, 'A tall man needs a tall house.' Dinish was seventeen when my wife died. She had breast cancer, but we made her comfortable here on this rooftop. The neighbours were unusually kind and allowed us to erect a tent, like an Ottoman prince's pavilion. I spent my days with her, and then worked when Dinish returned from school. She had precious hours with her little prince, reading and helping him with his studies. Our staff played their part too, adopting the white Moroccan tunic and red fez. Young Ari wears it now, like his mother and father did." On cue, Ari arrived and laid down a tray on an Indian hexagonal table, leaving a bottle of ten-year-old arrack, three glass tumblers and a brimming silver ice bucket with tongs.

"You still have it," said Mr Ashok, pointing at the ice bucket.

"Of course I do. I remember you showing me around your cellar when I first came to Kandy to meet my son's intended. You gave it as a leaving present. It's really treasured. How's Amelia doing? She must be finishing school this summer? She is an absolute delight, is she studying hard? Hopes to go to university abroad? She wrote that in her last letter to me. She working to win a place at either England's Oxford or Cambridge? You know I have money set aside for college fees."

"You've already been too generous."

"She writes me wonderful thank-you letters. I'd like to help her more."

This was the opening Mr Ashok wanted.

"Well, we need a favour. Which I believe has a lot to do with Amelia."

"Why?"

"I believe Amelia holds a flame for a young raft boy."

"Who?" asked Jacintha.

"It's a long story, but will you help us?"

"Of course."

"We need lots of turned stones."

"How many?"

"Hundreds."

"OK, what size?"

"The size and shape of a hen's egg."

"Come this way, my workshop is on the ground floor."

After walking down two flights of stairs, they moved through the hall to a small courtyard garden. Across it was a large white single-storey building, most of the facade enclosed by a large pair of turquoise-painted panelled doors. Jacintha took a key from his coat pocket and unlocked the blind doors, which protected a pair of sliding Crittle-like metal-framed glazed doors.

"I need big doors to get my lathes in. Some buy classic cars, but I buy old lathes."

When Jacintha switched on the overhead lights, the room sparkled with gleaming steel. Lionel had seen some workshops in his time, but this was up there with his Scottish clockmaker friend in Lewes, and like Bill's, this workshop was used, well-ordered and smelled of fine oil.

Jacintha walked past two lathes to the back wall covered in a random arrangement of wooden drawers and cupboard doors. From a shallow drawer, no more than 4 inches high, he took out not one, but two, malachite stones, exactly the size and shape they wanted.

"Perfect," said Mr Ashok.

"How many do you need?"

"Five hundred?"

"Give me a week and you will have your eggs. Would you like some wooden ones too? We have many woods that polish up well: teak, jack wood, palm wood and even Lignum vitae. I have trained Ari too."

"It's more than we expected."

"I'm happy to do anything for my granddaughter, and it gives me a project. Now come, let's go back up to the roof, and then you might tell me why I should be at my lathe for the next seven days!"

Chapter 24
Galle

Mr Ashok and Lionel breakfasted on the same raised terrace, in plain sight of his guarded car.

"You know the curd comes in those shallow earthenware pots," said Mr Ashok.

"Yes, lovely simple dishes, which would pass my weight test."

"Well, they are all made locally for the buffalo curd, or as you call it, yoghurt. In the supermarkets they sell them in plastic tubs. Important if you own a fridge, you don't want to scratch your white plastic-coated racking. If, like most Sri Lankans, you don't have a fridge, you want your curd in the earthenware pot."

"Why?"

"Well, when you dip the outside in water, evaporation will cool the dish, preserving the curd for three to four days. Here we have to work with nature."

"I really like them, they'd make great dog water bowls. If we like the taste of clay pot water, I'm sure Jack's dog, Clive, would like it too. I often see discarded ones by the side of roads. If I managed to organise their collection I could clean and reuse them and I'm sure I'd be able to sell them in England."

"Let's see how they're made first, you can then get the size you'd ideally want."

They left Galle and travelled east in the direction of Unawatuna, stopping outside a large roadside stall. There is something irresistible about repetition. Like the colonnades surrounding St Mark's Square in Venice. This stall didn't have one earthenware cooking pot, it had hundreds. A curry cooked in an earthenware pot has heart, there's a certain creaminess that comes from the very ground itself.

Both car and suit were greeted with much enthusiasm, and after a short exchange, they were led through the stall into a well-tended back courtyard. Mr Ashok spoke in Sinhalese to a smiley, tiny lady, who was in fact the owner, her young daughter running the roadside stall.

She was bird-like, no more than 4'8", and she wore a yellow cotton dress printed in the colours of her garden. She stood beaming in a courtyard peopled by pots. There were at least five large pots filled with still water, each holding beautiful lotus flowers alongside tiny tropical goldfish swimming amongst the visible roots. Then there were even bigger pots housing splendid red palms, the new growth as livid as a baboon's bottom. Amongst the palms was a large bow-fronted water cistern, containing two large black and white catfish. The courtyard was an oasis, speaking volumes about its owner. She was a successful artisan craftswoman who could garden, and Lionel would bet she could cook to the very highest standards to boot. More potted red palms screened a utilitarian area, where a large kiln stood, rectangular in shape, measuring some 8' x 8' with 4-foot-high walls. It showed old cracks, the scars of many firings. The bottom of this now empty kiln was divided by three small walls, and in these voids, dried coconut husks burned for days to fire the many different shelves of vessels. The larger pots were made for cooking, their rounded bottoms allowing an even heat for either gas rings or wood fires. Similarly sized were the globe-and-shaft-shaped clay water vessels used in Sri Lankan homes; these would stand on three-legged metal rings. The water from these pots is deliciously cool and, once tasted, never forgotten. Then there were the curd pots, heavy, simple straight-sided bowls with finger and thumb moulded rims, the ones Lionel had identified as making good dog water bowls. Perfect for British pet lovers.

Below the kiln, on the next terrace, were a string of five black 5,000-litre water tanks. The first one was being fed from a rainwater gutter, the remaining four linked with a 2-inch hose, keeping all five topped up to the same level, demonstrating that the power of the vacuum can sometimes rival Newton's gravity.

A potter must be resourceful, the margins are small, and any costs must always be saved. Between the string of tanks, and the neat white-painted bungalow, was an open shelter with short walls and overhanging tiled roof. This is where the electric potter's wheel was housed. It stood amongst a display of just-made small damp pots, presumably for sugar or salt.

Mr Ashok couldn't resist asking for a demonstration, whereupon the potter immediately grabbed a lump of wet clay, about the size of half of a football. She centred it on the steel wheel, stretching behind her to push the square-pin plug home into a rather kamikaze wall socket. She then drew her stool nearer to the wheel and with her bare right foot depressed the pedal. Within twenty seconds she had lifted off a perfectly formed salt pot, which she gently placed next to its fellows. Returning to the rotating stump of clay, she made another pot, another, and another. With no cutting wire in sight, she used her fingernail to release each one.

"What size do you want these dog bowls?" asked Mr Ashok.

"Nine inches in diameter."

"I think we've found our potter."

Chapter 25

Unawatuna

After agreeing a price of 250 LKR per water bowl, Mr Ashok and Lionel also commissioned the globe-and-shaft-shaped 'clay pot' water jars with associated metal stands. Her younger – sixty-year-old – neighbour made the stands, informing them that you need young strength for metalwork! Finally, rounded-bottom cooking pots were added to the order, the ones which produced earthy creamy curries and needed the rough brown twine doughnut ring stands to sit on, protecting tabletops from their hot bottoms and stopping them rolling over. A list of quantities was agreed, along with a 20,000 LKR down-payment. When the Rolls drew away from the stall, half the village was there to bid them farewell.

"I do believe we have filled our container," said Mr Ashok, moving into third gear. "Are you hungry?"

"Always," replied Lionel.

"Well, I know just the place. It's along the coast road and just over the railway line amongst paddy fields."

"Great, I have never seen growing rice. In Kandy, three-wheeler Chris showed me pepper on a vine. I've probably had pepper every day of my adult life, and that's the first time I've actually seen it growing. It's a bit like India, always in the news, but how many of us have seen its colour or smelt its smells? Very few Westerners, I'd imagine."

"Well today, I will introduce you to an Englishwoman who has lived in Sri Lanka for over twenty years." Mr Ashok fell silent and drove, entering that peaceful place of man and machinery in quiet union, with the gentle throb of the engine rarely heard above the calls of birds. As the high sides of his car kept the road noise out, the open roof allowed the overhead to be heard. Lionel marvelled at Mr Ashok's sixth sense; telepathy is often dismissed as coincidence, but as he got older he had begun to notice how numerous the incidences were. After the hustle and bustle of the coast road, it felt good to turn north over the railway track and into the countryside. As the roads got narrower, the other vehicles were replaced by bicycles and pedestrians, paddy fields and small villages. Mr Ashok sounded his horn and slowed the Rolls to allow a uniformed guard to open a heavy pair of blind gates. He successfully feathered the car through them and up a steep drive.

First to greet them was a small and noisy four-legged fellow. Standing no more than twelve inches high and measuring two feet in length, the smooth-coated dachshund lavished licks and excited barks at the new arrivals.

"Nigella, don't lick Ashok, he might have Kandy bugs."

"Rosemary, how lovely."

"What a surprise! No Sanchini or Amelia?"

"No, Amelia is studying hard for her A-levels. She wants to get into one of your English universities."

"Marvellous. Lunch?"

"Yes please. Rosie, I would like to introduce you to my friend Lionel from Hastings."

"Blimey, I'm not sure we allow people from Hastings at the Who."

The words were delivered with a poker face, which melted into a rumbling chuckle.

"Only joking, my favourite artist used to live in Hastings."

"Who's that?" asked Lionel.

"I'll give you a clue. During the 1980s I worked in London as a cook – directors' lunches and private parties. A good kitchen is laid out as a golden triangle, not too dissimilar to an Old Master painting, but in a kitchen's case it has a cooker, a fridge and a...?

"Come Ashok, while your friend thinks, let's find a drink."

Rosie slid her hand through Mr Ashok's proffered arm and walked through this tropical Eden towards a large white-painted pavilion.

"Bratby, John Bratby!" Lionel exclaimed, a little too loudly, as he was rather excited at solving her riddle, before adding, "The 'kitchen sink' realist."

"I like your new friend, Ashok. We are going to get along. Now, would you like beers or something stronger?"

"Beers, please," said a still pumped-up Lionel, trailing behind.

The draft beers were poured at the bar, located at the nearest end of this stunning pavilion.

"I'll leave you for a moment and scoop up any singletons by the pool. Let's have a lunch party," Rosie announced as she walked through clusters of black-painted Regency-style open armchairs, faithfully followed by her daxie.

"Cheers," said Mr Ashok.

"Bottoms up," responded Lionel. "Did you see the jewels on that dog's collar?"

"I did, it's the sort of thing Kandyan Kings would've done."

"How long have you known Rosie?"

"A long time, we used to stay when we came down to see Dinish and his father. Rosie is English, it's helpful to practise a second language, and the food here is the best."

Rosie returned carrying Nigella under one arm: the weight of the collar was obviously becoming too much.

"I have found some lovelies who are keen to join us. Now where's my gin and French?"

As they chatted about Bratby paintings seen and sold, they were joined by a tall man with an aristocratic bearing.

"Here is my handsome deb's delight, George," said Rosie, clutching his elbow. "It's so lovely to have a good-looking man about the place."

As Rosie enthused, George blushed. Minutes later, a rather glamorous dark-haired lady joined the party, followed by a blonde wearing more jewellery than the dachshund.

"Perfect," said Rosie. "We have our very own party."

She had the polish of an assured hotelier, coupled with the enthusiasm of a Sloane Ranger – those bubbly girls who had worked hard and partied harder, in a decade when London was awash with money and even the dull month of November was brightened with a Beaujolais Nouveau run. She sat at the head of the table putting Mr Ashok on her right, and 'Gorgeous George' on her left. Lionel sat at the other end next to glamour and jewels. The conversation had all the excitement and sprightliness of strangers making connections. Once mutual friends had been unearthed and they'd collectively decided it was a 'such a small world', the party settled into the afternoon. The end came just at the right time, with Rosie rising from the table, saying,

"Well, that was jolly, now I have work to do!"

Chapter 26

Mirissa

The drive from the Who to Mirissa should have taken an hour, but the roadside stalls in Koggala, Ahangama and Weligama proved too tempting; they found hundreds of coconut spoons costing all of 150 LKR each.

"Did you notice the island?" asked Mr Ashok.

"Yes, the one with the white-painted jetty."

"It was developed, or as we say 'colonised'," he winked at Lionel, "by a Burgher family. Historically, at low tide the family hosted elephant polo matches. I came once, quite a spectacle. The strangest thing was that there was hardly any noise. OK, there was plenty from the mahouts and players, you can just imagine the crowd, but when the elephants moved they turned with such grace and emitted no noise. You absolutely knew you were in the presence of graceful godlike giants, the ground shook, it was an honour to be a bystander."

This was the fabulous thing about Mr Ashok: every part of this island was the catalyst for a tale. A past visit, a home of a friend, or just the place where an object had come from. He didn't talk in the car, his special place at the helm, sailing through the multitudes. He liked hopping out of the unusual doors, which never failed to facilitate surprise. Once out, he took a couple of smart steps, then came to rest with feet apart, fists on hips and jutting elbows. Napoleon stood like that, but unlike Napoleon there was no scowl or menace.

"Now to business," he said, as he directed Lionel towards the many fish stalls.

"Does your man at The Papers Hotel have a barbecue?"

"I doubt it, vegans don't eat fish."

"I keep forgetting the food world has splintered. People were once vegetarians or not. If you weren't a vegetarian, it was meat and two veg with fish on Fridays. Then the meat was questioned, and shortly afterwards fish too. Now I hear milk, butter and eggs have been dropped. There is only one solution."

"What's that?" Lionel was expecting some grand proclamation from this tropical-suited Napoleon.

"We change hotels. No fish for dinner, or eggs for breakfast, isn't going to work for me. I will take you to a hotel that has a barbecue. Now, what fish would you like? Thin blue ones or fat fellows, red ones?"

"What should I look for?"

"Bright eyes and good colour mark a fresh fish, but all should be fresh here."

"You're the native, you choose."

"Less of the native, Lionel. Us Royal Kandyans maybe indigenous, but we're certainly not natives."

"I'm terribly sorry," Lionel turned crimson.

"You look just like that deb's delight George, you're blushing."

Lionel noticed a smile crossing Mr Ashok's face.

"You're too sensitive about words. Come choose a fish."

Lionel chose something matching the colour of his face, telling himself that it looked good against the green banana leaf. Mr Ashok chose not one but three creamy-coloured fish with deep chests. Some interesting bartering proceeded, involving a full armoury of actions: hands, arms, accompanied by a wobbling head. The fish were successfully bought for considerably less than initially quoted!

As soon as the car got into Mirissa's high street, Mr Ashok turned second right, ignoring the first to the harbour. Passing not one but two temples they turned through a pair of 8-foot-high gates. The Rolls filled the drive, and he wickedly pressed the horn; within seconds it was surrounded, and not by smart liveried bellhops, as had been the case at the Galle Face Hotel. The crowd here was more representative of the beach: shorts, T-shirts, sarongs, trunks, baseball caps and flip-flops. From the throng emerged a small man in a short-sleeved blue linen shirt, black shorts and a knee brace, all beneath a rather natty blue yachting hat. The man beamed.

"Mr Ashok, sir, how marvellous, what a car, sir."

"Good to see you too, Sunil. This is my friend Lionel and we would like to stay."

"Certainly."

"Two rooms please."

"Very good, I will get my very best rooms prepared. Come, come have a drink and enjoy our view. Ajith will see to your luggage."

They followed Sunil up three steps into the foyer, beyond which lay a large room with opposing floor-to-ceiling sliding glass and an open commercial kitchen to the right. At the far end, between a coffee station and a bar, was an open space, and through this they could see the bright turquoise sea. Like ball bearings to magnets, the two were drawn through to the beach; in less than thirty yards they had shed shoes and socks to paddle in the bluest Indian Ocean.

"Marvellous," said Lionel.

"Splendid," agreed Mr Ashok.

While they took in their new landscape, Sunil arrived with two beers. Mr Ashok and Sunil caught up in Sinhalese, whilst it dawned on Lionel that this was his previous beach coffee stop. Way beyond, to his left, past the land monitor island, lay Saman at The Papers Hotel. Now at the west end of the beach with a jungly headland to its right, and a bare rocky island to his left, was a surfer's bay within the greater bay. Perfect.

"We bought fish in Weligama hoping your chef might barbecue them?" said Mr Ashok.

"Do you have many? Would you like me to invite Claudio and Manuel?" volunteered Sunil. "They are both here at the moment, adding more rooms and a yoga pavilion to their hotel."

"I saw a shop at the entrance to Claudio's, is that new?"

"It is, and stocked with floaty dresses and tiny bikinis from Ibiza. They have done a lot of work there and Jackie, Manuel's son, is starting a restaurant. You have only just missed them. Claudio surfs here twice a day and Manuel swims four times a day and they then have tea afterwards. They've managed to establish a routine on a barefoot beach, just like the British brought us elevenses and tea. As we all know, routines are hard to establish, but once in place they're easy to follow. I go on. I will speak to chef now and get him making our special beetroot and green bean curries, yellow rice, and dahl. Dinner at 7.30?"

"Is that Sri Lankan or Greenwich Mean Time?" teased Mr Ashok. "You know me," said Sunil.

Lionel, Mr Ashok, Claudio and Manuel had drinks at 7.30 and dinner soon after, with Sunil never quite making it. Mr Ashok's butter fish was sublime, but Lionel's red fish tasted, well, rather red!

Chapter 27

Mirissa

As Lionel had done before, he woke to the sound of crashing waves, drank a glass of water first then looked at his phone for the time. Picking up his reading glasses and grabbing his book – *The Unmarriageable Man* by Ashok Ferrey – he swung a leg towards his white-tiled bathroom. On his return he turned off aeroplane mode, and almost immediately a message popped up from his friend Barty in Hastings.

"Please call, nothing to worry about. B."

When somebody says nothing to worry about, worry is exactly what one does. It was 8am in Mirissa which meant it would be 2:30am in Hastings. He would dismiss it from his mind and call at lunchtime. A swim before breakfast gets the blood moving and somehow clears the mind too. Lionel walked barefoot from his room on the first floor through a sand-covered garden, shaded by a mixture of trees, palms, and broadleaves – a bit like big magnolias with large glossy leaves. He stepped down from the fringe of trees whose roots divided the garden from the beach, turning left where swimmers were already in. Even on a beach there seems to be order. He knew from earlier attempts that the entrance to the sea was the most hazardous. Once past the breakwater point, swimming became easy. It's just getting past that break that troubled Lionel. As a tall man he presented a good target for a breaking wave. Steady progress was made through the white foam of smaller broken waves, and for the larger ones, he adopted his warrior pose, a take-home from yoga! Lunging with one leg in front of the other, he presented a smaller sideways target for the heavier waves. It was on the third use of this stance that Lionel got caught. He surfaced a good 15 feet from where he fell. After retrieving his trunks from around his knees and shaking the sand from his ears, he tried again and this time the waves were kinder. After a steady backstroke into the sun, he floated, letting the waves take him back to the shore.

Whilst Lionel started his day with a swim, Mr Ashok started his with a coffee.

"Jazzy here makes the most lovely cappuccinos, they have a bit of edge to them. Would you like one?"

"Thank you." Lionel, now seated and refreshed, ordered the same.

"What are your plans for the day?"

"Not a lot, I just need to ring home at about lunchtime."

"Good. May I leave you? I need to get back to Kandy and organise a container. What port would be easy for you in England?"

"The big one is Felixstowe, but Southampton and Port of London would work just as well."

"Would you WhatsApp them to me? Along with your business address."

"It's all beginning to feel very real now."

"Are you absolutely sure that you are 100 per cent happy to do this?" enquired Mr Ashok, looking seriously at Lionel.

"Of course I am, but we must have a very clear plan."

"Let's have a walk along the beach. I tend to think better when I'm walking."

Mr Ashok wore a pair of baggy sandy-coloured shorts that just touched the top of his knees. A scout leader came to mind. He started talking of his son-in-law Dinish, and his contact George in London, who would be key for the stone: cutting, marketing and sale. Firstly, he would go to Galle to see Jacintha and check on the progress of production of stone and wooden eggs. It was agreed that Lionel should stay in Sri Lanka until the container was packed and sealed; luckily he hadn't yet got a return ticket anyway. This would give him ample quiet time to decide what to do with his money, the real reason he had come. Mirissa wasn't a bad place to think, there was a huge bay to walk and a sea to swim in. Plenty of distractions: shops, good food, turtle-watching and surfing. The only problem was the wine and he still wasn't very sure about the beer.

"Don't let me go without giving you a little something from my car," said Mr Ashok.

After their walk and determining that bikinis had definitely got smaller whilst trunks had got bigger. Lionel, Jazzy and Ajith waved him off.

'A little something from my car' was a heavy cardboard box. Ajith kindly carried it to Lionel's bedroom. As he excitedly inspected the bottles he noticed how remarkably cool they all were. He wouldn't put it past that Rolls-Royce to have a cooler too. Mr Ashok had given him four reds, six whites and two bottles of champagne. Kindly included in the box was a corkscrew and a card from Amelia, "To Mr Lionel, Happy Holidays, Best wishes Grandpa, Ma and Amelia xxx."

He put two bottles of white Burgundy in his room's fridge and wandered down to the bar, ordering a large bottle of water, a chilled wine glass and some gazpacho soup. God bless those Portuguese invaders: wherever they went, they left gazpacho. Returning to his room, Lionel went to his large balcony, with its red epoxy-painted floor and over-engineered teak trellis railing. It sat in the middle of five rooms, all divided from their neighbours by stepped walls, providing him with privacy as he settled on his balcony with a cold soup and cold glass of the Burgundy.

"Morning, Barty. It's lunchtime here, and I'm sitting on my balcony looking at the most magnificent turquoise sea. Everything alright?"

"Yes, all good here, thank you. Jack has been updating me regularly, mainly to be fed, but also to report on your world of antiques. Sounds like he is doing an excellent job keeping your business warm. Do you remember the journalist from the *Antiques Trade Gazette*?"

"Yes, Mercy Penfold, how could we forget her."

"Well, she rang me yesterday, saying she wanted to tell me news regarding that stolen bronze. You know she paused – she actually paused – I think she was hoping I might fill the gap with something incriminating."

"You didn't, did you?"

"Of course not! You taught me the power of the pause. Which I practise almost weekly on Welsh Huw in Court House Lane."

"Don't tell me he's budging on his prices now?"

"Of course he isn't, his price is the only price, except he is being extremely kind to young Jack!"

"I'm not surprised, he's one of life's good eggs. Thinking about it, you're beginning to make me homesick. What did Ms Penfold say?"

"She wanted to inform me that the bronze had been recovered. Then she went on to say, and I quote, 'It had been returned to its original plinth.'"

"That's odd. Remember you left your business card with that donated raffle prize. You don't think she saw it, do you?"

"I'd forgotten about that, blimey, well that's why then. Anyway, sorry to tell you, but I couldn't share it with anybody but you. A problem shared is a problem halved. Now, tell me about your holiday?"

"It's amazing. Have you got the time?"

"Of course, it's Monday and I don't have to worry about the restaurant until Wednesday. The floor, as they say, is yours."

Chapter 28

Mirissa

Lionel took a sip from his glass of white Burgundy, and began. "It's hot," he paused.

"Is that all," replied Barty.

"Of course it isn't, but I knew sooner or later that you'd ask me about the weather. So I pre-empted."

"Very funny. How hot is it?"

"See, I knew you'd ask. Absolutely baking. Thank God for air-conditioning."

"Where are you now?"

"Sitting on a balcony overlooking Mirissa beach. I started at one end and now I'm staying at the other. It takes twenty-five minutes to walk from my first hotel, Papers, to the current one, Surf Sea Breeze. Mirissa has a lovely deep sandy beach and two islands. The nearest one to Papers is called Snake Island. It looks like dragon, with bare rocks for a head and a spit of sand for a tail. The beach is fun, lots of young action, what with beach volleyball, Instagrammers and turtles. The volleyball players wear trunks and Instagrammers wear 'look-at-me' thongs."

"Have you just stayed on the beach?"

"No, I've had the most amazing adventure."

"Tell all!"

"After only two days I got itchy feet. It was either a lack of eggs, as I managed to book a vegan hotel, or the absence of culture. Saman, the excellent general manager, arranged a taxi for me to go to the old capital Kandy."

"What's it like?"

"Really interesting, a bit like a hot Windsor, but instead of a castle you have a large temple complex. In one of those temples there is believed to be a holy relic of Buddha."

"What, a lock of hair or a finger?"

"No, it's a tooth hidden in a stoupa."

"What's a stoupa?"

"It looks like a muffin dish cover, bell-shaped with an elaborately turned finial, it's huge. They stand 20 or 30 foot high. Most are painted white, but the Sacred Tooth stoupa is gilded. I stayed in this super place, you would love it, the Royal Bar and Hotel in King Street, it's right in the action, no more than a ten-minute walk from all the temples. It's a lot like a hot London club with an open membership and a fabulous general manager, Lysanta. I've never seen so many Union Jacks, modelled in plaster, carved in wood, and even in cement render. When I settled down to my first curry on the balcony, he said to me, and I quote, 'Welcome home, sir.'"

"Sounds marvellous. Have you bought any antiques?" asked Barty, starting to make a coffee as he realised that he was in this for the long haul.

"Just the one bronze of a native girl. I bought it from a Sri Lankan version of me, a Mr Ashok, you would like him, Barty. Unlike me, he has an unbelievably beautiful daughter, Sanchini, and a granddaughter, Amelia. They live together in an incredible house. An old Dutch merchant's warehouse with a courtyard and cloisters. I've been on a buying trip with him. Remember our trip to East Anglia to find that replacement bronze?"

"Of course, we took my BMW."

"Guess what car we went in for this road trip?"

"No idea."

"Think big, think old."

"Bentley?"

"Near, a 1934 Rolls-Royce drophead coupe. It's magical."

"Wow, I thought you were going on holiday. You know, eating too much, drinking too much and sleeping too much. But I'm sure the wines are filthy; they normally are in the tropics."

"I'm currently sipping a 2016 Chablis."

"Blimey."

"I have to say it, Barty, Mr Ashok has a similar cellar to yours and what's more he has given me a whole mixed case. I think, I might be in heaven."

"You are, it was minus three degrees with a threat of snow here last night. I've ordered my veg seed and am looking forward to spring. When do you think you're coming back?"

"About ten days' time, but I've got to pack a 20-foot container first. I couldn't resist it! I've been buying: bamboo, rattan, teak and pottery."

"Wow."

"Well, you know that I have a penchant for bamboo tables and chairs? They're absolutely everywhere here and I couldn't resist. The Victorian-style pieces for conservatories and the Scandi '60s and '70s ones for contemporary homes. They make them to furnish all their hotels and guesthouses for a fraction of the price. You should've seen us. Mr Ashok in a splendid tropical suit which seems to be his uniform, and me."

"Send some pictures please? Jack, Clive, Pru and the girls send their love."

"I haven't even had time to miss you yet. Too excited about a stone."

"What stone?"

"It's a story that will have to wait ... involving a crocodile, a raft and a lost education."

"Sounds like a book, not a story."

"Toodle pip and look forward to seeing you."

Chapter 29

Mirissa

The following morning Lionel managed to avoid the indignity of retrieving his trunks from around his knees. The sea was oily and the sun was not yet too bright. A swim before breakfast must be the greatest luxury, and boy does it make eggs taste that much better.

He sat under the shade of a tree on a white plastic chair. It had all the things you need from a chair: a generous seat, arms and a concave back. Although plastic would never win any aesthetics awards, it quietly wins the comfort prize. It's the marginal flex of a plastic chair that gives every user a different experience, best suited to their own shape.

"Good morning, breakfast, sir?" questioned Ajith with his ready smile.

"May I see a menu, please?" replied Lionel, making an opening book action with his hands.

"Certainly sir." What arrived was a black-plastic-covered A4 menu.

They have the measure of me, thought Lionel. Under the 'Breakfast' section was listed various omelettes: Sri Lankan, English vegetables with chilli, plain or tomatoes and cheese.

Below this was the Israeli favourite, skakshuka, a simple dish of onions, peppers, tomatoes, and eggs lurking amongst tomato paste, mixed with chilli, garlic, paprika, cumin, caraway.

As he'd had an incident-free swim, he wanted to keep breakfast the same. "Tomato and cheese omelette, please."

Ajith smiled and removed the menu. Minutes later a folded omelette arrived. Its size would have happily fed three, but Lionel dug deep and made light of it. A Jazzy cappuccino followed, and he felt truly sated. Today, he would draft a list of beneficiaries to his new-found wealth. Barty's telephone call had been timely, reminding him of the people he most missed. He hadn't written a Will since his last divorce, the contents of which were probably coloured by hurt. The second Mrs Lionel had been great fun, probably too much fun, a fabulous cook and a great traveller. She and Lionel had once been invited to stay for four days at a house in the south of France just outside Antibes. The friend and owner was a man with a past, good looks, bedroom eyes and too many languages. When Lionel left, she stayed and as they had no children there was no need for contact afterwards. In fact, the last was a postcard wishing him a Happy Christmas from Tagazut in Morocco. A surfer's paradise with bad drains. It had smelt bad in the 1970s with few houses, one can only imagine what it smelt like now.

He checked his rambling thoughts that had unwittingly become spoken words. Thankfully, he hadn't ordered anything after his cappuccino; Ajith was not around to hear him mumbling to himself.

The pair of Chinese vases, God bless them, had made him £3.5 million. First on his list of beneficiaries, was course going to be Barty. His great friend, cook, customer and fellow gastronaut. He'd recently dropped everything to help him replace the stolen bronze. Like Lionel, he owned his own house and business premises and didn't need for anything, but Lionel knew that he had always dreamt of sailing around the Mediterranean. Once after a long evening service at his cellar restaurant they had shared a final glass of wine. It was then that he had expressed his ambition to sail around the Greek islands. They were both nearly sixty, still young and healthy enough to do it, so why not?

Lionel had once been interviewed for an antiques magazine. Trade had been slow, and he hoped it might drive some business his way. It was a 'Day in the life of' article with questions like, "What is the love of your life?" He had answered "the second Mrs Lionel". At the time, he thought the answer would be greeted with joy, but she had taken umbrage to the implied transience of 'second'. When asked "If you could go back in time, where would you go?" he'd replied ancient Greece. He remembered that years ago, Barty had taken him to the Southampton Boat Show. They'd looked at and boarded many different sailing boats and were invited to have a drink on one – below deck in the main salon. He'd thought it beautiful. It was completely made of wood with brass fittings which had particularly appealed to him. It had been made in a boat yard on the Orwell estuary in Ipswich and had been loaned as an elegant vessel for one of the James Bond films – for the closing scene in which Bond and the yacht made a lengthy exit through a crumbling Venice. As Barty had said on the way home from Southampton, "If a Spirit yacht is good enough for Bond, it's good enough for me!"

So, Barty equals a yacht, NB second-hand! Obviously.

Next on the list was Pru and her two daughters. Pru owned her own house, within walking distance of Barty in West Hill, Hastings. Her ex-husband had paid for the kitchen and bedroom extension, and he knew she and the girls were happy there. She had a good business, drawing pastel portraits of dogs, the four-legged family members of all the great and the good. He knew how much she enjoyed her painting, and fondly remembered the great pride with which she had shown her large abstract of Sir Roger Swotter's black Labrador Sampson. She had shown him the large canvas on an easel in her dining room, and before her big reveal she had voiced her wish for a real studio. He would find her a commercial premises in Old Town, ideally a shop with a residential flat above. The flat could provide an extra income that might cushion quieter times.

Pru equals studio/residential space.

Her two daughters, Polly and Phoenix, were easier. He would give them £50,000 each to cover their years at university and a £150,000 deposit for a buy-to-let house in their university towns. They could pay the mortgage from renting rooms to fellow students. This should work as long as they didn't go to Oxford, Cambridge or London!

Polly and Phoenix equal tuition fees and a deposit for buy-to-let house.

Then there was Jack, who he had only known for months, but who felt like the son he should have had. He had all the character that a father could have wished for, plus was the only person to have ever stayed at 69 Norman Road. Lionel would give him £150,000 as a deposit for something in Hastings and as he was working he could cover his own mortgage repayments. Jack didn't need a shop yet, far better he operated from the back of his van. He was already proving to be a good 'runner'. He had been buying from the back of Norman's Austin Maxi for years and had bought the stolen bronze from the back of Jack's Mercedes Sprinter van.

Jack equals deposit on a house.

After paying taxes he wouldn't get much change out of £2 million. The remainder would be his cushion, and Lionel required a sizable one.

Chapter 30
Galle

Mr Ashok sailed the Rolls-Royce back to Galle. His daughter Sanchini had tried many times to steer her father towards a newer car, perhaps a Mercedes estate with a boot — "I hear all English antique dealers own one." But losing his Rolls would be like stripping him of his tropical suit. They were more than props, they were him.

Turning into Pedlar Street, avoiding a poorly parked delivery lorry, he returned the courtesy, parking directly outside Jacintha's house. He stood in the shade of the colonnade and knocked, waited, knocked again, then tried the door. It was locked, and the windows shuttered too. He retrieved his phone from one of his bellows pockets and rang the landline: no answer. Then the mobile, no answer. In a final attempt to raise either Jacintha or Ari he sounded his horn. There was nothing ordinary about this Roll-Royce's horn. A klaxon airhorn is an instrument of great noise, and when originally fitted it was to compensate for slower and softer brakes. On this occasion it drew the stares of tourists clutching orange KK collection bags; it was a rather sheepish Mr Ashok who was finally admitted.

"I'm sorry sir, we were in the workshop. We didn't hear the phones over the lathes, but we did hear that horn! Mr J looked at his mobile and saw your missed calls so here I am. Please come this way."

"Thank you Ari. I was beginning to feel neglected."

Ari guided him to the garden and pointed out the metal-framed glazed workshop doors.

"Would you like some coffee?"

"Yes please, thank you."

As he slid the freewheeling door, Jacintha removed his goggles and raised a hand as the lathe slowed.

"Morning Ashok, are you checking up on me?"

"No, but I'm pleased you've started. I wanted to have a chat about Sanchini, Amelia and George."

"Good, so do I," replied Jacintha. "Let's do it at lunch. Ari makes a lovely curry. Can you stay?"

"That would be very kind."

At this point, Ari joined them with a tray of coffees.

"We both went beachcombing early this morning, before the soldiers started their exercises; they take a dim view of people taking shells and stones. We found quite a few suitable ones, and we're polishing them now, whilst I turn the softer stones on the lathe. I'm not mad about soapstone but it's perfect for turning. Ari's turning the wooden ones. Show Mr Ashok what you've done so far."

Below his lathe, Ari picked up a wooden fruit box and placed it on the low bamboo table. Inside were two layers of random-coloured patterned eggs. Mr Ashok picked up one in each hand.

"They are perfect. This one is palm wood, but what's this one?"

"Jack wood," replied Ari.

"There must be at least fifty in this box."

"In a week we should have about a thousand. Will that be enough?"

"More than enough. Thank you," said Mr Ashok. "They are just the right size."

"Thats good, it's been our pleasure. Come to the rooftop and tell me all about your new friend Lionel."

"The other night, I didn't want to say too much, as I hadn't had a firm commitment from him," Mr Ashok said as they climbed the four flights of stairs to the roof.

"I understand."

Under a canvas canopy on the roof stood four low chairs around a 1960s rectangular teak coffee table.

"I like these chairs."

"We have eight. My wife found them in an antique shop near the fruit market soon after we bought this house. She thought they had the hand of Geoffrey Bawa about them."

"They do. Funnily enough, we've just visited his house in Colombo, and they had similar chairs there. I like the zigzag pattern under these wide arms, generous enough for resting glasses?"

"Was that a hint Ashok?" said Jacintha, ringing a bell.

Two minutes later Ari arrived. He had removed his apron and restored his white tunic and fez. He placed on the coffee table a galleried tray holding a jug of iced water, limes and cashew nuts. Jacintha also requested two glasses of beer.

"The restaurant over the road has draft beer. Ari takes a jug and I settle the slate when I eat there. Good neighbours should work together, right? Now who is this Englishman?"

"He came into my shop and had the manner of somebody who knew what they were looking for. We started talking and found mutual ground in Rye. He lives just along the coast in Hastings and I had an aunt who worked for a family in the town. I visited it as a child, it was full of antiques, sort of 'around the world' in one drawing room. Anyway, the chatting hasn't stopped, similar minds I suppose, and then Manoji happened to appear."

"The raft boy?"

"Yes, Amelia was at school with him."

"What makes you think our granddaughter should hold a flame for him?"

Mr Ashok ignored the question, demanding, "Where do most of the gemstones come from in Sri Lanka?" and, before the former mineral surveyor could answer, announcing, "They are mined in Ratnapawra, and are found not far from the surface, eight to fifteen yards down, and when they strike a horizontal seam they follow it. Well, in Kandy the Mahaweli river sometimes cuts into gem-bearing seams. The loosened stones are generally topaz, and generally small. These stones are found by the raft people. Families who dredge the river from large floating platforms. Their principal income is from river sand sold to the building trade, but every raft will sieve the sand to clean it. Well, on this raft a royal blue sapphire the size of a hen's egg plopped on to their sieve!"

"Wow!" After a moment's pause, Jacintha pointed out, "But you're an antiques dealer, not a gem dealer like Dinish. Why did this raft boy bring it to you?"

"Amelia's first school was a Montessori one a street away from our home. Well, in her class was this very bright boy. He was poor, but his extended family collectively helped him to get the best out of school. He was so bright that the teachers started ignoring his second-hand uniform and third-hand shoes. He was soon thriving, reading well before the rest of his classmates had even mastered their alphabet. Amelia stayed at that school for only two years, as she then left for Sanchini's old girls' school. Years later she heard that Manoji, this boy, had left his secondary school because his father had been killed by a crocodile. She felt desperately sorry for him as she knew what it felt like to lose a father. It was he who brought the sapphire to us last week."

"A tragic story that needs a happy ending. Still, my question remains: why did he bring it to you?"

"Because he and his family trust us. We all know our society can be snobbish and restrict a person's mobility, but sometimes luck can change a family's path. The boy's intelligence had once carried his family's hopes, now it's this extraordinary sapphire."

"So what's your plan, and how does this Englishman fit in?"

"Well, he has kindly agreed to export a 20-foot container to England, which we have been busy filling with cheap items for him to sell in his shop. Earthenware cooking pots, dog bowls, bamboo furniture, cane wastepaper baskets and the like. Amongst it all will be this sapphire, loose amongst hundreds of stone and wooden eggs."

"Like a needle in a haystack."

"Exactly."

"You've mentioned Amelia and Sanchini, but why George?"

"Do you think he would help us with the stone when it gets to England?"

"I don't know, but I could ask. We're still in contact. He calls me every year on the anniversary of Dinish's death. It's a call I both dread and look forward to. He is a leading jeweller in London now. I'll call him tonight. Can I help in any other way?"

"Well, I need to pack this container. The bamboo furniture manufacturer offered his yard, but I would like to do it away from prying eyes. We have bought all the items from either the north or east of Galle."

"I've just the place. I don't know if you're aware that my wife inherited her parents' cinnamon farm, which I have kept. Her parents were great gardeners, and it's in their memory, and my wife's, that I maintain it. After Dinish died, I no longer needed so much help here, so Ari's parents moved in to look after the farm. Ari and I go there when Galle gets too busy or too hot. It's just north of here – only 2 km from the main coast road."

"Perfect! That's very kind, would you WhatsApp me the address."

"I do remember your courtyard garden with its spectacular traveller palms. At this farm we have a long drive planted with red palms. Let me know when you are expecting the container and deliveries, I'll alert Ari's parents. I might even go there myself. Better still, why don't you bring the girls to stay. It's about time I started spending time with them."

"That would be lovely, and on home ground it might be easier for you. You will see Amelia has turned into a lovely young lady."

"I'm sure. Now we have a plan, let's have lunch, and then I must get back to my lathe."

Chapter 31

Kandy

Mr Ashok made good time back to Kandy, stopping only once; the petrol attendant agreed that petrol rationing shouldn't apply to a 1934 Rolls-Royce. He tooted as he passed the big three aluminium pans on the pavement outside his shop, turning into the small side street which served his property. Sanchini slid the large garage doors open and guided her father in. Much like Geoffrey Bawa's house in Colombo, the car was part of the interior. It lived on a stone paved floor, which was originally the main 'goods in, goods out' area of the warehouse. Beyond the bonnet was an open lightwell in which stood an arrangement of large pots planted with exotic flowers. No part of this building was missed by Sanchini's 'tropical' fingers. After hugging his daughter, he put on a pair of gloves and slid the oil tray under the car's engine. This being Sri Lanka, the galleried tray wasn't made of plastic but teak.

"Come, come father, tell me all about your trip! Did you call in on Jacintha?"

"Of course I did. He is well and sends his love."

"I do miss him."

"He knows and is ready to be a part of our family again. He

would like us to stay on his cinnamon farm. I didn't know he even had one, did you?"

"I do remember Dinish talking about it. I never went there. I got the impression it was a memorial to his mother. I'd have thought Jacintha might have sold it by now, but I'm glad he hasn't. Dinish said the gardens were out of this world." She paused. "Did you and Lionel fill a container?"

"Of course, it was easy. He's as good a shopper as I am. We found the smallest potter, aged seventy-four, bird-like and so quick, she made even me look like a giant. Lionel thought he could market the buffalo curd pots as dog water bowls in England. He said his young friend Jack's dog, Clive, prefers drinking out of an earthenware bowl. He came up with this idea to organise the collection and cleaning of the used and discarded pots that you see by the roadside; I suggested we got somebody to make them to his design, and dimensions, rather than taking potluck."

"Spreading the love."

"Precisely. Now is your father allowed a drink before Amelia comes home? Where is she?"

"Exam revision, until six. At least she no longer has three hours' prep. Tonight, she is going to a friend's house for a swim and supper afterwards. I've organised three-wheeler Chris to pick her up at nine, so it's just you and me for dinner. We've a simple vegetable curry, I thought you might have overdone the food."

"We had the most excellent crab at the Galle Face Hotel, and barbecued butter fish at Surf Sea Breeze in Mirissa."

"Well, it's thin soup and vegetable curries for you now, otherwise you will become even rounder. How's my father-in-law?"

"Impressive, hasn't really aged. He and Ari are turning the eggs for us. He has quite a workshop there."

"I don't remember a workshop in Pedlar Street. It must be a retirement hobby."

"He is busily turning the stone eggs, and Ari is turning the wooden ones. He's calling George tonight."

"Who's George?"

"Dinish's buyer in London."

"Oh yes, George, that's a name from the past. I never met him, but I know Dinish thought highly of him."

"Jacintha said he will call us tonight. You know what he's like?"

"I certainly do. I learnt early on in my marriage if I said I'd promised to do something for my father-in-law, it had to be done there and then. Dinish had that same earnestness, but thankfully he was generationally more relaxed. Is Lionel happy?"

"I'm sure so. We had great fun on our road trip. He thanks you for the swimming trunks, it was hot in Colombo. We went to Geoffrey Bawa's house. I wanted to see his car, as I knew he owned a very similar one. It's almost an exact match. The only noticeable difference is mine's a runner; I bet Mr Bawa's hasn't left Number 11 since his death!"

"Where did you leave Lionel?"

"Mirissa. He said he had some things to work out before he got back home to England. A little 'thinking time' he called it."

🦎

While Sanchini organised their supper, her father made them both a gin and tonic. His mobile phone rang as he was handing her the glass.

"Ashok," he answered.

"Ashok, it's Jacintha. I have just spoken to George in London."

"What did he think?" Mr Ashok demanded as he put his mobile on loudspeaker.

"He thought the stone had a great story. Which turns out is important."

"Will he help us?"

"I think so. He was reserved at first, but he's come round."

"I have Sanchini here with me, and you're on speaker."

"Hello Jacintha, my father says you're well."

"I'm really well, lovely to hear your voice."

"And yours too. I understand you're turning lots of eggs?"

"I've had a lovely catch-up with London George and fingers crossed he's willing to help us. He said the cutting of the stone will be key, it's just the marketing that might be more problematic; towards the end of the conversation he kept calling it a name."

"Oh?" chipped in Mr Ashok.

"The Crocodile Stone."

Chapter 32

London

George hadn't spoken to Jacintha for almost a year. Dinish had been his main Asian supplier. Mines aren't for the faint-hearted, being generally in remote and often hostile places. Dinish had bought all over Asia, but principally in Sri Lanka and Burma. He had a particular eye for colour, finding sapphires only of the deepest blue: never inky, always saturated. His Burmese rubies were pigeon-blood red. A dying bird's last action ... producing a colour so intense that it becomes a benchmark.

George remembered teasing Dinish how he must have looked so out of place amongst those tiny Burmese miners. He would retort, "My height is my calling card. When I arrive in town everybody comes to stare at me. I'm the Michael Jordan of gems."

He would come three times a year to London, booking an economy seat with Sri Lankan Airlines, always presenting himself early at the check-in desk, smiling and fluttering his big dark eyelashes. Hey presto, he found himself in business class. After his third trip, the Colombo desk manager took him aside and gave him a card in return for a direct debit of 100,000 rupees per month. This way, at least Sri Lankan Airlines got something out of it.

On arrival at Heathrow, Dinish would go through 'Items to Declare', and produce a shabby pouch of uncut gemstones, agree they were all different coloured topaz, and pay some arbitrary sum. On passing into the arrivals hall, the first face he would notice would be Derek's.

"Good trip, Mr D?" Derek would ask, as he took over Dinish's trolley and handed him a cappuccino.

"Excellent, thanks."

"Good grub?"

"Milk rice and fish curry."

"You're joking!" Derek would reply. "No fish and chips? It wouldn't be for me or the Mrs."

Derek's job was to look after Mr George, his boss. He did this to the letter. Mr George had almost forgotten what a door handle felt like. Derek walked ahead, opening the way and keeping watch. Not that anybody came near.

It's hard to describe Derek, but if you stripped a well-built West Ham football supporter of his home strip and then sent him to a Savile Row tailor, stipulating that the dark grey flannel cloth should be able to resist both bullets and blades, you'd have Derek!

No smiles, just focus. Keeping Mr George and his jewels just so. Derek didn't do driving, that was his nephew's job. Where Derek went, Tommy was nearby. As Dimish went through the last set of sliding doors he knew Tommy and the navy-blue Mercedes would be waiting. Once Mr D was in the back, and the cases were in the boot, Derek would take the front passenger seat, fasten his seat belt, and say, "Let's go, Tommy."

Everything was always pre-arranged. Derek didn't do spontaneous, that was for other nationals. Dinish sort of knew, if he ever had a problem in the 'Items to Declare' channel, Derek would have a brother, uncle or aunt who would come to his aid.

Tongue in cheek, Dinish would ask George, "When you employed Derek, did you get the whole family?"

He'd reply, "Just the curly tops." All Derek's family had thick black curly hair...

"We will arrive at 7pm. Mr George is at the office. It's a new car, Mr D."

"I can see that, Derek. It's a great colour."

"Like sapphires, Mr D. Mr George didn't want to change the car until Tommy showed him this new extra." With that, a small spotlight picked out the back of the front seat's central armrest, now moving, firstly revealing a pair of cut-glass champagne flutes held in a chrome frame, then a drum-shaped lidded bucket.

"The glasses are Baccarat, Mr D."

"They're beautiful, but they're empty," replied Dinish.

"See the drum, Mr D?"

"The ice bucket."

"Take the lid off," said Derek, almost-smiling with his eyes.

"Wow. No ice."

"Everybody thinks it's an ice bucket, but it's a cooler. Help yourself."

Dinish took one of the three half-sized bottles of champagne.

"It's lovely and cold."

"Mr George said you like champagne."

"I do. Especially Perrier-Jouët. My father-in-law in Kandy has some of this in his cellar."

"Fire away, it won't be fizzy. Tommy never drives over sixty."

Tommy didn't respond. His uncle did the talking and he did the driving. 'Chain of Command,' as another of his uncles would often remind him.

Dinish turned the bottle and held the cork. Mr Ashok had taught him how to open a bottle of champagne.

"It's delicious, Derek. Perfect temperature."

"By having three bottles, Mr D, they only touch once, and slip nicely into a circle. Clever, those Germans."

The conversation stopped. Dinish relaxed with a glass in his hand and watched the best of London go by.

As soon as they arrived outside Mr George's office in Albemarle Street, Derek went through the same routine, just in reverse. He unfastened his seatbelt, removed the bags from the boot, and then opened the rear passenger door for Dinish. Pushing the door to, he said, "This way, Mr D."

Dinish knew the way, he'd been here many times before, but there was a protocol with Derek. Every person must play their part. After all, when the stones were cut, most would be worth millions.

Mr George had his office on the first floor. "More secure than ground. Derek, head of security, doesn't like ground or shop windows," George had once told Dinish.

Through the doors they walked into a cubed-shaped hall, and up a shallow flight of stone steps. Derek didn't like lifts, too many surprises. At the top of the stairs, the large landing was lit by a row of three astragal glazed windows. The walls were panelled and white-painted. A young receptionist picked up a desk phone whilst they waited. Moments later, a pair of mahogany double doors opened, and out came a tall man with a broad smile.

"Dinish. Come, Come."

Once through the doors, Derek closed them from the outside and sat down.

"What have you found for me?"

From a frieze drawer of his large library table George took out two velvet-lined trays, one for rubies, the other for sapphires.

"It's like Christmas, just more often."

George had two talents: he could see the cut jewels within rough stones, and he had the right private clients to buy them, clients who would alter their plans if he rang. He was sharp enough to deal with the trade, and smooth enough to woo wily tycoons. He would instinctively pick up a stone and say, "That'll be a cabochon ruby, set as a pendant drop necklace."

"What a fabulous colour," a client would say. "Where did you find it?"

"We have a buyer who travels to source and will only buy the very best, from the people who actually own and work the mines."

Chapter 33

London

When Jacintha rang, and spoke of a very large sapphire, George had immediately thought of three clients: one in Switzerland, another in London and an actress in LA. Very large stones are comfortable in crowns, but very few people can wear them as jewellery. The best place for a large stone is on a necklace.

He was universally known by both the trade and his clients as 'Polished George': not only on account of his gleaming gemstones, but also his immaculate turnout. He had the figure for bespoke suits, Turnbull & Asser shirts, and Shipton & Heneage whole cut shoes. He didn't do gyms – too much sweat and Lycra – instead staying trim with tennis: he played three times a week at The Queen's Club, once with his regular four, once with the club coach and then at the weekends with his wife. His home was in Kensington, near enough to the club, and also close to Derek and Tommy in Hammersmith. Everything was interconnected and everything worked. When the commercial world changed in the 1980s, George was in the thick of it. As a young man he had sold engagement rings and Rolex watches to City traders. As they got more senior they started buying more expensive bracelets, necklaces and earrings. Then when they got divorced, the cycle started all over again. He had grown with his clients and as he approached sixty he was now steering them towards investment pieces.

People liked George; he had this knack of making everybody feel special. He called on them, inviting them to his office, enticing them with his recent purchases followed by a lunch. He didn't keep a large stock of finished jewellery, but he did keep a sizable stock of large stones; it's hard for people outside the trade to get excited about gems 'in-the-rough'. He tried it once with a commodity trader. Who had exited saying, "I haven't left the floor to look at a beach!"

He and his wife Julia had no children but had been happily married for thirty-five

years. George had his gems, and Julia had her art. Like him, she was at the top of her field – portrait painting. Her works hung in many public spaces including the National Portrait Gallery. His nickname for her was Singer, after the great Singer Sargent, whose work she much admired. Her brush strokes could lighten even the most autocratic tycoon. Whilst he went to the office, Julia stayed at home. They had converted their basement into a large studio, and by installing bigger grilled windows to its north-facing side and screening the garden windows with plants, 'Singer' got sufficient light. At home she was kept company by Dougal, a Parson terrier and Hamish, a short-haired dachshund. Both were comical in their respective ways. Dougal, since a puppy, had adopted an angled look. He would sit on his hindquarters, look intently at a visitor and then cock his head 30 degrees left or right, the cocked head exaggerated by extended ears. Julia would often return from her kitchen with a cup of coffee to find her sitter with cocked head too. Hamish on the other hand had no comic device, just his size. George found it endlessly amusing to watch him keep up with his longer-limbed companion.

The only young person in the couple's life was George's godson, Ollie Croyd. Where George's office was in Mayfair, his godson's was over in Piccadilly. They met every week for lunch, either at Murray's in Albemarle Street or The Austin in Piccadilly. If they were too busy, Ollie would have supper with them at home. His father had been George's best friend at boarding school. Ollie's family were coffee farmers in Thika, Kenya, and when they were teenagers George had enjoyed fantastic holidays with Ollie in Africa, either at the family farm or at their beach house in Malindi. Regrettably, all good things come to an end, and often in Africa it's in tragedy. Ollie's parents were killed in a road accident near Mombasa. They were driving at night and didn't see a lorry with no headlights on. It was then that George and Julia stepped up as Ollie's guardians. They paid his school fees and encouraged him to read History of Art at Exeter University. On graduation, it was George who got him an interview with the international auction house, and it was he and Julia who gave him the keys to a flat in Notting Hill. It was small but perfectly formed and, most importantly, it was just around the corner.

George had an enviable life, and it was all of his own making. He had worked hard, made many contacts and never burnt bridges. In the early days he would scooter around his golden triangle, the points being the West End, Hatton Gardens and the City. Over the decades these points had spread to Albemarle Street, Switzerland and Los Angeles.

Ollie had recently held a record-breaking oriental sale in Hong Kong but George had little traction in China's expanding economy. He had once sold some fabulous Art Deco jade jewellery to an elderly Hong Kong banker, but that connection had faded, or rather died. He knew he couldn't ignore this market and would ask Ollie which Chinese clients he should be wooing.

At Murray's, the private members' club in Albemarle Street, George liked the food and wine, and Derek on the other hand liked the security. He always insisted on walking George the fifty yards from his office. As he had informed his boss in the early days of his employment, "If you have security, it's no airy-fairy business. You're either in or out." George had decided he was 'in'. Derek would make sure that 'Mr George' was safely in Murray's before having a coffee over the road. If there were any obstructions in the street, delivery lorries or paparazzi, Tommy would bring the Mercedes around, and double-park to give Derek a nearer sight-line. There were no such problems today; everything was just so.

Ollie found George at his usual round table, looking onto the small courtyard garden. "Great to see you," said George as he gave his godson a big hug.

When Ollie's parents had died, Julia had said, "If we are going to do this properly, it's hugs, not handshakes. He will need all the love that we can give him."

George always did as Julia said. He had loved her since the first day he saw her. That tall, fair girl, carrying her portfolio down Cork Street on her way to life-drawing class. It didn't take him long to find out her timetable. He was 'accidentally' there when she came out of her classes, handing her a takeaway tea. After two weeks, he asked her out for dinner. That dinner never really finished, and within six months they were married.

George ordered a bottle of white Burgundy.

"How was Hong Kong?"

"Hard work but incredible."

"Any highlights?"

"Lots, but can we talk about those later. I have some exciting news – *I have met somebody!*"

Those all-important four words, so much greater than the sum of their parts.

Chapter 34
Sri Lanka

Mr Ashok had been busy, arranging the delivery of a 20-foot steel container to Jacintha's cinnamon farm, and contacting the bamboo furniture man and accepting his offer to deliver to the farm on Friday week.

Jacintha had also been busy. On Mr Ashok's departure, he had pinned a piece of foolscap paper to the workshop wall to record the numbers of turned eggs, like a cricket score card. With an engineer's eye for detail, he had noted the numbers in different stones and in different woods. He and Ari had worked continuously, scouring the tide line for suitable stones at first light and then remaining glued to their lathes. They had completed 1,002 eggs – two for luck – in six days and both had loved every minute of their joint endeavour. Jacintha had also found a man and a van in Galle who would collect the pottery from the old lady, and had cut two new keys for the farm's old front door. All before arranging a taxi to take him, Ari and the eggs to the farm on Thursday, to help Ari's parents prepare for their weekend visitors.

It had been arranged that Mr Ashok would drive Sanchini and Amelia down on the Friday evening, so they could be woken the following morning by the jungle sound of the magical garden.

Ari called his parents as the taxi turned off the tarmac road onto the farm's red earth drive. This was walled, not loosely edged, with exotic red palms. No kerbstones, just broad-leafed lily plants. The coolness was immediate. The drive's front circle had the same feel as a woodland clearing. At its centre was a large oval earthenware cistern, decorated with stylised lotus flowers in a yellow slip glaze. It was the size of a small bath and was planted with living and breathing star-shaped purple lotus flowers.

Ari's father and mother were waiting for them on the porch, and led them up a sloping corridor to the large sitting room. It had been some time since Jacintha had last been to Mamboz, and it was still as his wife had furnished it – pairs of low open armchairs, with jack wood frames and cane seats and backs. She had made the square cushions, sewing the heavy blue and red linen covers on the heavy black japanned sewing machine with 'SINGER' written in gilded letters that been her mother's. It lived on its own table in a small north-facing room that served as both laundry and sewing room. Dotted beside every armchair was a drum-shaped table, designed by her and made by Ari's father, a talented and keen metalworker. She had embossed each circular ceramic top with leaves from her favourite trees and plants, and he had cut and welded the metal rods to form a repeating 'Y' shaped pattern to form the sides. There is a beauty to a repeat pattern, as any miscalculation or irregular welds are lost in the repetition. It was on one of these drum tables that Ari's mother, Keshini, placed a cup of tea and left Jacintha to sit and survey his late wife's special place. To his left was a long open veranda with a terracotta paved floor enclosed by a trellis railing. The railing was both broken up and supported by robust cylindrical teak posts. The pattern of the trellis was as depicted in all Chinese blue and white plates – painted with Boxer children and attendant mothers. The top rail was three foot high with a plank top, perfect for books, drinks and casual seating. When Dinish had been a child he had loved walking along this rail, holding his mother's hand for balance.

The railing terminated at the southwest corner and here, the veranda gave way to two shallow steps and a sloping grass lawn beyond. To the right of the steps was a roofed area, a sort of large hall, which led to a more intimate garden room beyond. This open room was furnished with a large teak dining table, its circular top raised on eight gun-barrel-shaped legs united by a handy foot rail just high enough for slouching feet. This had been Dinish's special place as a child. The eight-legged frame become his tent and the home of all his favourite toys, made by both his feather and Ari's. As Jacintha sat and drank his tea he patted his coat pocket for the two replica keys. It was his intention to give them to Sanchini: the farm needed a female owner, she was its missing ingredient.

The next day, the bamboo furniture arrived. Ari and his father intercepted the manufacturer's delivery lorry before it tried to come down the main red palm drive. Its roof would have torn the palm fronds, and its twin tyres would've crushed the lily kerbs. They led the lorry to a service road, shielded from strangers by a great stand of yellow bamboo. There, on the farm's old drive, stood the steel container. The lorry was accompanied by a classic old Nissan car. It was white, highly polished and housed the beaming owner of the bamboo manufactory. He was small with a splendid tummy restrained by a batik shirt. Without prompting he had thoughtfully wrapped the legs, rails and other extremities with corrugated cardboard. Jacintha and the owner checked off the purchase list, while his four men carried the goods to Ari and his father inside the container. They packed as they went, only stopping when a different style of chair came off the lorry.

"Come, come, sir."

The seller would bid Jacintha to lower himself into yet another chair, before promptly squeezing past him and sitting in the same chair: "See, it fits 'normal' people too!"

After an hour Keshini brought tea and ginger cake. Like a greedy child, the seller slurped his tea and guzzled his piece of cake. On finishing it, he stared at the remaining slices, willing an offer of more. Ari's mother had seen this all before. The bamboo man's mother must have been indulgent, even weak, to have allowed this sort of behaviour to seep into adulthood, she thought. Maybe it was his beaming smile that dissolved discipline. She offered the last two slices first to Jacintha, who took one – a man of his height needs the calories – and then to her husband and son, who, fortunately for the seller, declined. The bamboo man's face lit up as he took the last slice; she knew his sort only too well ... spoilt.

Within two hours, the operation was over, with four-fifths of the container filled with tightly-packed bamboo furniture, light shades, wastepaper baskets, coconut spoons and the like. As they waved goodbye to the owner and his Nissan, Galle Fort's man and van arrived. The carrier had taken 'just in case' flat-packed cardboard boxes for the pottery. These remained flat, as the lady potter had packed her items in straw-filled wooden fruit boxes. Just the eggs to pack now, but those could wait.

Chapter 35

Sri Lanka

Sanchini hadn't been so excited for years. She had the same butterflies she remembered getting when first courting Dinish. Normally, Mr Ashok and Amelia did their own packing, but she decided to lay out their respective clothes in good time for the weekend.

She desperately wanted it to come, as she had always been fascinated by Dinish's stories of his mother's gardens at Mamboz. Their final preparations for the weekend included presents. She selected three plants for Jacintha; her father had already boxed up a magnum of champagne, along with a mixed selection of red and white wines. Whilst in the cellar, he retrieved the 'egg' sapphire. The banana leaf that it had arrived in had now been upgraded to a drawstring green baize bag. Sanchini had made it whilst her father and Lionel were on their road trip. He put it in his right-hand coat pocket, and as he patted it, he said, "Here's hoping you have a safe journey."

Once all was loaded into the Rolls-Royce, Sanchini pulled back the sliding warehouse doors and Mr Ashok released the handbrake, allowing the mighty car to roll out. Once the garage doors were secure, they drove to Amelia's school. Although excited, she insisted he parked a street away from it.

"You stay here, and I'll go and collect her."

Mr Ashok knew all the various intonations in his daughter's voice. Not surprisingly, they were the same as his wife's. He knew when a 'no' was a no, and when a 'no' was a maybe.

As he waited, he felt the stone in his pocket. In all his recent busyness, he had forgotten to ask Sanchini what was said at the meeting with the raft boy Manoji. Hearing excited chatter from his two girls, he looked in the rear-view mirror. In it he saw the slow grace of his approaching daughter, and the long legs of his granddaughter. Amelia was like a baby giraffe still exploring the extremities of her limbs. She had the looks of her mother, the height of her father, and he hoped the brains of her grandfather! Sanchini climbed into the front passenger seat and Amelia the back.

"Good day?" Mr Ashok questioned, smiling from beneath the black lacquered peak of his grey chauffeur's cap.

"Why do I need to learn the periodic tables in chemistry, if I want to read English literature in Britain?"

"Because all Sri Lankan parents want to say that their daughters read chemical engineering."

"Surely there is enough paint in the world by now," Amelia retorted with rolling eyes.

"What, with our climate?" he riposted.

"Father, take off that cap before Amelia's friends see you. Everybody knows we don't have a driver."

"All the government ministers and doctor's daughters have drivers, but we have a chauffeur. The difference, my dear, is the uniform. The English have a rule that Bentleys may be driven by owners, but Rolls-Royces are only driven by chauffeurs. Remember, it's very important to keep up appearances in Kandy."

"Don't be so silly, father. Everybody knows that Amelia's grandfather is the antique dealer in his ridiculous tropical suit with the three large pans outside his shop. Amelia used to be called 'missionary pot' and was teased: *how many missionaries has your grandfather cooked today?*"

"Thankfully I grew to be twice their size. No trouble now," said Amelia.

"You never told me that you were called 'missionary pot'," said a suddenly-less-chipper grandpa.

"We only tease the people we love," said Sanchini, smiling at her daughter.

Amelia changed the subject. "I'm so excited to see grandpa Jacintha."

"It'll be lovely and we'll get to see your grandmother's gardens. I can't wait."

"How far is it?"

"Just over three and a half hours."

"Three hours, nooo!"

"Why don't you have a sleep, and I will wake you just before we arrive."

Amelia moved her schoolbag to make a pillow and within five minutes she was fast asleep.

"Oh, do look father, she's out for the count. That's one of the few good things about this car, its suspension."

"One of the many. Tell me, how did you get on with Manoji?"

"He's actually such a nice boy. He came to the shop with his uncle, a quiet man who let his nephew do the talking. I told them that the Englishman, Lionel, would take the sapphire back to Britain to sell. They seemed very happy that it was going far away from the dealers here. They have total trust in you. I told them to come back after the third new moon and we should have some news. They were very keen that I should pass on their thanks to you. How much do you think it might make?"

"It all depends on the saturation of the colour. We know it has some good colour, but it is all about the consistency. It might be very valuable. One thing is for certain."

"What's that?"

"The young man, and his family, will soon no longer need to work amongst those pesky crocodiles."

Three hours later they turned off the highway into a drive marked by lit coconut torches. Ari and his father had wanted their arrival to be special so they had staked thirty 5-foot-high torches down the red palm drive and circle. In his excitement Mr Ashok sounded the horn.

"Father, we aren't in a three-wheeler, you can't sound your horn!"

"I can, and I just have."

Jacintha, Ari and his parents had been hovering on the veranda nearest the hall. To say they were excited would be an understatement. Jacintha allowed Ari's parents to open the front door before bounding out. He really was tall. He first hugged Sanchini. Then Amelia, the young 'giraffe', leapt out and hugged her other grandpa for the first time in a very long time. Mr Ashok supervised the removal of the luggage whilst Jacintha led the two girls into the house.

"It's more beautiful than I had imagined," smiled Sanchini, reaching out for Jacintha's free hand.

"Now, who's hungry?"

"We all are," said Mr Ashok, becoming to Ari, who was carrying his case of wine. "Jacintha, a present from Kandy."

"Thank you, there is really no need to be so generous, Ashok. Now come to the dining room. Ari's mother Keshini has been cooking all day."

He led them to a large circular table in an open-sided dining room. It was laid with four place settings: on each mat was a tightly-rolled steaming flannel beside a tall glass of lime and soda. After all were settled, the food was brought in, Jacintha opened a bottle of champagne and said gently: "Amelia, your father, as a boy, made under-this-table his special place. Probably because as adults we weren't small enough to get between its eight legs. He would sit for hours playing with his toys, while your grandmother and I were working on projects in the garden. Tomorrow, when we have light, I will give you a full garden tour."

Chapter 36
Sri Lanka

Jacintha had temporarily moved from the master bedroom that he had shared with his wife. It was on the ground floor with its own courtyard garden – within its walls were a cooling mixture of plants and water. Ari's parents had separated the double bed to form a pair of singles in readiness for Sanchini and Amelia. Mr Ashok was put in the guest room and Jacintha moved into Dinish's boyhood bedroom. He really wanted them to like his late wife's special place.

Whilst Mr Ashok and Jacintha snored in their respective rooms, Sanchini and Amelia talked into the small hours about the sapphire, the farm and university abroad.

🦖

Sanchini was eventually awoken by Ari's mother drawing a bath outside in the courtyard. It wasn't a white enamelled affair on claw and ball feet, but more like a fountain. The water spouted from a smiling wall mask and fell into a bow-fronted stone cistern. Beside it was a teak box step and table with folded towels and glass jars.

"I don't normally sleep in so late," said Sanchini in Sinhalese.

Keshini didn't reply but beckoned her towards the cistern, and held out her arms for her nightdress. The last time Sanchini had stood naked in front of somebody was with her late husband, but this seemed somehow fine, courtly. Like a Kandyan Queen might once have done for her attendant ladies. She stepped naked on to the box step and sat on the flatted edge of the cistern, swivelling her bottom around and slipping into the water. It was deep, about three feet, deliciously covering her shoulders with cool but not cold water. Keshini placed one of the folded towels behind her head and left, allowing Sanchini to enjoy the morning birdsong. She could get very used to this, she thought. After some twenty minutes she rose from the water, wrapped herself in a fresh towel and went in to wake up her daughter. While Amelia bathed in turn, Sanchini wandered around the courtyard. There were numerous teak seats, trellis screens and temple-like roofs offering shady spaces. In the centre of the courtyard was a circular pool planted with purple lotus flowers. Swimming amongst them were tiny goldfish whose job it was to eat the mosquitos.

The girls found Mr Ashok and Jacintha drinking coffee on the veranda.

"You both slept well," said Jacintha.

"We have just had the most luxy outside bath. How are my two grandpas this morning?"

"Hungry," replied Mr Ashok.

"Good, just how we like our guests. Come into the garden, the west side is cooler in the morning."

Jacintha led them through a pair of swirly-patterned wrought iron gates, surrounded by a bed of inky black lilies and finally through a perfect moon-shaped gate to another courtyard. On a paved area stood a rectangular black-painted table with tub-shaped bamboo and rattan chairs. Once seated, a succession of jugs arrived: coffee, water, mango and passion fruit juice and coconut water, followed by dishes of egg hoppers, dahl, fruit and curd.

"Who wants a garden tour?" said Jacintha.

Two hands shot up.

"Leave me here," said Mr Ashok, "I will only hold you up."

"Are you sure?"

"Perfectly. I'd like Ari to show me the container, and see all your good work turning the 'eggs'."

"I will get him to come and find you shortly. Let's go girls."

Jacintha guided Sanchini and Amelia back through the 'moon' gate and open dining room onto the grass in the cool shade of a large frangipani tree. As they walked towards a set of steps, the garden dropped away. To the left was a rill feeding a flight of small ponds, and in front, the grass sloped steeply to a perfectly flat croquet lawn.

"Dinish said you used to play croquet here."

"We did. His mother was very keen, and also frustratingly good at clearing hoops. I don't think she ever let me take a game from her. Let's play this afternoon when it's a little cooler."

"What a fabulous position and so big too. It makes my courtyard garden look tiny." "Size doesn't matter, I remember it as exquisite."

"It is. Come on grandpa, which way now?"

"Down the slope, if you dare, over the lawn and then you will find a mystical path which runs around the bottom of the garden. Go and explore, lunch at 1pm sharp."

Amelia was off.

"Come through here, Sanchini."

Jacintha walked towards a gap in a giant stand of bamboo. The stone-paved path picked its way through a twisting corridor of yellow stems, each one fat and clean of any side-shoots.

"Your mother-in-law was a stickler for order, verticals must be plum, and horizontals should bear the scrutiny of a spirit level."

"It's beautiful Jacintha, an earthly paradise. How many gardeners do you have here?"

"It's maintained by a head gardener and his son, but when I'm not here, which is most of the time, Ari's parents help too."

On emerging from the cool of the paved bamboo trail they found themselves at the foot of the falling ponds.

"Wow," said Sanchini. "This pond is the size and shape of our one in Kandy, but here you've got nine! Dinish made our pond in Kandy."

"I knew, he told me you designed it. Just like his mother would've done. It's lovely for me to have you all here."

The four reunited for lunch, which turned into a slow affair. Ashok was put in charge of wine and Amelia entertainment; she chose to give impressions of animals she had spotted in the garden. Her monkey was good, but top prize went to her mime of a slithering snake. Both men were loving seeing their only granddaughter so animated. After lunch they moved under the frangipani tree for coffee. Unknowingly, Sanchini sat in Jacintha's late wife's favourite rattan chair and for the first time in decades he felt truly at peace.

Croquet was followed by drinks at 6.30pm, with Mr Ashok opening another prized bottle of champagne from his Kandy cellar. Tonight was another special night and Ari and his parents chose to wear the white tunics and red fezzes Dinish's mother had so loved. The table had been laid with the best china and flowers from the garden, and at Sanchini's place setting Jacintha had left an oblong teak box. When they took their seats Jacintha urged her to open the lid. Inside was a large key.

"I would like you to have this house, gardens and farm. It was my wife's love and I hope one day it will be yours too."

Sanchini didn't get up and hug her father-in-law. She didn't dare, such was the generosity of the offer. She took his hand, squeezed it, and mouthed, "Thank you."

Chapter 37

Sri Lanka

Six in the morning found the occupants of Mamboz apart. Jacintha was dreaming of his late wife beating him at croquet. Mr Ashok was snoring; not the loud rumble of a water buffalo, more the settled rhythm of a wild boar. Amelia was dreaming of oak-panelled dining halls in Oxford. Only Sanchini was awake and walking around the noisy jungle of her new garden. She had slept clutching the key of the very first home she'd ever owned: she couldn't bear to leave her father upon marriage, so Mr Ashok had converted a set of rooms on the east side of the cloister. That was the great thing about the old Dutch warehouses, there was ample space for everything. Dinish never resented this; it worked well when he was away on his many foreign buying trips. Her father had offered to buy them a house, but she wouldn't hear of it, and he'd quietly loved the arrangement, especially when Amelia was born.

Sanchini decided to view her gardens as a visitor might do, so she started at the very beginning: walking up the red palm drive, turning left onto the lower boundary path. At numerous intervals there were smaller angled paths, some paved and some just bare earth, but all led to something of interest: a seat, a viewpoint, a specimen tree or a sculpture. Not only had her mother-in-law been a keen gardener, she had also been a sculptress. Maybe there was a studio on the farm? She took photos and made sketches. Her father had taught her to draw as soon as she could hold a pencil.

"A picture paints a thousand words," he had said.

On her return she found a full breakfast table, with her daughter snugly seated between her two grandpas.

"What would you like to do today?" asked Jacintha.

"Absolutely nothing thank you, I have a garden to enjoy."

"Excellent. Ashok, I think you and I should check over and close the container."

"I think it would be sensible to invite Lionel to join us too. After all, it's being shipped to him, so he should know what's in it."

"Well, don't ask me. Your daughter is the owner of Mamboz now, you must ask her."

"Any friend of my father's is welcome here. Jacintha, I hope you will continue to stay. You've been most generous, and there will always be a bedroom for you here."

"Father, why don't you invite Lionel for lunch, Mirissa is no more than an hour away. Amelia, you will need to get to school for nine tomorrow, and I think I would like to stay here for a couple of days just to get to know the place. Would you mind taking Amelia home tonight father?"

"Of course."

"Jacintha, I'd like it if you stayed for a couple of days?"

"It would be my pleasure; we have lots to catch up on. Go and tell Ari's parents what you would like for lunch. I would imagine your English friend may not share the same tolerance of chillies!"

After breakfast, Mr Ashok called Lionel.

"Morning, where are you?"

"Still at the Surf Sea Breeze, but temporarily seeking refuge at my first hotel, Papers."

"Why so?"

"The next-door restaurant decided to throw a party, involving beach scaffolding, and the largest speakers you have ever seen. A pop-up hunting ground for the beach boys and tuk tuk drivers. The music was simply dreadful, the bass could have found you in Galle and it went on all night. I'm tired of watching these bamboo-legged boys constantly stroking their frizzy manes into hair ties. Preening and strutting along the beach in their quest to open the legs and bank accounts of foreign girls."

"Come for lunch? I have lots of exciting news and the container has arrived and is awaiting your inspection."

"You have been busy. Should I pack? I think I've had enough of the beach."

"Pack away, dear friend. I will message you the address. You have a taxi number?"

"I don't, but Saman will, I should be with you before 1pm."

Saman arranged a tuk tuk for Lionel back to his hotel with the promise of a taxi in forty minutes. He packed, paid the bill, tipped and hugged the staff goodbye.

"What a place, so lovely and quiet."

"Was the beach that awful?"

"It's a beautiful beach, but the music! If that's what they like, I'm glad I'm no longer young."

"Relax, there is none of that here, only jungle birdsong. I have got some leftover champagne; would you like a glass?"

"Yes please. I finished your wine two days ago. I'm gasping. So the furniture man fulfilled his order?"

"Miraculously, yes he did, and we have all the pottery too. After lunch I think we should place the stone in the container. Were you successful in Mirissa?"

"Yes I was, it was the reason I came to Sri Lanka in the first place, a long story about a bit of luck."

"Save it for tonight."

"How did it go with Dinish's jeweller friend, George?"

"Jacintha had a long chat with him, he's on board. The ball is rather in your court now."

"All I have to do is take delivery of the egg..."

Mr Ashok interrupted: "You mean the Crocodile Stone!"

"What?"

"That's the name George has given it. He says it's all about the marketing. I must warn you, he does work quickly. You'll enjoy meeting him, he's very polished."

Suddenly three generations walked across the lawn: Jacintha followed by the human goddess Sanchini, and her baby giraffe, Amelia. Lionel watched the evolution of a genetic code enter the veranda. He leapt to his feet and became immediately tongue-tied.

"Lovely to see you again, Lionel."

Lionel seized Jacintha's outstretched hand as a drowning man might a lifebelt. Sanchini awkwardly smiled and said something about checking on the kitchen.

Time tripped away merrily at lunch, with Mr Ashok assuming the role of butler and Jacintha entertaining them with tales of foreign lands and iron ore found. For Lionel, though, it was a testing occasion. The presence of Sanchini was overwhelming.

He looked, trying not to stare. He didn't dare speak for fear of his tongue, once released, letting him down.

After lunch Mr Ashok led the 'container party', waving a wallet of shipping papers. As they turned the corner they saw two men just inside the container looking amongst the crates.

"Stop. What the devil do you two think you are doing!" Jacintha shouted as he and Ari broke into a run.

They took one look at the party, simultaneously jumped off the back of the container and bolted.

"Do you think they took anything?" puffed Mr Ashok.

"That confirms we will need someone here until it leaves for the port," replied Jacintha. "We cannot afford to take any chances, especially with our Russian friends, you don't think this is their doing? They must have only just opened the doors as everything appears to be in order. Hopefully just curious men looking for tools. I very much doubt they will be back, but Ari, will you and your father do a 24-hour watch?"

"Of course, sir."

The cardboard-wrapped bamboo and rattan furniture consumed most of the space, amidst crates of pottery and the wooden fruit boxes. In the latter were the turned stone and wooden eggs, loosely packed in three layers, each wrapped in a single sheet of newspaper. Mr Ashok took the drawstring bag from his coat pocket.

"You choose, Lionel," he said, pointing to the fruit boxes.

"I like this one."

"Why?"

"I like the paper label, 'Produce of The Sunshine State, California'."

"That's exactly why we will not choose that one."

Mr Ashok pointed to a box that didn't have an attractive label. Ari pulled it from the stack, and placed it on top.

Mr Ashok handed the sapphire to Lionel, who promptly passed it to Sanchini.

"I would like you to place it in the box."

She looked at Lionel, and held it up to the light. His heart missed a beat.

"May this stone fulfil many dreams." And then she gently kissed it, wrapped it in newspaper, and tucked it inside the box.

One amongst many. The container doors were closed and secured by four latches; the nearest to the vertical seal was fastened with a plastic-coated steel bolt.

Chapter 38

London

Since the 'after-works drink' Mercy Penfold and Ollie Croyd had become inseparable. So much so that Mercy's father had had to remind his wife on occasion to breathe. She was beyond excited. It didn't matter that she hadn't even met him. Her daughter was in love. Yes, in love and, for Rose, that was enough.

Mercy caught her mother staring at her.

"What's the matter?"

Rose couldn't reply, she just clasped her hands together, smiled, wept, smiled and repeated. Mercy sighed. Even her sister was behaving oddly, not asking one question!

Luckily her Pa, the mathematician, seemed totally unchanged by her new relationship status. From never having a boyfriend to an all-consuming relationship was quite something for the family to take in. But as Albert had reminded his wife, "We knew when we first met, I'm pretty sure your parents did too. It must be in the genes."

When Ollie had said he would like to introduce her to his godfather, Mercy knew things were going to the next level. He had told her he was an orphan, and that his godfather George and his artist wife Julia were effectively his parents. She also knew that his godfather was a jeweller in Mayfair. When it came, the invitation wasn't to lunch but to supper and in their home. That would mean meeting his family, and for that she knew that she would have to enlist the help of her own family. This was new territory and required a little preparatory role-playing. Her parents had always impressed on Mercy and Grace the importance of preparation.

At supper that evening, she announced she was to meet Ollie's guardians. In fact his 'sort of parents'.

"Oh?" enquired her Pa.

"They were killed in a road accident in Africa."

This was too much for Mercy's mother, who burst into tears yet again.

"Come on Rose," said Albert standing up from the table to give his wife a hug. "This is a happy occasion."

"I know," said Rose through tears, "I'm so happy."

"You could have fooled me," said Grace.

"Now, how can we help?"

"Thank you Pa, and before anybody says 'just be yourself', that's not helpful."

"What night are you going?" asked Grace.

"Saturday at 7pm, and the dress is casual."

"Well let's start with the outfit," volunteered Grace.

"Great idea. You girls take your mother upstairs and I will bring a pot of lemon and ginger tea."

"How lovely," gasped Rose from behind a tissue, "I'm so happy."

"We know you are, maybe it's time to show it," he said, hugging his wife again. "Upstairs with you all and go and find a killer outfit."

This was all so new. Mercy's parents were only children, there were no uncles, aunties or cousins. Rose hadn't worked, she had concentrated on her daughters just as Albert had concentrated on his career. They were a tight-knit family unit of four that now could become five!

The sisters settled their mother on Mercy's bed, where she sat amongst plumped-up pillows and cushions, watching her two daughters offer up trousers, tops, dresses, jackets, boots, shoes in every combination. Once Mercy's wardrobe had been exhausted Grace brought in alternatives from her own bedroom.

"More colour," Rose urged. "Your colouring can take it."

After considerable time the outfit was settled on: the geometric dress that Mercy had never worn but knew she just 'had to have'. It was cinched tight at the waist, mid length, sapphire blue and burgundy, 'not-trying-too-hard' they all agreed.

Their father finally turned up with the promised ginger tea.

"Left or right, Pa?"

"Your left," he replied. "Darling, you look fabulous."

"The burgundy boot it is. These boots are made for walking..."

Saturday came and the morning moved slowly into afternoon. Although Mercy was only going five streets away, Albert insisted driving her in his car. She didn't protest as she wanted somebody on her team outside.

Hair washed, a light brush of make-up and Mercy was ready. She arrived at a very similar 'wedding cake' white stucco house to find Ollie lurking outside.

"Mercy."

"Hi, have you been waiting?"

"I have. I thought it would be less scary to go in together."

"You lovely thoughtful man," she said, reaching up to kiss him.

The front door opened. Mercy was immediately ambushed by both dogs, plus Julia and George. Julia watched Ollie guiding

Mercy to the table and pouring her a glass of water. She smiled. There was no doubt Ollie was in love and the girl was stunning.

Mercy soon relaxed into this family. Similar houses, but very different worlds. Her father and sister lived in and breathed finance: margins, derivatives and futures. George, Julia, and Ollie lived in an older antique world: before stocks and currencies, there had been silver, gold, spices and jewels. Powerful kings and queens displayed their wealth in gemstones, objects of awe which were traded across the world. Julia might have painted those monarchs, but in today's modern world she painted portraits for institutions, presidents of corporations, politicians, benefactors and film stars. Worthy people who had excelled in their chosen fields. She spoke of the process of portrait painting, the sittings, the sketches, the chats, the teas and coffees. It was an intimate process where an artist endeavours to add layers to an image. Something with a little more heart, something of the person. George was charming and fun. His stories ranged from the clients who came from all over Europe, Hollywood and beyond, to remote mines in faraway countries. He bought rough stones for their size and colour, then commissioned their cutting and setting. He did this with particular clients in mind. Once a large cabochon ruby was polished, set amongst diamonds and given a green jade hanger, it became almost impossible for somebody to resist. He favoured the Art Deco period: the geometry and colour of that era worked so well with coloured gemstones. The conversation bounced to Ollie's last sale in Hong Kong.

"It was a record breaker," Mercy reminded them proudly.

"I'm interested in your buyers, Ollie. If they can spend millions on vases..."

"The answer is, I don't know, but what I do know is that porcelain is in their DNA; who knows, maybe in a couple of generations it might be deemed old-fashioned."

"I can't wait generations, I'm hoping to get a very important stone in a couple of weeks. A huge royal blue sapphire found by a boy who lost his father to a crocodile. If the colour is as they say it is, and I get a big stone from it, I'm going to market it as 'The Crocodile Stone'; it might be a little squeamish for my European and Hollywood clients, but I hope this may be the jewel that introduces me to a new Chinese market."

Chapter 39

Sri Lanka

Mr Ashok checked the serial number on the plastic bolt cap, and passing the shipping papers to Lionel said, "It's in your court now. Don't look so worried. The stone will arrive and George will be there to help you. Tonight, Ari and his father will ward off any curious locals. Come on, let's all have tea."

Beneath the frangipani tree, Amelia tried to persuade Sanchini that she should travel back home in the morning.

"Grandpa's eyes aren't up to bus headlights, are they grandpa?"

Amelia didn't mention that she had double chemistry first thing on Monday mornings. She always hoped for bad traffic so she might miss some of it, but, alas, Sanchini had a sixth sense concerning her daughter.

"Amelia, your first lesson is chemistry, and I always have to drag you to school on Mondays."

"I've told you I want to study English and be a journalist. I don't want to wear a lab coat and centrifuge things."

"I know, but you will need top marks in all subjects to get a place at a British university."

"What are you studying in chemistry?" asked former geologist Jacintha. "I know a bit about minerals. Maybe I can help? When

I was at school, when Kandyan Kings still reigned, we started with the periodic tables."

"Oh no, it hasn't changed then," said an exasperated Amelia.

"I remember them well, and in my day, we had the threat of the cane, it must be easier now?"

"No cane now, but still not easy."

"You like words?"

"Yes."

"Do you like history?"

"Of course."

"Well from now on then, it's the history of elements not chemistry. Would you allow me to teach you the history of elements?"

"I'd love that, yes please."

"Come on, there is no time like the present, by tonight I reckon I will have given you the key to chemistry."

"That would be cosmic."

"That's where they come from."

"Very funny." Amelia took Jacintha's hand.

"What are you two going to do this afternoon?" Sanchini looked at the two antique dealers.

"Ari's father is showing us how to make these drum-shaped metal tables."

"Father, since when have you been interested in making things?"

"Since Lionel expressed an interest, that's when."

"No more wine until dinner," Sanchini looked sternly at her father and then at Lionel. "Don't make me be the policeman."

"Scouts' honour," replied her father in his own tropical uniform.

As her father and Lionel left to find Ari's father, Sanchini went in search of her never-met mother-in-law's studio. Jacintha said that she was, like his late wife, an 'early morning bird'. He had explained there was a blue door in her bedroom courtyard. If she went through she would find herself in a secret courtyard. The studio had a big north-facing industrial window, the sort used by tea factories. In fact, this one had been salvaged from a former tea factory in Nuwara Eliya.

Whilst Sanchini explored, her daughter was getting the lesson of her life. Like most old engineers Jacintha kept up with tech. He erected a large iPad on its easel, adeptly folding the cover back and brought up the all-too-familiar periodic table.

As Amelia tried not to groan, he pointed to the first element.

"Number one hydrogen, it's a gas discovered by Henry Cavendish in 1766, its name comes from the Greeks, 'hydro' and 'genes' meaning 'water forming'. Number one on the periodic chart will be our future. Hydrogen gas can be generated from water and returns to water when used, your teacher probably uses the word 'oxidised'."

"Yes, how did you know that?"

"Well, when our teacher says oxidised, you must think 'used' and that Henry Cavendish went to Peterhouse College in Cambridge."

"I would love to go to there. Or Oxford."

"I'll come visit you if you make it. How proud your father would be to have a daughter studying in England. Now who was on the throne in England in 1766?"

"A George?"

"Spot on, George III, he reigned for 60 years. So what's the first element of the periodic table?"

"Hydrogen, and it's our future."

"Why?"

"Because it's all around us and when used it's still clean."

"Unlike coal or oil. Are they elements?"

"I don't think so, but I know the world is concerned about carbon and that's a waste product of use."

"Yes and it has a number."

Amelia looked at the chart.

"I'm going for number six."

"Yes, yes, yes, my clever granddaughter."

Amelia and her grandfather criss-crossed their way through the periodic table, discussing relative facts that finally began to bring the elements alive to her.

The new chatelaine of Mamboz decided to enlist the help of Ari's mother. Keshini had produced her one son when she was only sixteen. The marriage had been arranged, but her husband was kind and capable and she grew to love him. They lived near the fruit and vegetable market in Galle. He had got the job with Mr Jacintha when he married and she later joined her husband, primarily to look after Mrs Jacintha when she became ill. It was her husband and Mr Jacintha who had made the Moroccan tent on the roof, and it was Mr Jacintha's idea to adopt the traditional white tunics and fezzes. It became their livery, which extended beyond the confines of the house in Pedlar Street. The perk of their service was to come to Mamboz. On Mrs Jacintha's death, her husband had decided to keep the farm going for Dinish. The farm's ownership was again threatened when he had died, because Jacintha chose to stay in Galle Fort. His needs were simple and well covered by their now grown-up son. It was their dream come true when they were asked to look after Mamboz, airing and maintaining the house, working with the gardeners and generally being there. This weekend had been enjoyable and busy, the house and gardens had come alive again. Mamboz's days as a living memorial, with luck, might now be nearing an end. Keshini was so thrilled to be told by Mr Jacintha that he had given the house and farm to Sanchini; she hadn't worked for a vibrant young mistress for a long long time.

Keshini lifted the key off a labelled board in the kitchen and hurried to the front circle, from which she guided her new mistress behind the red palm wall to the studio. The key opened both the studio and the blue courtyard door. They stepped up into one large single room, pavilion in feel, studio in practice. It was sparsely furnished with wooden flooring and a large central worktable, surrounded by a collection of easels, a potter's wheel, a white sink with a grooved wooden draining board and a partially screened bed.

"This is where my mistress used to take her rest in the afternoons."

"You and your husband have kept this place immaculate."

"Thank you madam."

"Now will you show me the door to my bedroom courtyard please." A tiny dancing smile crept upon Sanchini's lips as she said 'my'. Keshini carefully locked the main door – screened from the drive by red palms – and opened a small door abutting the industrial window leading her down three stone steps towards another blue door. As Sanchini walked, she reflected that she'd thought she'd created an earthly paradise in her cloistered courtyard back in Kandy, but this was so much better. She imagined her late mother-in-law's daily routine; up early wandering through the door to her studio, working on a picture or carrying on through the red palm curtain into the garden beyond.

🐊

It was a relaxed household that met for drinks on the veranda. Lionel and Mr Ashok were telling everyone how simple Ari's father's drum tables were to make.

"Good design is always simple," Mr Ashok infrmed Jacintha, "but the devil is always in the detail."

As Sanchini and Amelia approached, Jacintha rose from his seat and said, "May I introduce our granddaughter, the chemist."

"I think I've finally got it," beamed Amelia.

"What's changed?" replied her mother.

"The language. Grandpa has phrased it more simply, oxidation is now 'used' and hydrogen (H1) he thinks may be our salvation."

"Let's raise our glasses to Jacintha, our most generous of hosts," Mr Ashok then looked at his granddaughter, "and a brilliant teacher."

"Here, here," cried Amelia, "to my other brilliant grandpa."

Once they were settled at Dinish's table, the curry arrived.

"This is superb, not too hot."

"I gave instructions to Keshini that Englishmen don't like it too hot."

"Some do," said Lionel, who then awkwardly blushed.

"Come on Lionel, tell us why you came to Sri Lanka. It wasn't just a holiday, was it?"

"No, it wasn't. It's a long story."

"We've got all night," said Sanchini with a 'do tell' smile.

Mr Ashok filled everybody's glasses.

"I came to Sri Lanka to get away, not for a bad reason, but for a good one. I knew that if I stayed in Hastings, I'd spill the beans."

"What's spilling...?"

"Saying too much. I have a great friend in Hastings called Barty, he's a chef and he helped me recover a stolen bronze. 'Recover' isn't really the right word, maybe more 'replace'. During this adventure I was asked to clear a pub. Not as splendid as your Royal Bar and Hotel, but a typical traditional English pub that had just been sold. Well, in an upstairs bedroom I found two old cardboard boxes and inside these, wrapped in 1960s newspaper, were a pair of 18th-century porcelain vases. They were large, pink and perfect. I consigned them to an auction house assuming that they would be sold in London, they weren't. Instead, they were flown halfway round the world to Hong Kong as late entries in an important oriental sale." Lionel paused.

"And," interrupted Mr Ashok, "they sold for?"

Lionel paused again.

"Too much money. When you have two wealthy bidders, well the sky tends to be the limit and things can get very out of hand!"

"Oh," said a collective table.

"How much, is too much?" asked an intrigued Mr Ashok.

Lionel tried to bat this away by lifting his water and taking a couple of thoughtful draughts.

"Come on, how much?" Mr Ashok teased.

Lionel now lifted his wine glass. He was going to need more than water.

"Over four million pounds."

It was as if a main electricity cable had fallen on the table, everybody around it became stiff with the pulse of revelation. It was only Lionel who now felt a wave of calm, maybe it was the relief of finally saying the figure out loud.

🐊

After Sanchini and Amelia had gone to bed, Jacintha, Mr Ashok and Lionel had an arrack.

"That's a lot of money," Mr Ashok finally said.

"With it, of course, comes responsibility too," volunteered Jacintha.

"I know and that's why I came here – to decide what to do with it. Like you, Mr Ashok, I have a happy and settled life. I buy and sell antiques, eat and drink with friends, but unlike you I have no family. My family are my friends: Barty, Pru, her two daughters Polly and Phoenix and my young apprentice Jack. I will share the money with them, so that they can live their lives free from day-to-day concerns. That's the reason why I'm keen to help your raft boy, I know only too well how a little bit of luck can change lives."

"Good for you, and on that note, I must bid you farewell. It sounds like you will do the right thing. I'll have gone before you're up as I have a granddaughter to deliver to double chemistry tomorrow. I've truly enjoyed meeting an English antique dealer, and if Amelia wins this university place we will come and visit you. Won't we, Jacintha?"

"Yes, we will."

"Safe travels, Lionel."

"I can't tell you how much I have enjoyed our road trip. Thank you for including me."

"Likewise, you have been such a tonic." Mr Ashok shook Lionel's hand and left.

"Come on Lionel," said Jacintha, "I think we have been deserted. As an unattached single man we have put you in the studio."

"You're making me sound dangerous."

"Men with too much money generally are!"

Chapter 40

Sri Lanka

Ari's father and Jacintha settled Lionel into the studio. The moonlight fell through the large window. It was furnished as a studio should be, sparsely with the necessaries for painting and pottery. After pointing out the single bed, hidden behind a closeboarded 4-foot-high screen, Ari's father showed him how to operate the outside shower and badly tempered loo.

"You must check for scorpions and snakes," were his parting words.

Jacintha had stayed in the studio and conjured up glasses, ice, and a bottle of arrack.

"Did he give you the creepy crawly talk?"

"He did."

"He's always had a dark sense of humour. It's a Sri Lankan thing. Good should always be balanced with the misfortune!"

"I do feel that I've seen much more of the country with Mr Ashok than I might have done as a tourist."

"As a tourist you get to see the sights, but with a native you get to meet the people."

One glass became two, Lionel asked about his only son.

"Had Dinish been alive do you think the sapphire would have taken another route to Europe?"

"I doubt it, Dinish never showed me a stone this large. As a geologist, I've seen many large stones: amethysts, aquamarines, topazes, but I haven't seen a sapphire that size, other than in a book! When I spoke to George, he thought it was unusually good, but we will have to wait."

"Have you met George?"

"No, he hasn't come here. He is a retailer and by all accounts a very successful one. The only time he takes a plane is to see a buyer, and luckily for him, most of his clients come to London. I know Dinish loved going to see him, he took him to clubs and restaurants not even Hollywood stars know exist."

"As soon as I open the container back home and have got the stone in my hand, I will message Mr Ashok."

"I know he'd like to be informed of progress. Remember, important stones attract attention and often misfortune. I wouldn't let it out of your sight."

"Should I go with George to the cutters?"

"Definitely, you will find it a fascinating process and it will be the most amazing part of the stone's story. When it's cut and polished it will take on its new identity. Who knows, it may yield more – a whole 'float' of Crocodile Stones!"

"Did Dinish say whether George used cutters in London or Antwerp?"

"Both. I'm sure this one will be cut in the UK, as he might be wary of crossing borders. Now, I must get to my bed and hope that the next time we meet it will be in England."

"With her periodic tables licked, she's sure of a place."

"Now here is the key, it locks both the studio door and the blue door in your courtyard. Good night, Lionel."

Lionel wasn't ready for sleep. His brain was whirring;

Sanchini, sapphire, George, Sanchini, cutters, Sanchini... It was just too hot to sleep. Maybe a shower would slow down his brain.

It wasn't a big courtyard that served the studio, think Japanese outdoor space without the raked gravel and manicured moss. The shower was mounted on a wall, with its rose a good foot above Lionel's head. He turned a copper lever anticlockwise from 12 to 9 o'clock and the cool sweet water cascaded down his back. He was just about to turn the tap off when he noticed the mosaic on the wall. It was of a female nude with tiny waist and legs almost twice the length of her torso. The lever tap sprang from her bellybutton. So engrossed was he in the intricacies of the coloured stones that he leapt when he felt something on his left shoulder. Was it a snake? He turned his head, brushing his shoulder and caught not a snake, but a hand!

The hand belonged to a naked Sanchini. It was as though the gilt bronze of Tara had sprung off her British Museum plinth and was now in the shower with him. On her head she wore a crown of white frangipani flowers, made pearlescent in the moonlight. Above her tiny waist her breasts shone like gilded stupas. It was the hands of a Kandyan Princess that glided down Lionel's arms from his shoulders to his hands. He took those hands and kissed her. It was she who turned off the tap and led him to the small studio bed, lay him down and kissed him slowly from his nose to his toes.

🦎

Lionel awoke with a start in the dawn light. He had had the most vivid tropical dream. He'd been enticed by a siren in a deluge of water and lain on his studio bed and been caressed like never before. As he rubbed his sleepy eyes and swung his legs from the bed, his bare feet fell on a discarded string of flowers.

Chapter 41

London, Heathrow

Lionel settled into his business-class seat with a glass of champagne and reviewed his stay in Sri Lanka. He had come for a holiday to sort out his new-found wealth, but the way Jacintha was talking, this sapphire could be worth well over five million, what are the chances of that... Like a baton in a relay race, as one problem is solved another presents itself. He'd never given much thought to the expression 'only the rich get richer', but he was beginning to see why now. After a non-stop flight he disembarked into Heathrow's miles of connecting corridors. A cold shiver passed through his spine at the thought of customs. Thank the Lord, the stone wasn't actually on him.

🦕

Jack had called Barty regarding Lionel's return flight and they'd decided between them to take Jack's van rather than Barty's BMW. It would be more fun if the three sat up front as conversations between front and back seats are wearing; the endless turning of heads, missing vital words as the initial excitement of returning quickly wanes and exhaustion sets in.

Jack and Barty stood in the arrivals hall of London's Heathrow Airport. Lionel's flight from Colombo airport was to arrive at 7pm. They had allowed forty minutes for their friend to clear passport control, baggage reclaim and customs but were unaware that at least half the flight was delayed in the immigration hall. It's an easy passage if you have a UK biometric passport, but if you don't and you're on a connecting flight starting in Cochin, India, it's considerably longer.

Lionel watched the same cellophane-wrapped bags go round and around the reclaim carousel. Finally, he picked up his bags and headed towards the Nothing to Declare channel. With heart pounding he held his breath and almost had a heart attack when he felt a tap on his shoulder.

"We'll have this one."

He turned to see a smiling customs officer and then recognised him as one of Justin's cousins. Justin was a well-known 'man and van' in Hastings, and when larger jobs required more hands, his extended family helped out.

"Very funny," Lionel said as he made quick exit towards the arrivals hall.

What was beginning to fascinate the many waiting relatives and professional drivers was a man in a full clown's outfit. He wore an orange-coloured wig and oversized boots, carrying a large bunch of flowers ... not garage carnations, these were more Mayfair flower stall. Within a short time, the crowd resembled spectators at a tennis match: as the automatic doors revealed a new person, the crowd's heads turned to the clown then swung back to the doors. When it finally happened, the woman didn't disappoint. She was tall, dark and impossibly glamorous. The now well-rehearsed heads switched to the clown whose expensive bunch of flowers rose as his feet started moving. Her trolley accelerated before being abandoned for an unselfconscious embrace, and as his flowers fell to the floor the crowd erupted in clapping, cheers and whistles.

It was just at this dramatic moment that a heavily-breathing Lionel came through the automatic doors. All eyes including Jack and Barty's were still on the clown couple. Confused and befuddled, he wondered why he was being clapped back into the UK. Then Jack spotted him.

"Welcome home," he said whilst taking over his trolley.

Barty gave Lionel a big hug.

"Coffee?"

Before either could say, "How was it?" Lionel launched into a panegyric. "It was incredible. I walked into an antique shop in Kandy, hoping to buy something. The owner, Mr Ashok, recognised me as a man 'of similar minerals' and before I knew it, he invited me into his amazing home, an old Dutch merchant's warehouse, tea turned to lunch and then dinner the next day. Before this amazing island was known as Ceylon or Sri Lanka, its old name was the island of Serendip. It's an island where you can find anything, it has so many riches when you go looking for something you often find something better. And that's exactly what happened to me."

"Serendipity, the rule of happy accidents," ventured Barty.

"Exactly! I walked into a shop in search of a bargain and stepped into an adventure."

"Wow," said Jack, "but can we continue this in the van? Short stay parking costs a fortune here."

As all happily squeezed into the front of the van, Jack said, "Tell us all about this Mr Ashok?"

"He's just like us, essentially an antiques dealer and house clearer but, unlike us, operates in a far less crowded market. If someone dies in Kandy and had antiques the family will call him, he'll arrive in his 1934 Rolls-Royce wearing a tropical suit. His enormous warehouse is full of silver, wine, antiques and curios. One day, Jack, you might find a big live/workspace and then you can start syphoning away goods that you don't want to sell. It's just like a bank: it's an alternative store of wealth."

"You spoke of a stone, a crocodile and a raft," Barty reminded him. "You said it's a long story and not for the phone? I'm dying to hear."

"Well, he and I had just had lunch at the Royal Pub in Kandy and we're walking around the Sacred Tooth Temple when he takes an urgent message from his granddaughter, Amelia, to return home as soon as possible. On arrival, we are introduced to a young man of about eighteen, very much like a Sri Lankan you, Jack, he had been at primary school with Amelia. His family dredge the Mahaweli River for building sand. It's difficult and dangerous work as the river and its banks are home to hundreds of crocodiles. In fact, this boy's father was killed by one. Anyway, he unwraps the most unbelievably huge sapphire, at least the size of a hen's egg, from a banana leaf! It was so big it should really belong in a royal crown and what's more, its colour is extraordinary. I know that I'm prone to exaggerate but I am truly not in this instance."

"Blimey," said Barty.

"Now, not a word to anybody. I have been warned with a stone like this comes serious potential danger. I mean it when I say not a word to Pru, Polly, Phoenix, anyone at all."

"Do you have the stone with you?"

"No, I don't, it's coming in the container, it should arrive in a couple of weeks. Oh, and I've met somebody. A living goddess, someone finally seems to be smiling on me!"

Barty and Jack were speechless and then simultaneously asked:

"What, a woman?"

Chapter 42

Hastings

After the deep, deep sleep only ever really achieved in one's own bed, Lionel pottered up to his kitchen. There was no 'Clive monitoring' movement in the house: he and Jack must be worrying wildlife on the beach. He peered out of his window over the descending roofs to the shingle beach and twinkling sea, dotted with the odd dog walker along the tideline. He couldn't make out either Jack or Clive. He put on the kettle and popped a teabag in a straight-sided mug. After probing and pressing, he removed it and bent down to open his under-counter fridge. It was a very different fridge to normal. His usually housed lemons, eggs, wine and milk; now he found cheese, mackerel pâté, a cooked chicken, ginger beer, orange juice and, thankfully some milk. He intended to put some bacon or sausages in the oven but there were none. He had marked Jack as a grab-it-on-the-road 'pasty' sort of guy, not the wholesome fellow of the fridge take-over. He sat in his chair and picked up his trusty *Antiques Trade Gazette* newspaper; upon opening he heard the ring of the shop bell and the racing ascent of paws. He just managed to put down his mug before Clive burst through the door and joined him in his chair. The last kiss Lionel had received came from his dream of a goddess Sanchini; in contrast Clive's was cold, slathering and wet.

"Down, Clive," Jack said. "Morning Lionel, sorry about the sand, the tide was out today."

"No worries, that's why I have never bothered to carpet the wooden floorboards. I have always found hoovers such a wrestle, they're inevitably on the wrong floor and I find the hoses have a mind of their own. The only time I use mine is when I break a glass or have flies at the window."

"I don't own one, the nearest I get is a dustpan and brush in my van."

"What time are we going to Pru's?"

"After one, she thought you might like a lie-in."

"I've been on Eastern time for three weeks, five hours ahead."

"Norman is coming to see you this morning."

"If he comes at his normal 11, would you mind running me up to Pettit's warehouse before we go to Pru's?"

"Of course, where is it?"

"They're on the top, along the ridge, off Ivy House Lane. Will you give Norman a call, we need to leave by eleven, is your van close?"

"Yes I've managed to find a good spot by the Horse and Groom."

"Have they missed me?"

"What do you think? June wanted a regular update."

"I can taste it now, her chicken and ham pie. Pastry, God how I've missed it."

"Well, you look all the better for it. You've lost some timber."

"Not lost, just tightened."

"I hope Pru is doing her quiche?"

"Ah, the famous quiche, I had one over there in your absence.

I've seen quite a lot of Polly and Phoenix."

"Oh?"

Norman arrived buzzing with gossip: "You missed a bronze incense burner."

"Didn't you keep it for me?"

"Couldn't, cash flow," he said with a shrug, "but I've got you something in the car." Lionel needed no persuading to follow him and watch as Norman performed his bamboo cane boot prop ceremony. Why he didn't just get a new pair of gas struts was beyond Lionel, but we all have our foibles. A blanketed item was removed, righted and gently placed on the tarmac. Norman allowed himself a theatrical pause and slowly plucked and then discarded the grey blanket covering. Before them stood a bright pink enamelled barrel-shaped Chinese porcelain garden seat.

"May I?"

"Be my guest."

Lionel lowered his bottom onto the pierced seat. It was just the right height, not too low as the cheaper ones often are. He stood up, rolled it over on the blanket and inspected its base. Regrettably, no painted or impressed character marks. As he rolled it about on the blanket, he checked for any damage. When a piece of porcelain is heavily decorated, it's sometimes hard to spot, better to use your hands to feel for cracks and chips. He executed a more thorough feel and then balanced it to check how heavy it was. It passed his weight test.

"Is it sound? No damage?" He knew to ask for future come-back.

"It's perfect, no cracks or chips."

"How much?"

"I bought it well and thought of you. I know you like a garden seat, fifty quid to you. Welcome home."

"Thank you, Norman. See you tomorrow?"

Lionel gave him a pink £50 note and Jack picked it up.

"Would you take it up to the kitchen please. I'll retrieve my presents for Pru, are you ready to go?"

Twenty minutes later they found themselves in Pettit's yard.

"Have you rung?" asked Jack, turning off the engine.

"No, I wanted to remind myself of the unit and its outside space first."

As they walked towards the up and over door, Mr Pettit emerged, cupping his hands to light a cigarette.

"Ah, the antique dealers, how did you get on with that scrap metal?"

"Well, thank you very much."

"Good. I always try to leave a little something for the next person."

"Hear, hear," said Lionel, remembering the Chinese vases. "You certainly did that," he added under his breath.

"More scrap?"

"No, not this time. I came to ask if I could unpack a 20-foot container here?"

"We have four large parking spaces and we only use two."

"It's not for long, as the shipping company only allow 2 hours to unpack the container. Might I have a small space in your warehouse too, only for a week? Would £400 cover it?"

"It certainly would," said Robin Pettit promptly, shaking Lionel's hand.

"I will let you know about delivery."

"Good. I will get my son to put some railway sleepers here to protect the tarmac."

Barty had rung Pru the day before and invited her to a

'welcome home Lionel' lunch; she had kindly offered to cook instead, knowing from her daughters that Barty was too busy at his restaurant.

"Come to me. I have only one commission this week, I'll do a quiche."

"That would be lovely, we seem to be fully booked at the moment, thank the Lord for your girls. It's not just the service, it's the prep and the shopping. It all takes time. Oh, and thank you for the salsa verde, Polly made some yesterday. It does more for a vegetarian dish than any amount of that veggie gravy."

"It's addictive, it must be the vinegar and lemon zest. I think lemon zest is the new anchovy, once used you can't stop."

Pru had missed Lionel and his little presents. There was rarely a week when she didn't return home to find a box or a bag at her door. A piece of kitchenalia: a colander of just the right size, or a horn-handled knife with a razor edge of soft steel, a pottery mixing bowl, or once a first edition cookery book. Items found for pounds on his daily rounds. Lionel, Jack and Barty were coming at 1 o'clock, but no girls today, as Polly and Phoenix were at college. Pru, like all organised cooks, made the sauce first, that famous salsa verde. She roughly chopped a large bunch of parsley and scooped it into a small six-inch glass mixing bowl, another present from Lionel. Then she weighed and added 40 grams of Panko breadcrumbs, 75ml of best olive oil, a garlic clove, 40ml of her own red wine vinegar, along with a tablespoon of capers, a pinch of salt and the vital lemon zest. She blended it and put it in the fridge. Done, now the pastry. She sifted 175 grams of plain flour, half the amount of cubed butter, a pinch of salt and Magimixed it all with one egg.

"Cold hands, warm heart," she thought, setting her oven to 180°c.

Pru brought the flour and butter together with a sprinkling of thyme leaves and lemon zest, then into the fridge to set: not all cooking is done in an oven. Whilst it cooled, Pru stuck two sheets of cling film together on her island, lightly dusted with flour, and prepared another two sheets to go on top. Twenty minutes later she removed the pastry from the fridge, flattened it onto the centre of the cling film, covering it with the other two floured sheets. By using this sandwich method, she was able to minimise adding more flour to stop her rolling pin sticking, which would make her pastry too dense. When almost translucently thin, she removed one side of cling film and gently shaped the pastry into a buttered fluted dish. Once happy, she pulled off the top layer of cling film and poured in her jar of 'baking' rice. She placed the dish in the top of the oven for 12 minutes, removed the rice and returned it to the bottom of the oven for a further 15 minutes. As a failsafe, she brushed the pastry case with an egg yolk to seal any cracks and returned it to the bottom of the oven for a couple of minutes. She now had her thin and lightly tanned pastry case. She would add the custard of eggs, milk, double cream, parsley, smoked bacon, cheddar and mascarpone cheese, and cook it at the lower temperature of 150°c for 40 minutes, ready for when her guests arrived. This would allow her both time for drinks in the kitchen and afford her the ceremony of removing a freshly baked quiche. After all, she had her reputation to uphold. She made a companion green salad; her pudding would be a lemon drizzle cake, which she'd already done yesterday along with the yoghurt and stem ginger.

Barty arrived first and was promptly put in charge of drinks. Ten minutes later there was another ring at the front door. A tanned and slimmer Lionel stood carrying two bags. "This one is for you and this one is for the girls. Textiles are so much cheaper in Sri Lanka. I couldn't stop buying."

"That's very kind."

The chatter of old friends flowed. Although Lionel had the most news, he was careful to allow others to speak. The quiche was sublime.

"Possibly your best, Pru," said Barty, raising his glass and toasting, "To the best pastry in Hastings."

The party broke up with Jack and Clive leaving for Epsom and Pru walking to meet her girls at the station. Lionel needed no persuasion to walk back to Barty's house for one more glass. Two streets later and he was in Barty's light-filled sitting room.

"I have something to tell you."

"Sounds ominous," said Barty, handing Lionel a glass of red Bordeaux.

"Do you know why I went to Sri Lanka?"

"No, though you did go rather quickly now I come to think of it."

"I left because I sold something at auction. Do you remember when we were in Norfolk at the Beccles street market and I dropped my takeaway coffee?"

"Yes, you took a call and then whispered to me 'my luck has turned'."

"Well, the item, more correctly a pair of items, sold for a lot of money."

A certain stillness fell over Barty's sitting room.

"Oh!"

"I knew I couldn't stay here, I knew I would blabber. I just wanted to work out what I was going to do with the money first."

"How much is a lot?" ventured Barty.

"Over three million pounds."

Barty didn't reply.

"I have decided to share my windfall with you, Pru, the girls and Jack."

Chapter 43

Hastings and London

Lionel only had a couple of weeks before the container ship was due to dock. He decided to ring George, Dinish's London jeweller friend, who immediately asked whether the sapphire had been pre-formed? "No," he replied, the stone had remained in the same egg-like shape as he had first seen it in Kandy. George had suggested involving an experienced English gem hunter, highly respected, and he also had a strong relationship with a stone cutter based in England. The thought of taking the sapphire over another international border had just been too terrifying; he'd done enough smuggling for now. George had recommended that, once the container was open, Lionel should get a friend to drive him to London. George would need the make, model and registration plate, and then his assistant would arrange the parking, congestion charge and all other frustrations associated with modern motoring. Barty was happy to be his getaway driver, as long as it didn't clash with a lunchtime service, but if it had to be on Friday or Saturday he was prepared to allow Jack to drive his precious BMW. After travelling to and from Heathrow, Barty was impressed with the younger man's road-craft: he pre-empted possible danger by allowing a gap of at least two car lengths, and not the more commonly adopted five feet from a rear bumper. In congestion, he kept moving by maintaining an even larger gap, no Mexican wave of brake-and-throttle; in fact, Barty had noticed he rarely touched his brakes. A skill much appreciated by his co-pilot Clive, whose favourite position was upright next to his master.

For advice on containers, Lionel had approached a fellow antiques dealer, Peter, who filled much larger 40-foot containers with furniture and objets d'art bound for the US. Once dispatched, he hoped his containers would land in New Orleans, but informed Lionel that they could be dropped almost anywhere along the shores of the US. He had provided the name and number of a firm of hauliers based in Liverpool who regularly collected from the southern ports of Felixstowe, Southampton and London.

"Give them a call now to register your delivery address and payment method so when the shipping agents email you, you can move quickly, as your container has only three to four days' grace 'on the floor' at the docks, before the charges start."

"What do you mean?" asked Lionel.

"Well, anything over the allotted period of time is subject to penalties. Beware, if your container is held by customs for inspection and you go over your allotted time, you will be charged demurrage."

"Blimey, I hope it doesn't get stopped. Have you ever been charged fees?"

"I have once, I stupidly listed an item of furniture as having 'shell' inlay. This single word 'shell' flagged a customs inspection, which cost me dearly. As soon as you receive the email stating that your container has cleared customs, ring the haulier, also don't forget to take some bolt croppers when the container is delivered to you – you'll need them."

"Why?"

"Remember the seal with locking pin and plastic cap?"

"Yes."

"Well, that's how you break the pin. You shear it off with the croppers."

"A whole new world. Sounds painful."

The very next day the email arrived and Lionel sprang into action, first ringing the hauliers and then George.

"Once you've got your hands on it, weigh it and send me lots of photos."

"How do I weigh it?"

"Use a set of digital kitchen scales set to grams. As the more information I can give Guy the better."

Two days later an excited Barty and Jack and an anxious Lionel awaited the container's delivery in Pettit's yard. Once neatly settled on railway sleepers, Jack was handed the bolt cropper. Despite his wiry strength, it took him some doing. Once cut, he lifted the catch and pulled the long handle through 180 degrees to release the doors. First was the sight of bamboo, followed by an earthy tropical smell, a heady mixture of bamboo, rattan, pottery and cardboard wrapping.

"Where is it?" whispered Barty.

"Sshh, it's in a fruit box. Jack, if you could start moving the furniture to the warehouse we'll start on the boxes." On removing the bamboo furniture, they discovered that some of the lower boxes had split and contents spewed onto the floor, some of the stone eggs remaining wrapped but many rolling loose.

"Oh God, I hope nobody has been in here."

"But the seal was intact," ventured Barty.

"Would you like a cup of tea?" asked Robin Junior.

"Yes please, milk and we'll need one sugar each," replied Lionel, looking worriedly at the hundreds of loose eggs.

"We have less than ten minutes before he returns. I remember the box was below the 'Sunshine State' label, so if we remove these four, we will limit our search."

"How many in each box?"

"Jacintha packed one hundred in each box. We need to get a wiggle on."

"How will I recognise it?"

"After taking your breath away, you will not be able to stop looking at its blueness."

As they both worked, they got faster at unwrapping each egg from its newspaper. After five minutes Lionel exhaled loudly, stood up and tapped Barty's shoulder.

"Here's the fellow!" He passed the stone to Barty, who automatically held it up against the sunlight of the open doors.

"Put it down," said Lionel in a stage whisper.

His friend whistled. "I see what you mean about the colour. That deep blue reminds me of the sea in Sicily."

Lionel whipped out his mobile. "I promised I'd message Mr Ashok the moment I had it in my hand. He should understand this: 'The eagle has landed.'"

Chapter 44

London

Barty drove past the Conquest Hospital and turned north on the A21. Lionel was determined not to look at the stone until he was safely on the Pembury bypass but then he remembered George's request.

"We must stop. I need to weigh and send photos of the stone."

"I'll pull into the farm shop in Hurst Green. It's more secure than a petrol station and I'd love a coffee."

On arrival he avoided the parking spaces in front of the Hampton's-style fruit and vegetable tables, choosing a space tucked far away in an empty corner of the car park.

"Coffee?"

"Cappuccino, please, and one of their excellent almond pastries?"

"Here, take the key and keep the car locked," said Barty.

Duly locked, Lionel opened the glove box to form a temporary table and took a set of digital kitchen scales from his Brewing Brothers canvas bag. He then twisted the newspaper wrapping into a ring shape stand, placing the egg upright, just as you would in an egg cup. He turned on the scales and set them to grams, removed the egg and reset it to zero. It weighed 174 grams. After taking several photos, he carefully replaced the sapphire in his coat pocket before sending them to George. Within seconds, he received simple confirmation, "It's over 800 carats!"

A knock on the driver's window made Lionel jump!

"All done?" asked Barty as he passed a lidded takeout cup.

"Yes. Any pastries?"

"Patience, I've only got two hands."

He passed the white paper bag over before starting the engine.

They had a good run up and once on Hyde Park Corner, Lionel rang George.

"Hello, we are nearly with you."

"Great."

"What's my instructions?" asked Barty.

"We'll be met by his security, Derek and Tommy. I think this might very well be a welcome to another world."

As he drew adjacent to the parked cars in front of George's Albemarle address, Lionel's passenger door was opened by a polite, thickset man in a grey flannel suit.

"Good afternoon, my name is Derek and I work for Mr George. Would you please come with me?"

"What about my friend here? Can he come too?"

"Of course, Tommy will park your car. Leave the engine running and come this way."

A wiry young man with thick black hair and flannel suit opened Barty's door. He would normally give instructions regarding his precious BMW, but he got the feeling that this fellow knew more about driving than he did. Derek held a plastic card to a wall-mounted digital reader and a glossy black door opened.

"After you."

They walked into a large empty hall with a geometric-patterned limestone floor. The only piece of furniture was a circular specimen marble-topped table with a gilded triangular stand; on it stood an oversized vase of expensive tropical flowers. Derek led them up a set of shallow stone steps with black-gloss-and-gold-painted metal balustrade and highly polished mahogany handrail, on to a light-filled landing. He knocked on a pair of double doors and entered. Standing by a mahogany library table was a tall handsome man in a well-cut navy-blue suit, and beside him, an older man in a well-worn dark flannel suit.

"Good afternoon, how lovely to meet you. I'm George and this is my friend Guy."

As George moved forward to shake their hands, Guy held back and smiled, not with his mouth but with his eyes. There was a stillness about this gentleman.

"I'm looking forward to seeing the stone," he said in a quiet, smart English accent. "I understand from George it was found in Kandy's Mahaweli river, a place I know well. May we see it?"

Lionel brought the unwrapped stone from his coat pocket and handed it to George, who weighed its heft in his right hand before holding it up to the light with his left. He didn't say a thing, just smiled at Lionel and passed it to Guy.

"My word, you would expect a stone tumbling down a riverbed to be small but this isn't. It's without doubt the biggest sapphire I have ever held and I have been in the business over forty years! George, have a closer look."

They all watched as George sat down and raised a jeweller's loupe across the bridge of his nose to his dominant left eye. As he kept rotating the egg with his left hand he started smiling.

"Well, I doff my hat to you. I have been up a lot of mountains, cut through many, many jungles and sweated at too many militia checkpoints, but I have never held a gemstone like yours. I think it's called beginner's luck?"

George reached towards a set of digital black scales. "Let's pop it on."

The display read 870.68 carats.

"I believe a bottle of champagne is called for."

Either by telepathy or prior planning, the double doors opened and in walked a young lady, wearing a blue-and-white-patterned Diane Von Furstenberg wrap dress.

"Jackie, may we have a bottle of Ruinart?"

Lionel and Barty watched as she about-turned in her knee-high caramel suede boots and strutted from the room. The only eyes that didn't follow her were George's; he couldn't take his eyes off the digital display. Jackie returned with a tray of tall fluted glasses followed by Derek, trying not to look too uncomfortable carrying an ice bucket and bottle. Without a smile or a word, she took the bottle, removed the wire cage and then the cork. She brought an air of professionalism that wasn't normally expected of a personal assistant, more of a sommelier. After handing out the glasses she left.

George stood up, lifted his glass and toasted, "To the Crocodile Stone!" He continued, "Never has an awaited stone exceeded my imagination as this one has. The next step, if you agree, is for Guy to take it to his cutter friend in Norwich. Lionel, are you happy to leave it with us?"

"I am, but I promised Mr Ashok and Manoji that I wouldn't let the stone out of my sight."

"That's fine. I half-expected you to say that. You should go with Guy now. Tommy and Derek will drive you both. Would you like to go too?" George asked Barty.

"No, I must return to Hastings. Thank you."

Derek took Barty to his car and returned for Guy and Lionel.

"Lionel, you take the stone. You will be amazed at how Guy's cutter approaches this, I believe he uses a traditional cutting technique. Jackie will send you details of your accommodation and ensure you have toiletries and other necessaries. Good luck, safe travelling and I will look forward to an update."

Chapter 45

Norwich

Derek led Lionel to the waiting Mercedes and issued the simple instruction, "To Norwich, Tommy."

As the car made its way to Green Park, Lionel was reminded of Mr Ashok's 1930s Rolls-Royce, which sailed ... this glided. Once through Piccadilly Circus and Trafalgar Square, the car settled on the Embankment, travelling east past the Tower of London towards the City. The central elbow rest suddenly started moving towards them.

"Drinks are now being served," said Derek as he turned to smile at Guy.

"This is new."

"Help yourself, Mr Guy."

"I will," he said as he took one of the three small bottles of champagne, "they are cold. Lionel would you like a glass?"

"Of course. This is my sort of travel."

The two and half hours swept by with tales from Guy's gem-hunting in Africa, Asia and South America. What struck Lionel was that it was all about the colour.

"What my friend Akram will be looking to do is to preserve the colour, size and shape of the finished stone. The obstacles are inclusions which are, I'm afraid to say, locked into the stone. You always hope these faults lie just under the skin rather than at its heart. If you are forced to cut a once rich blue stone too thinly it may lose its hue."

"How many stones will your cutter get out of it?"

"At this stage it's impossible to say but the fewer you get the better. It will all be up to any flaws. Akram is world class – we are exceptionally fortunate he resides in the UK. I should caution you the process isn't quick. First, he will want to carefully assess the stone before he starts cutting: once he starts there is no going back."

Tommy slowed the Mercedes whilst Derek found the house. It was large and not too dissimilar to a Decimus-Burton-designed villa in St Leonards or Royal Tunbridge Wells, the only difference being that this was made of a regional white brick instead of the ashlar block sandstone of the Sussex and Kent Weald.

Once through the Indian-looking metal-studded hardwood gates, with their rather painful-looking spiked cresting, the men were met at the front door by two of the jeweller's sons. Most new homeowners choose to modernise their interiors – this one had been 'Mughalised'. The hall was bejewelled with alternate green and purple Moroccan tiles to dado level, with incredible raised and geometrically carved tadelakt plaster above. It was like stepping into Alhambra. They were led from this beautiful and empty hall through a mihrab-shaped doorway into a small anteroom furnished with French Louis XV-style gilded elbow chairs upholstered in emerald-green silk brocade and a large wall-mounted screen showing a matrix of live security camera feeds. Another mihrab-shaped door opened into a large kitchen, filled with talking and laughing women dressed in saris, through which they were finally taken into Akram's workshop. As Guy was greeted in Sinhalese by his Sri Lankan friend, Lionel took in the room. It must have been converted from an adjoining outbuilding. The roof timbers were open which gave it greater height. At the top of the brickwork were a string of modern landscape windows that gave a diffused light and were set far too high for prying eyes.

"Security is key. What you can't see..." said their host Akram, "and it would take a brave man to get through my wife and aunties in the kitchen. I have seen many a hardened thief in a market brought up short by a hot spoon!"

At this Guy and his friend started laughing.

"Where is this stone then?"

Lionel took it from his coat pocket.

"You weren't exaggerating, it's weighty," said Akram, sitting down on one of four wheelie-legged desk chairs.

A jeweller's workshop is universal, whether you are in Bangkok or London. They sit at scalloped benches hung with skin aprons, to catch the lemel, the bits of filed gold or platinum too precious to discard. Normally, beside each well hangs a pendant motor drill, similar to those found in old-fashioned dentists and two lit torches for soldering gold and platinum. This room had different work benches; Akram and his sons were not setting jewellery but cutting and polishing coloured gemstones. It looked like four washstands had been joined together and placed in the middle of the room. They were all made of the same material, mahogany, with distinctive three-quarter galleries, but instead of marble tops each table had a crank handle and circular copper turntable, just like a record player except that the decks were a good inch thick.

Akram took a cloth and rubbed the stone, giving it an oily sheen, then he held it under an industrial lamp above a sheet of white paper. First, he used his naked eyes to inspect the stone, then a jeweller's loupe. After what seemed like ages he spoke.

"It's going to be a long night. Normally, with a crystal-shaped gem there is an obvious table or heel to it. This generally determines how I will pre-form or cut the stone, but you have given me an egg, and eggs don't have tables or heels, just girdles. Can you leave it with me?"

Guy looked at Lionel.

"I'm happy to."

"I hope you release some good stones. I will call you in the morning," said Guy.

"Not too early please, my friend."

On leaving, one of the sons handed Guy a brown paper bag.

"From my mother, Mr Guy."

"Thank you."

Once in the car the smell became intoxicating.

"Who wants a samosa?" said Guy, passing the bag to Derek in the front.

"No thank you, Mr Guy. Tommy has firm rules about food in his cars. I will keep these until we get to the hotel then."

"Is it near? I'm starving."

"Jackie has booked you both into the Gunton Arms, it's half an hour away near Cromer on the coast."

"Ah, the crab," said Guy.

"Why the crab?" asked Lionel.

"Off Cromer and Sheringham is a huge shelf of chalk, the chalk sort of filters the shallow tidal water, making the brown crabs a touch sweeter."

"Why not Sheringham crabs?"

"Alliteration, dear Lionel, alliteration."

"You will like the Gunton Arms, lots of crab there. Mr George and Julia sometimes escape there for weekends. He describes it as Longleat without the entry fee."

"Why so?"

"It has a huge deer park, sort of out of Africa feel, right up your street, Mr Guy."

Chapter 46

London

As soon as Guy and Lionel left, George called his godson. "Hi Ollie, are you busy? I need some help."

"I've just got a couple of calls to make then I could come to your office?"

"That would be kind. I want to pick your brains. I've just held the biggest uncut sapphire I've ever seen."

"OK, I'll come around as soon as I can."

He called out to Jackie, laughing: "I think your catwalk strut was a little too much for Lionel and Barty."

"I couldn't stop myself, it's these new boots, they don't do normal walking."

"Ollie's coming around and I'm starving. When he arrives, would you get us something from Ben and Dan's deli. Nothing too heavy, no meat please."

"They do a great lentil lasagne."

"Would you arrange shirts, underwear and sponge bag for Guy and Lionel?"

"Thong or full coverage?"

"Jackie, now now!"

George chuckled as his mind went straight back to the carats –

and not the ones in his impending lasagne. Guy had spoken often of Akram in Norfolk and his traditional jamb peg polishing. If he could release some big stones from the egg he had just held, he would be a lucky jeweller. He knew that once the stones were polished the form and setting would become obvious. The soft square of a cushion cut stone would be perfect for an important gem and would be best set as a pendant. A ring would look ridiculous. His musings on halos of diamonds and jade hangers were interrupted by approaching steps. He stood up and hugged his godson.

"Thank you for coming, are you hungry?"

"Starving."

"Good, Jackie has gone to the deli to get us something."

"Less food, more news. It sounds like the stone was all you hoped for and more?"

"Definitely yes," said a smiling George, "the colour is magical. Think of the best blue sea, not the sandy shallow bit, but the deep stuff over the reef, the bit with mystery and menace."

"How can I help?"

"I need a buyer who won't blanche at the backstory."

"Why, is it bad?"

"It involves crocodiles. The finder's father was killed by one in the same river that the stone was found. That's why I want to name it the Crocodile Stone."

"Is that wise? Surely, it will narrow its appeal."

"Maybe, but it could also work in my favour. To the right person a predator is emblematic of strength. Take Damien Hirst's *The Physical Impossibility of Death in the Mind of Someone Living*... the shark in the tank. I bet it made more than the sheep and the cow?"

"OK, I get what you're saying," conceded Ollie.

"Your last sale in Hong Kong, was there a buyer who might fit the bill?"

"There was, come to think of it. New to us, a bit scary."

"How?"

"He didn't come alone, he had four bodyguards and a very firm PA, who had negotiated that they should view the sale alone after we closed for the day. We don't normally do private viewings for people that we don't know, but this PA had very good English and assured me that his boss was extremely keen. Well, when he arrived that was not the impression he gave. He didn't speak. I tried to greet him, his PA intercepted, charmingly but firmly. He was fiftyish, wore a well-cut suit and didn't remove his black gloves. They were such an odd party that you couldn't resist watching them. The strange thing was he didn't touch anything. The PA picked up and inspected the lots whilst his boss carefully watched. I got the feeling that there was a story there."

"Did he buy anything?"

"He bought one of the star lots: a pair of pink porcelain lidded vases."

"How much?"

"Over £4 million."

"Good, do you think he might be a contender for a large sapphire?"

"He might, he certainly fits a collector's profile. When I delivered the vases to his offices above a casino in Macau, the PA asked me to keep him informed if anything special came up for sale; it turns out his boss wants to fill the casino with items of interest. Think British Museum meets Vegas casino.

"I did like his PA. Straight-talking and very interested in the provenance of the vases. Of course, they knew from when and where they were made in 18th-century China, but were also keen to know from whom and where they came from in England. All I was able to tell them was that they were from a house clearance in Hastings, on the south coast."

"How funny, that's exactly where the sapphire has come from. Lionel and his friend Barty drove up here this morning."

"Are they jewellers?"

"No, Lionel is an old antiques dealer and Barty his friend is a chef."

"I would love to meet them. Anyway, back to the jewel in hand, do you have any photos?"

"Not for a couple of days. It needs to be cut and polished first. If the stone is really big I may not even set it. Guy said he would call me tomorrow from the cutters. Do you know anybody else who might be interested?"

"What about US buyers, they have a lot of money at the moment with all that tech and oil."

"My American buyers are mostly Hollywood actresses and they wouldn't wish to be associated with predatory crocodiles! Though they'd fall for the raft boy story."

"Hang on, remember the stand at Battersea where you bought me that amazing Art Deco bar. The horseshoe-shaped mirrored one, which I have in my flat."

"Yes I do. I'd have loved it for our kitchen but Julia put her foot down. As soon as they gave us a glass of champagne, I knew I had to buy it."

"They read you like a book. They're called Martin and Paul. Not only did they deliver it to me that very evening, they also re-arranged my sitting room and I haven't wanted to change the layout since. I remember they told me their best customers were in the States. They might know somebody."

"Will you give them a call? If you can find me two bidders I'll give you a commission."

"I'd rather have an offcut from this stone. Something ring-sized?"

"A ring? Well, well, well..."

Chapter 47
Norfolk

There is something lovely about staying in a smart country pub. They generally feel like country houses filled with comfortable furniture, dogs, rugs, wood smoke, books and art. Whether you're smelling them, stroking them or just looking at them they aggregate into a gloriously calming whole. Lionel's room had an overstuffed bed with heavy eiderdown, blankets and crisp white linen sheets. He slept like a top, even falling straight back to sleep after a 4am visit to the adjoining bathroom. His morning bath with a black Earl Grey tea had further pushed him into a blissful stupor, so it was with some surprise when he entered the dining room that he saw George sitting with Guy.

"Good morning Lionel," said George, standing up to shake his hand. "Surprised?"

"Very."

"Let me explain," said Guy. "You know the call I took at supper from Akram, well just as I was drifting off to sleep, he called again. He was rather keen that I should ring George. It seems that this sapphire just keeps on giving. Akram is grabbing a couple of hours' sleep and has asked us to come for coffee to tell us his findings."

"I'm hungry, let's get stuck in," said George, passing the breakfast card to Lionel. "Bed and breakfast, the bedrock of hospitality. It's a full English for me," he responded.

"Scramble, fried or poached?"

"Scramble every time," said Lionel.

Once on the move, the chatter in the Mercedes was of 'what ifs'. What if there were just too many flaws. What was the final colour going to be like?

On arrival a rather excited Akram sat George, Guy and Lionel in front of his worktable. He held the partially-ground and wetted egg under a strong light.

"I have marked the surface as a guide to where the internal flaws are," he said.

"There is a small fracture suspended right in the middle which I will cut through and then I'll use these two new surfaces as my tables. Hopefully, the cutting will remove most of the flaws, but what is left, I will polish out on the wheel." He tapped his thick copper lapidary wheel. "This is the big cut, but before I begin, do I have your backing?"

Guy looked at George.

"What are you looking at me for, Guy? It's not my stone."

Guy turned to Lionel.

"It's not mine either. George, it's your call, as you're the one selling it."

"Every man has a job and it's not mine to cut. You are the professional here, we are in your hands. Cut away, Akram," replied George. With that, Akram scuttled his wheelie chair to a bench-mounted circular saw, pressed a button to start it and lowered an industrial light just above the whirring blade.

"Here goes," he said, as he placed the egg on a metal guide and started pushing the stone against the wetted revolving saw. Surprisingly quickly the egg was sliced in two. Akram propelled his chair back to the table and handed a piece each to Guy and George.

"Colour is key," said George, "and these have the blue we all hoped for. I can just see bits on the surface here," pointing them out to Guy and Lionel on either side.

Akram took the stone back and brought it up to his jeweller's loupe.

"The flaw's not too deep. It will polish out well. Now I have got a lot of pre-forming to do before we start cutting and polishing on this copper wheel. The one in your hands, Guy, has quite a few flaws to navigate around. It's cushion cut stones you prefer, not pear-shaped ones?"

"Cushions are best for me," confirmed George.

"Why don't you go next door to the kitchen? I know my wife is keen to feed you and we can then get on with the basic shapes."

On this prompt, the three were guided out of the workroom. Lionel held back, keen to keep Mr Ashok in the loop — 'The eagle is now two, all good' — before joining a beaming Derek and Tommy at the large pine kitchen table.

"You're not going to believe these samosas."

"It didn't take you long to get inside," said George.

"It would be rude to stay in the car and you know Tommy's views about crumbs in cars."

The five were soon drawn together by another plate of samosas. Lionel noticed a busyness about the kitchen; the chatter had dropped and the cooking had ratcheted up. There were a lot of gas flames, large pans and hot spoons. It reminded him of his cookery lesson with the spice seller in Mirissa. When the curries started to come, the remaining samosas were taken to the workshop. They were just tucking into a ginger pudding when one of Akram's sons beckoned them back next door.

The workshop had a different feel to it now. The sound of a bench-mounted disc-cutter had given way to the rhythmic sound of the hand-cranked wheel. Akram had fixed one of the large stones to a stick-like rosewood dop which he held in his right hand, pressing the stone against the revolving copper lapidary wheel. The other end of the dob was fashioned as a sharp point, located in one of a line of vertical holes drilled into a large turned knob held on a steel spike adjacent to the thick copper wheel. It had the rough look of a record player, with the dob replacing the arm and the stone the stylus. The whole set-up looked and sounded Dickensian, with the exception of Akram's Rolex 'Pepsi' wristwatch.

"I managed to get a good table on this one," he said, removing the stone from the wheel. "Now it's the girdle and the heel of the stone to facet. Remember, cutting a diamond is a science; but cutting a coloured stone is an art."

He returned to cranking the handle; once started, it's hard not to put another facet on.

"When I finish cutting, my eldest will start polishing on a different wheel."

"When do you think you'll finish this one?" enquired Guy.

"By the end of the day. As soon as I do, I'll start on the other one. I don't know for sure how many offcut stones I'll get, as there are a number of flaws to negotiate."

"I'm really happy with the progress but a little anxious about the other one. Would you preform it for me now so I roughly know what weight it'll be? I can then leave it to you to decide the sizes of the smaller stones," said George.

"The offcuts could be at least 5 carats," said Akram.

"Did you weigh the first stone before you fixed it on the dop?" asked George.

"It weighed just under 300 carats, but I will lose another 20 per cent in the cutting."

"Shall I say around 240 carats for the final weight?"

"That hopefully would be about right," said Akram, itching to get on.

"Can I leave Guy and Lionel with you? I need to catch a train back to London. I'll send Derek and Tommy back here to pick them up."

"Don't do that, it's a short journey to the Gunton Arms. One of my sons can drop them off," replied Akram.

"Lots of photos and please, remember to record the weights. Good luck."

Chapter 48

London

On leaving his godfather, Ollie Croyd walked over Piccadilly and down Duke Street towards his office. It was a sunny afternoon and the traffic was quiet. He slipped in his AirPods and rang the mobile number he had saved for the antique dealers Martin and Paul. It rang five times before the call was caught.

"No room too large, Martin here," he said over the hum of the road.

"Hello, my name is Ollie Croyd, I bought..."

"An Art Deco bar. I remember you. I do wish I had it now, do you use it?"

"Yes, I do."

"This is a call out of the blue. How can I help?"

"I wanted to pick your brains regarding buyers. American buyers."

"OK."

"When you delivered the bar..."

The call disconnected, Ollie checked his screen, full signal. He resumed his steps to his office with the intention of calling from his landline, thereby doubling the chance of maintaining a call. His AirPods suddenly jolted with an incoming call.

"Ollie Croyd?"

"Hello Ollie, we're in a difficult area, may I try you when we stop in ten minutes?"

"Of course, speak then."

He was settled at his desk when the call came.

"Hi, I just caught, 'American buyers'?"

"Yes, it's not really for me, more my godfather, whom you met with me at Battersea."

"I remember, the jeweller and his wife, the portrait painter?"

"Yes, George and Julia. Well, he may have a rather unusual gemstone for sale. Sort of controversial."

"Why?" Martin's voice lowered in interest.

"Are we speaking in total confidence?"

"Of course."

"My godfather is hoping to sell a large sapphire named 'The Crocodile Stone'."

"Unusual, why crocodile?"

"The boy who dredged up the stone lost his father to a crocodile in the same river."

"How awful."

"Yes, the stone is a remarkable blue, a blue only nature can make. I remember you saying you had some good American customers."

"I do, especially Texans – hold on, Paul is mouthing something to me. Yes, John Julius. One of our stateside interior designers is furnishing a holiday home in Miami for an oil man, John Julius III. Would there be commission?"

"Of course. Why would your Texan buy it?"

"Our friend Franc, their interior designer, who incidentally messages us continually, says that the Florida home is for his new wife, the fourth Mrs JJ. She's a Florida girl who finds the dry heat of Texas a little too much for both her skin and hair and needs a sea breeze. He also informs us that JJ says 'yes' to anything his wife wants, as he's not getting any younger and knows he needs to hang on to this one. Would you like us to message Franc?"

"Yes please."

"Paul is trying to do it now, if our dog will allow him. Ben has just spotted a squirrel from the passenger window."

"I will let you go. Many thanks."

In for a penny ... thought Ollie as he then sent a WhatsApp greeting to Macau, Hong Kong. A message came back quickly.

"Midnight here, lucky our business is nightlife. My boss is here until 2am."

"Have something of interest, an important gemstone."

"A lucky ruby?" came the reply.

"No, even better, a Sri Lankan sapphire, colour of the bluest blue sea, size of a quail's egg, called the Crocodile Stone."

"Photos?"

"To come shortly."

"Will notify you on receipt of photos."

"Thank you."

Unbeknown to Ollie, the PA's boss was in front of him at his normal encroaching distance of a foot. It would be intimidating for most people, but Wen Saang had known his boss since birth, being his nephew on his father's side. Most found his boss sinister but Wen liked the silence. His uncle had a remarkable brain, a combination of pure maths and on-course bookmaking which saw the beyond: cards, backgammon boards, dice and roulette wheels. He saw just the numbers, never in isolation but in endless strings, running in many combinations and making patterned shapes. Their relationship was mutual and self-sustaining; his uncle may have the numbers but Wen had the words, which came in many different languages. He was his uncle's voice outside the casino penthouse; by only speaking in private, the boss was able to reinforce his sinister and elusive image. He knew he wasn't good at words, so better that his nephew did all the talking. They made a strange pair, with the young man over 6 foot tall and the boss under 5 foot, the oddness compounded by the fact that he always wore black rubber gloves of the sort normally used in chemical spills. There was much speculation over why he wore them, but never an explanation.

Wen spoke. "I liked the English auctioneer."

After his uncle's customary silence came, "So did I."

"The pair of vases we bought from him add class and status to our entrance lobby. Have you noticed how they draw a crowd, just like Leonardo's Mona Lisa."

"I've noticed the crowds on the security cameras."

"If we play our cards right this Mr Croyd may be our Mr Lucky?"

His uncle abruptly changed the subject. "I have a Japanese Meiji period bronze of a crocodile in storage, it stands 45 centimetres high. The crate is barcoded as 8 232376 888001. Can you arrange delivery here."

Wen instantly messaged an employee on the mainland, knowing the barcode would be correct.

In London, Ollie was messaging George. "One American and one Chinaman on notice. Both need photos soonest. Love Ollie. PS Thank Jackie for lunch."

On receipt, George rang Guy in Norwich. "Guy, George here. How is Akram getting on?"

"Very well, but there has been a setback."

"Why?"

"As you asked, Akram paused cutting the first stone and starting pre-forming the other half of the stone but as he cut it on the saw he found colour patches around its girdle. Problems under the table or the pavilion of the stone can be cut away without too much loss, but around the girdle losses can be much greater. He does, however, believe that he can still cut a flawless stone, but it may now be under 100 carats."

"That's a shame but for the stone to be important it does need to be flawless. Are any of them finished?"

"Not yet, both stones are still on dops. Akram is now cutting the facets on the smaller stone, and his eldest son is polishing the big one. They say they won't stop until they're both done."

"Did they get any smaller stones?"

"They got three of note when Akram reduced the girdle of the second stone. All over 5 carats."

"When do you think they will be finished?"

"Let me ask." George could hear Akram over the rhythmic sound of the hand-cranked wheels.

"Another three or four hours for the two big stones and they haven't touched the smaller ones."

"Don't worry about them. Just get the two large ones back to me, I really need them in my hands to sell them properly. It's 3pm now, so if you're in the car by seven, you could be back by 10pm. Are you happy to come straight to my home?"

"Of course."

"I'll make the arrangements with Derek. Is he with you?"

"Yes, next door in the kitchen. He and Tommy have almost eaten their bodyweight in samosas. We are being far too well looked after here."

"I can imagine. Would you take some 30-second reels of the stones being cut and polished, they'll be useful in the stone's story."

"I'm already on it, you'll get them shortly."

"No more than 40 seconds, and can you please ask Akram questions. How many facets has he cut? Do you have a name for the colour? What's their carat weight? All the usual stuff."

"I will."

George rang Derek and briefed him, then summoned Jackie. "Guy is sending me some reels of Akram cutting the stones, can you edit them? We could use them as a taster for Ollie's buyers. Too late for Hong Kong now, but Texas will be waking up soon. Our midnight is their 6am."

When the reels arrived, Jackie deftly turned them around: brightening the light, saturating the colour, cutting out the pauses and adding subtitles. It's always good to have the carat weight in numbers.

"Excellent, Jackie. Would you WhatsApp them to Ollie."

Chapter 49

London

Just after 10pm, Tommy pressed his boss's video entry buzzer. George checked the screen carefully and only then pressed the door release button. Before anybody could say hello, his two dogs rushed through Guy and Lionel to greet Derek. Whilst Dougal licked his stroking hand, Hamish stood his ground barking until scooped up. Once calm was restored, George led Guy and Lionel to a circular table beyond the island at the back of the kitchen. They had no sooner sat down than Julia walked in. Standing up, George made the introductions.

"I have smoked salmon, any takers?" said Julia.

"That would be lovely, poppet. Anybody like a drink? I've got just the wine for nibbly bits."

Guy then produced two zippered navy-blue silk bags.

"Smart pouches," George said.

"Back in Sri Lanka Akram's wife was a seamstress, and when she isn't cooking she's sewing."

Before George could say, "Let's see them again," Guy unzipped the bags and placed the two sapphires on his folded white handkerchief.

"Oh my God, they are enormous, nobody is going to believe the colour," said George taking out his jeweller's loupe, "Any flaws?"

"You tell me," said Guy. George inspected both stones.

"Have they been weighed?"

"Of course," said Guy, "The smaller one is fractionally over 68 carats and the big fellow is just over 90."

"A toast to Lionel's friends in Sri Lanka, Mr Ashok and the all-important very clever raft boy."

"To Mr Ashok and Manoji," Lionel replied. "That reminds me, I must get them up to date."

"Guy, well done. Without you, we wouldn't have Akram and his jamb peg cutting wheel. You should see the reel Jackie sent to Ollie. It's late, would you like to stay in London or get home?"

"I would like to wake up in my own bed," said Guy as Lionel nodded.

"Are you happy, Lionel, to leave these two stones with me?"

"Of course."

In Texas, interior designer Franc had already shared Ollie's reels with John Julius III's new wife, who had become beyond excited at the chance of owning a Sri Lanken sapphire normally worn by royalty.

"Darlin', you always say I'm your queen, go get me the jewel."

JJ was hot and restless but praise the Lord the price of a barrel of crude oil was rising. He rang the number given and the first thing he asked was, "Is it rainin'?"

When George reluctantly admitted, "It hasn't stopped," he wasn't expecting: "Perfect, haven't felt rain in months, save me the biggie. I can be in London the day after tomorrow."

The starting pistol was well and truly fired. Ollie now needed to sell the smaller one to his casino owner in Hong Kong. He hadn't sent the reel to the PA, but had sent some high-resolution photographs with precise measurements of the smaller stone.

In Macau, the Japanese model of the crocodile had been delivered to the penthouse where it now stood on a temporary plinth. The crocodile was rearing up on its tail, giving it height, presumably before it fell on its unfortunate prey. Its jaw was open, and in its gaping mouth a craftsman was setting a blue glass model of a 68 carat replica stone in a frame with a microlight behind. The whole procedure was being closely watched by Mr Saang and his nephew.

"It fits well," Wen said to his uncle, motioning for the jewel and light to come further forward. A brief smile registered on his face when the jewel sparkled between the crocodile's teeth. The real thing, he thought, would dazzle.

"That's perfect, it should work. Would you message Mr Croyd – we need to know price?" When the message arrived Ollie didn't need to ring George, as they had already settled on the prices, the big one at £8 million and the 68 carat at £4 million.

He crossed his left fingers and sent: '£4 million UK sterling for 68 carat Crocodile Stone sapphire.'

The reply seemed to take an age and then the message popped up, '3.5 million UK sterling, final offer.'

Ollie referred to George before sending:

'Done at 3.5 million UK sterling. Congratulations.'

Wen had never seen his uncle properly smile before.

George, Jackie and Derek had planned what they might offer John Julius. Should he come to the office around 11am it would be coffee; any time after midday, champagne. Jackie had everything in readiness, including blinis and caviar. George would gauge it. He'd been retailing long enough, but this was a big stone and he wanted to get it right.

JJ called in the morning saying that he would be over just after noon. Jackie checked the temperature of the Ruinart champagne and gave the Russian silver-gilt caviar bowl another buff with a dry tea towel while Derek waited in the hall watching the security screen. When the buzzer sounded he checked the TV monitor again before opening. John Julius III looked like a bear and walked like a bear. Even Derek didn't fancy his chances against this Texan. He had come dressed for Britain, wearing a large sand-coloured Burberry raincoat.

"I was hopin' for rain," he said as he handed his coat to Derek.

"Yesterday, you would have seen plenty, it didn't stop all day. Mr George is upstairs, please follow me."

"Sure thing. What's your name?"

"Derek."

"No Dereks in Texas. The only Derricks we got in Texas are in oilfields. How're you spellin' yours?"

"Two e's and one r," replied Derek.

"Well, there you are. I think it was your George Bernard Shaw who said we're 'Two nations divided by a common language'."

JJ double-took as Derek introduced Jackie. "Mighty fine boots you have there."

Jackie was tempted to reply, "Why thank you, sir," in her best

Gone with the Wind accent, but George interrupted her, fearing that the four-times-married JJ might forget why he had flown all this way.

"Come into my office." Once seated, they chatted about flights, Florida, Texas and inevitably the weather.

"You Brits are lucky with your changing seasons, it gives you small talk for strangers. In Texas all I can say is it's hot! Anyhow, where's this jewel?"

George took the silk pouch from his coat pocket and placed it on the desk.

"It's a loose stone, only just been cut, which means you can choose any setting."

JJ unzipped the bag and tipped the sapphire into his left hand. When he held it up to the sunlight it sent out beams of blue light.

"It's got some life in it. I know a lot about oil but I don't know nothin' about jewels."

George started telling him about how it was cut and polished, but he was interrupted by Jackie strutting in with caviar and glasses, followed by Derek bearing champagne and ice bucket. George stopped as JJ watched her first open the bottle and then spoon out the caviar.

"Mighty fine," he said as she left.

George handed JJ a glass, nudging him back to the sapphire.

"Franc, my wife's interior designer in Florida, mentioned a crocodile?"

"Yes, it was dredged up by a boy on a raft in a river full of crocodiles."

"My granddaddy started his working life on a gator farm, in the days when skins were prized for shoes and handbags. I remember him telling me he and his brothers used to feed them whole chickens. They'd throw 'em into their gaping jaws and watch 'em swallow 'em whole. My Daddy did a great mime, but he could never gulp anything bigger than a new potato. The Great Depression killed the gator business, luckily for me it pushed him from gator farms to oilfields. Praise the Lord," he added, raising his glass. "Why should I buy this stone?"

"Because you'll never see another. Every sapphire, in fact any coloured stone, will have a unique colour according to its formation and size. This stone is the full ticket, the granddaddy of sapphires."

"What's its price?"

"The Crocodile Stone is 8 million UK sterling."

"That's a lot of barrels of oil," he paused. "I bid you 6 million sterling, and before we start dancin' around figures, is my money safe in this stone?"

"As you have just thanked your grandfather for changing his business, your wife will thank you for buying probably one of the largest sapphires outside the Tower of London."

"Tell me, what do you call this type of cut? Is it one of those 'step cuts'?"

"It's called a 'cushion cut', with a small table and soft edges." George paused. "As you are the one who's done the travelling and will take possession this side of the pond, it's yours for 6.5 million UK sterling."

"Let's keep it to a round 6 million," he countered.

JJ had spent a lifetime trading oil in bundles of many hundreds of million dollars and he could easily recognise the 'Yes' in George's eyes. He paused and pressed,

"Are we done?"

George was just about to say, "Yes," when JJ took the stone, pushed it into a blini and swallowed it whole.

"As my Daddy always said, possession is nine-tenths of the law."

Epilogue

Guy was at home and under the weather, but he just managed to reach his mobile before the call transferred to the answer machine.

"Guy, George here. Good news."

"I could do with some. I'm feeling a little poorly."

"Well, this will make you better. Sold both stones."

"And ... and, for how much?"

"Just under 10 million." George continued, "I will take the usual commission plus the smaller stones, I will pay you and Akram out of this. I'm going to invite Lionel and his friend Barty for a celebration tonight; would you like to join us?"

"I better stay here. I'm all shivery."

"I will get Jackie to send you some of Lipman's Special Chicken Broth. It's like blood plasma with a few stem cells thrown in. It's sorted me out more than a couple of times. Get better, you're far too valuable."

George rang Lionel next. "Are you seated?"

Lionel instantly recognised the caller he'd been waiting for.

"I could tell you now or would you and your friend prefer to come to London for dinner at Murray's in Albemarle Street for a little celebration?"

"I know Barty has always wanted to go there."

"Hop on a train to London Bridge, it connects with Green Park tube station. I'll book a table for 7.30 but come soonest and then we can get the business side out of the way."

Next, Lionel placed a call to Kandy.

"Ashok speaking."

"Mr Ashok, it's Lionel."

"Good timing, I'm in the car with Sanchini waiting for Amelia to finish her final chemistry exam."

At the mention of Sanchini Lionel blushed and managed to say, "Give them both a kiss from me." He paused. "I have got some good news. Both stones are sold. Manoji and his uncles can now beach their raft for good."

"Fabulous, how much?"

"Just over 5 million after George's commission of 40 perecent. He will keep the money in the UK until you and Manoji decide how best to employ it. Remember there will be taxes to pay, please do get careful advice. I hope Manoji will now go to university."

"He can, he had top grades before he left school and the chancellor of Peradeniya University is a friend. He will now have the education he deserves."

Next, George messaged Ollie: 'Celebration dinner at Murray's tonight. Please bring Mercy, Singer is going to join us.' He received a thumbs-up emoji.

Derek walked the short distance with George to Murray's. Once inside, he secured his favourite circular table beside the fireplace and below the large lantern. Derek had instilled in him the merits of a corner table, keeping solid walls to his back. Not that either of them anticipated any trouble in this private member's club. Ollie and Mercy arrived shortly after seven and were halfway through an Aperol Spritz when George waved at two men being shown into the bar. As they turned to greet them Lionel double-took. "Oh my god, It's Mercy Penfold," he whispered to Barty.

"Keep going," Barty replied through a gritted smile.

George extended a hand. "May I introduce the heroes of the hour, Mr Lionel Thompson and Mr Barty Hix, my godson Ollie Croyd and his girlfriend Mercy Penfold."

Both Lionel and Barty froze as Ollie Croyd recognised his client's name and Mercy Penfold finally put a face to The Stolen Bronze.

Passing around glasses, George said "I'd like to make a toast to The Crocodile Stones."

Mercy looked at Ollie and then with a broad smile replied, "To The Crocodile Stones, and the ... Chinese vases."

The End

BARTY - A TALE OF A STOLEN BRONZE

JAMES BRAXTON

The first book in the series

When a garden bronze is stolen from a Norfolk country house, and embarrassingly sold to a private collector in Hastings the hunt is on to find the thief. Leading the search party is Barty a chef, Lionel an antiques dealer, Mercy Penfold a journalist, Jack a young antiques dealer, and a dog called Clive! Not to mention the police! A warm and humorous story for those who love food and antiques.

In a word, fulfilling!

In Barty - A Tale of a Stolen Bronze, we are introduced to a colourful cast of characters, none more so than Barty, a chef, and his good friend Lionel, an antiques dealer. Written in expansive style, the pair undertake the search for a stolen statue, the tale ranging between Hastings and Norfolk, via Brighton, London and Essex all the while collecting engaging characters and memorable culinary moments along the way – you could almost say Barty is a tale in 47 courses! James' warmly engaging style is sprinkled with delightful insights into the antiques' world that left this reader with a satisfying glow and a sense of having comfortably indulged. Highly recommended.

Richard Knight

Amusing Romp with Barty and the hunt for the stolen bronze

One of the most amusing starts to any book I have read will keep your attention on the jolly intriguing voyage of discovery. An English gem taking the reader on a gentle journey including idyllic Hastings by the channel to Norfolk and beyond, the tale of Barty seeking the stolen bronze and its "handlers" is well worth the read from the well known BBC expert and personality James Braxton as seen on "Antiques Road Trip", "Bargain Hunt" and "Flog It"

Rupert Cutler

Great Read but not so good for your waistline!!

A great read and very atmospheric!

James has natural ability of taking you to places through your imagination, you can almost taste and smell Barty's journey. Be pre-warned not so good for the waistline!!

Helen Bryant

A Thoroughly Enjoyable Read

There is no-one better placed to write about the antiques trade than James Braxton. In this book he gives us a flavour of the trade from an insider's perspective, but the book is far broader than this. It combines humour, old school crookedness, good friendship, community spirit, and an epicure's delight in food; all of which is wrapped in a joyous bundle of easy reading, solid plot, and a delightful finish. Buy it, read it, enjoy it ... and await the next book with eager anticipation!

A Mitchell

"I am really enjoying your book – finding it difficult not to just sit down and binge read."

Philippa Judd

"What Ian Fleming is to a spy novel, James Braxton is to an antiques mystery."

Peter Cottrell, Man about Town.

Like mint sauce to Lamb... Red current jelly to ham... Marmalade to toast... This wonderful book has been the perfect accompaniment to my holiday. If you love food and Antiques, this book is for you!

Christina Trevanion

JAMES BRAXTON

BARTY - A TALE OF A STOLEN BRONZE

ISBN 978-1-0686480-0-7

www.jamesbraxton.com